THE ORANGE GROVE

Kate Murdoch

Regal House Publishing

Published by
Regal House Publishing, LLC
Raleigh, NC 27612
All rights reserved

ISBN -13 (paperback): 9781947548220
ISBN -13 (epub): 9781947548237
Library of Congress Control Number: 2019940528

Interior and cover design by Lafayette & Greene
lafayetteandgreene.com
Cover images © by NemesisINV/Shutterstock

Regal House Publishing, LLC
https://regalhousepublishing.com

Printed in the United States of America

For David, with love

Don't take the manners of the time so hard!
Be a bit merciful to human nature;
Let us not judge it with the utmost rigour,
But look upon its faults with some indulgence.
Our social life demands a pliant virtue;
Too strict uprightness may be blameworthy;
Sound judgment always will avoid extremes,
And will be sober even in its virtue.

Molière - *The Misanthrope*

CHAPTER 1

Blois, 1705

On a winter morning, Solange saw the mist of her breath. She blew on the windows, making a cloudy canvas for her finger.

The maid had come just after dawn to stoke the fire and bring hot chocolate. She had swished open the silk drapes, letting in muted light.

Solange's mother, Henriette, disliked mornings and was attended by a number of maids, who helped her through the early hours. Solange slept in a small anteroom next to her mother's, their rooms at the rear of the château, reached by a narrow, twisting staircase. After the maid had opened the drapes, Solange would rush to her mother's dressing table, eager to be included in Henriette's morning routine. For her mother would spend hours in a gilded chair—her hair coaxed into ringlets, powdered and pinned, her cheeks rouged, her lips painted.

Solange stood at the window and stared out at the private courtyard, enclosed by tall hedges and visible only to her and her mother. Gardeners kept the hedges trimmed but left the potted plants to wither, their leaves shrivelling over their terracotta surrounds in search of water. Frost sparkled on the hedges in the weak sun. Solange wondered if Tomas might chase her through the hedge maze as he had the day before, or if they might skate together on the frozen canals. She rubbed her arms against the chill as she sidled closer to her mother's skirts.

'Go and play. This can't possibly interest you,' Henriette urged with a smile, reaching over to tuck a stray lock of her daughter's hair behind her ear.

'But it does interest me, Maman. I want to learn how it's done.'

'I'm sure if you go and find Tomas, he'll play with you. Your eyes are boring into the back of my head.'

Henriette raised her eyebrows as she turned to examine her daughter. Solange's dress had been chosen for its comfortable fit and plain blue linen. Her hair, barely contained by a white ribbon, was tangled and unruly.

'I'll have to speak to your maid. You're not dressed appropriately. Again.'

'It's my fault, Maman. I insisted on this dress. Lots of playing to do today,' she said with an impish smile.

'Let me kiss you.' Henriette leaned over and kissed Solange's forehead. 'Now you may go. Try not to get so dirty.'

Solange let herself out and climbed the staircase to a vast hallway. Creeping along, she placed her feet with care in the middle of the parquetry flowers on the floor. She had been reprimanded by the duc's valet for galloping, causing the glassware in the hall cabinet to tinkle.

The silk sash of Solange's dress trailed behind her, having escaped her mother's attention. Above was a curved ceiling, where cherubs cavorted, their delicate wings as light as clouds. Solange imagined they watched her as she twirled on each blossoming flower and stood on tiptoe on each leaf. There was no need to hurry.

Solange knew where to find Tomas. He was currently preoccupied with fountains and could be found either throwing coins into their depths or, on warmer days, immersed completely, coming up to open his mouth and spurt jets of water.

The main fountain depicted Zeus and Hera, their arms entwined. Zeus's profile was formidable—the sculptor had meticulously carved each hair of his beard. Hera's sinuous form was swathed in a clinging robe, her refined features a mask of tranquillity, save for a determined stare. No less than fifty jets of water gushed from the statuary into the pool below. Tomas had been locked in his mother's rooms for days after climbing onto Zeus's shoulders. Once released, he had discovered the less spectacular fountain of Apollo, near the orange grove, visible only to servants. Here the children could play in privacy.

2

Once outside, Solange followed the gravel path to the grounds bordering the orchard. The stones crunched beneath her feet and a citrus-scented breeze caressed her face. Tomas sat on the edge of the marble fountain.

'Hello, Tomas. Too cold for a swim?'

Tomas swivelled around and smiled, his blue eyes glinting in the early morning sun. He had removed his stockings and undone his shirt ties. The wind had tousled his brown hair, which curled to his shoulders.

'Maman was crying this morning,' Tomas announced. 'It's been a week since the duc called for her. There's a new mistress, have you seen her?'

'No. Is she younger than our mothers?'

'Yes, she looks barely five years older than us. From the north. Calais, I think.'

Solange seated herself next to Tomas, her sash trailing in the water. 'The duc wishes for a son. I heard the duchesse tell Maman so.'

Tomas frowned. 'But an illegitimate son, it's not the same.'

'A bastard son is still a son.'

Solange pulled her ribbon from the green-tinged water and flicked it at Tomas's face.

'Don't! I'll throw you in!' he lunged at her.

Solange ducked out of the way, jumped to her feet, and ran. Their laughter echoed through the grounds as he gave chase.

Solange's footsteps reverberated as she dashed through the hallways. She could hear Tomas counting in the distance as she searched for a hiding place.

Duchesse Charlotte's rooms were full of pretty objects and she slipped inside. The low desk in the corner held a display of mother-of-pearl snuff boxes and hand-painted fans depicting lovers. Solange picked up a fan, giggling under her breath at the watercolour of a bewigged man kissing a lady's neck. Hearing footsteps, she ducked behind a screen. She held her breath, her heart thudding in her chest.

Two voices spoke softly, one Solange recognized as the duchesse. Peering through a tiny gap between the screen partitions, she saw the duchesse's companion, Madame Céline de Poitiers. Both women were dressed for dinner, their hair twisted into braids and ringlets, the skirts of their silk dresses billowing beneath bow-trimmed bodices. The duchesse's indigo dress was elaborate, the bodice embroidered with multi-coloured flowers and the sleeves embellished with lace.

'We must work this out,' Céline said urgently, the words escaping from lips that barely moved. 'My husband cannot support me. I would be an outcast, a sullied woman. I have gone against the tenets of my faith to be his mistress. I can no longer take the sacraments without feeling a hypocrite.'

'Céline, I understand your distress, but what can we do? I cannot control the feelings of my husband, and believe me, I have tried every argument possible.'

'It's simple. The new girl is young and naïve, ignorant of court ways—how we speak to one another, the courtesies, the conversations. We must befriend her, show her how to navigate her way. She will be grateful and confide in us. In this way, we shall learn her weaknesses and undermine her. Show her up or trip her up, whichever comes first.'

The duchesse was silent, examining her hands. She did not lift her head for a long moment. 'It is a vague plan, Céline,' she said at last, 'and I'm not sure where it will lead us. But it's something we may begin at least. Who knows what we may discover. I cannot befriend her, however, my husband would be suspicious. You must do it, and tell me what you find out.'

'Yes, of course.'

Solange held her breath as she listened, gripping the handle of the fan. She committed the words to memory and waited for the right moment to escape.

❧

Madame Céline de Poitiers was the second eldest mistress. Her husband permitted the arrangement and lived in the nearby town of Blois, content to drink *vin sec* all day and play faro with the income provided by his wife.

The words of his last letter were fresh in her mind as she stood outside the gilt-edged doors of the duc's rooms. Her husband had reminded her of his mounting debts, requesting that she visit. Céline tried to banish all thoughts of him as she prepared herself to meet with the duc. She had dressed with care in her most expensive white dress and dabbed perfume behind her ears. The duc had been distant for weeks—she would remind him of her worth. She pinched her cheeks and undid the ribbon at the top of her bodice. Poised to knock, she froze, hearing the low rumble of the duc's laughter from within, followed by a high-pitched squeal. A thud and she imagined both of them tumbling to the Persian carpet beneath the canopied bed. He had often done the same with her. Céline stepped backwards with a faltering step and pressed her palm against the wall. Her limbs felt weak, as if they might not hold her upright.

The man's presence beside her did not register until, with a ragged intake of breath, she inhaled a woody scent and her eyes fell on a pair of highly polished shoes with gleaming silver buckles. Her gaze travelled up the man's slight but muscular form, clad in grey breeches, an embroidered waistcoat and navy coat. He adjusted the sleeves of his coat and smirked, enjoying her attention.

Céline frowned as she studied his features. Wide-set flint-blue eyes and full lips, his jaw more oval than square, and brown hair lightly powdered and pulled back. A Roman nose prevented his face from being overly feminine.

'Good morning, madame, are you feeling well? Or would you like me to find you some smelling salts?'

'Blessed Virgin, who in the world are you? And what are you doing sneaking around the hallway?'

'Forgive me, madame, for startling you. My name is Romain de

Villiers and I'm an old friend of the duchesse. She has kindly invited me to stay at the château. May I ask your name?'

'Madame Céline de Poitiers. What is the purpose of your stay, monsieur?'

'I am a master of the tarot and will be giving readings to whoever would like them. The duchesse would like the château to be blessed with divine guidance.'

'Divine?' Céline snorted. 'That would be the prerogative of God or the king himself. Do you place yourself on that level, monsieur?'

Romain's face remained a mask of calm. 'Perhaps an unfortunate choice of words, madame. Earthly guidance maybe, or just guidance. What would you suggest? You have intelligent eyes but sensuous lips. I imagine these two aspects of your character are often in turmoil. Piety, the desires of the heart, and the urges of the body. All equally pressing, I imagine.'

Céline's eyes widened and she flushed. Romain's gaze did not waver as he stepped back. Her pale brown hair had not yet been dressed and was pinned loosely. An unremarkable face was made pleasing by astute dark eyes. She was proud of her slender white arms and hands, her fingers long and elegant. She knew she lacked beauty, yet compensated with wit, her show of devotion to God, and her powers of seduction. She was accustomed to achieving her objectives, carnal and otherwise.

'You have surely been sent by the devil, monsieur. I look forward to your readings. Now, I must go.' Céline suppressed a smile and turned, feeling his eyes on her back as she glided away.

CHAPTER 2

From the window of Duchesse Charlotte's private drawing room Henriette could see the wide avenue, lined with plane trees, that led to the château. Geometric plantings of peonies and neat squares of lawn were dissected with precise hedging. The perfection was comforting. The gardeners knew where to cut and did not deviate. Only the colours changed and the blooms, which appeared in summer, withered in winter.

The duchesse sipped hot chocolate, her Bichon dogs nestled around her voluminous silk skirts. One lay spreadeagled on its back, waiting patiently to be scratched. Charlotte's cheeks were flushed pink and she tapped her foot in a rapid beat.

'Well, have you met her?'

Turning from the window, Henriette feigned ignorance. 'Have I met whom?'

Charlotte sighed. 'Letitia. My husband's child concubine. I know your rooms are tucked away, Henriette, but you're the most senior mistress. Are you truly unaware of what's going on?'

'There may have been whispers, among the maids. It's just another young mistress; what is it about her that disturbs you so?'

Charlotte pulled a lace handkerchief from her sleeve and dabbed at her eyes. 'She is ravishing and virginal,' the duchesse said. 'Her voice is sweet and she possesses an uncommon wit for a girl of eighteen. But these virtues are the least of my concerns. My husband…he appears…'—her voice quavered—'to be in love with her.'

Henriette drew in her breath and lowered herself onto a chair, giving Charlotte her full attention. 'And how do you know this? Love, are you certain? I did not believe him capable of it.'

The duchesse was silent, head bent to her hands, white-clenched in her lap. Tears fell on her fingers, rolled off, and soaked the rose-coloured silk of her dress.

'He *is* capable of it. Despite you, Céline and the others, it has always been me he loved,' Charlotte insisted. 'I have prayed to the Virgin every day for the past three years that I may bless him with a son, but she has been deaf to my pleas. Now this child will deliver a bastard, who will be made legitimate. He has been courting her for six months and I did not know of it. You will see.' Her startling blue eyes were red-rimmed, glistening with tears.

Henriette reached out and took the duchesse's hand in her own. 'He is close to Estelle. You will not lose your status, as that would hurt his daughter.'

The duchesse composed her face and tucked her handkerchief beneath her sleeve. She pressed her lips together. 'You're quite right. He is very fond of the girl. You are a dear friend, Henriette—you must promise to keep our conversation to yourself.'

Henriette patted her hand. 'It will not go beyond this room.'

Romain de Villiers waited in the drawing room near the entrance hall, shifting on a brocade armchair. A clock whirred on the mantel and faint peals of laughter could be heard from upstairs. The room was dim, save for a shaft of golden light streaming through the window and pooling on the polished parquetry. The scent of lilies hung in the air.

Pressing his fingers to his temples, Romain tried to forget a memory from the day before. The thickset man, with bulging bloodshot eyes and snarling lips, had pummelled Romain as he cowered against the wall of the tavern. 'Give me the money, I know you have it, you dog!' the man wheezed between punches, spittle showering Romain's face. An entire container of powder had been required to disguise the livid bruises decorating Romain's cheekbones and the puffiness swelling one eye.

The swish of skirts sounded Duchesse d'Amboise's arrival, and

Romain rose stiffly to his feet, brushing down his velvet coat and sucking in his cheeks.

'Monsieur de Villiers, it is a pleasure to see you again. It has been a long time.' The duchesse held out a tapered white hand and motioned for him to sit down.

Romain bowed and sat, keeping his eyes fixed on the duchesse's face, as she sank with a rustle of silk into the chair opposite him.

'I am also honoured to see you, Your Grace.'

'There is no need for such formality, monsieur. You may start with 'madame,' and we will see how things progress. I have heard you show great accuracy with the cards.'

'I do not wish to be immodest, madame, but I am yet to be wrong in my predictions.'

Perched on the edge of her gilt chair, the duchesse leaned forward, her pinned-up blonde hair backlit like a halo, her features as delicate as a porcelain doll. Her lips curved in a smile. 'I'm pleased to hear that. I have some questions and lack the patience to wait for answers.'

The drawing room glowed as the fire leapt in the hearth. The orange-gold flames mirrored the fading light outside as the sun dipped behind the hills surrounding Blois. An imposing portrait of a younger duc dominated one wall. Hugo stood in hunting clothes, the carcass of a fox draped over one shoulder. He was flanked by a group of salivating hounds, the forest a forbidding smudge of green behind.

Henriette stood at a slight distance from the other women, who huddled around an ebony-topped table, their skirts rustling. Some had arrived from the court at Versailles, others were members of the local aristocracy. They had come to hear the great tarot reader reveal their fortunes. Romain de Villiers bent over the cards, resplendent in a scarlet cloak and a silver turban with a peacock feather. A curlicue of smoke wove from a brass incense burner and two blue and white ceramic dragons stood guard at each corner of the table. A guttering candle illuminated a glittering display of coloured crystals and two golden pentacles wrought from brass. Céline sat opposite Romain, studying his expression as he gently caressed the vivid illustrations that decorated the tarot cards. His eyes were half-closed and his lips moved but he did not speak.

Tomas and Solange had been instructed to keep their distance, but inched ever closer. They craned their necks to catch a glimpse of the tarot reader between the silk-clad shoulders of the court ladies and their elaborate hairpieces that glittered with gold and feather. Their mothers had been unable to speak of anything else for days, the lure of readings surpassing any talk of the new mistress. The women murmured and leaned forward to catch Monsieur de Villier's low tones as he delivered his verdict to Céline.

'You wish fervently for love and it is denied you. You search in the wrong places and seek affection from people whose attention is elsewhere. This card, the reversed King of Swords, speaks of someone in your life who delights in rejecting you. It is up to you to take your power back. The Seven of Swords suggests underhanded dealings. Deception. I cannot tell whether this is done unto you, or if it is a result of your own actions.'

With his index finger, Romain tapped a third card—a man with a hostile expression, fleeing from a campsite with an armload of swords.

'This card'—he turned over another that featured two people in ragged clothing, heads bowed as they trudged through snow—'the Five of Pentacles. I'm sorry, Madame de Poitiers, to be the bearer of bad news. This usually means financial difficulties to be overcome. It can also indicate emotional loss, which may tie in with the King of Swords.'

Céline shivered, feeling the cards' message of suffering and loss. She exhaled a nervous laugh, her eyes darting around the room at the women, their eyes wide. 'Do we allow these cards to make our futures, or do we make them ourselves?' she asked, her voice shaking. 'Perhaps someone else might like to hear their own sorry tale?'

'I'm sorry to disappoint you, madame, I merely interpret what the cards tell me.'

Céline scowled and rose to her feet in a majestic sweep of skirts. Settling into a corner chair, she retrieved her embroidery hoop and began to sew with intense concentration, ignoring the titters of amusement that followed Romain's pronouncement. She flinched as she pricked a finger.

Henriette sighed. She wondered what the man would say about her, but knew she would not ask for a reading. The women were like schoolgirls at a puppet show, jostling and exclaiming. The doors creaked open and a young woman entered. She held herself with regal poise. Her pale hair was fastened with braids that twisted in an intricate knot around her head and she wore a simple dress, the blue of seawater. A natural blush flowered on her cheeks. For a fleeting moment, Henriette wondered if she were an angel.

The girl seated herself at the table, acknowledged the women with a nod, and turned her attention to the tarot reader.

'I am Letitia du Massenet and I would like you to tell me about my future.'

Romain shuffled the cards with a languid motion as his eyes traversed her face, shoulders, and chest.

'Romain de Villiers, mademoiselle. I'm delighted to meet you. You may have upset the Baroness de Villeneuve, who was next, but your lovely face may charm her out of her displeasure. Am I right, baroness?'

The baroness stood with a rigid posture, glancing at the door. 'It's quite all right, monsieur. I'm waiting for the duchesse to arrive and I will, as is appropriate, take my turn after her. These *ladies* should really do the same.' She raised one greying eyebrow and pursed her lips. 'Clearly, it is too much to expect courtesy when it has not been taught from the cradle.'

Henriette stepped forward, her green eyes glinting. 'Baroness de Villeneuve, if your own manners were so impeccable, you would be above insulting these women, who have shown you nothing but respect.'

The baroness drew herself up, staring down her nose at Henriette. 'I've not insulted them, just observed their display of bad origins.'

Romain spread three cards out across the table, his tapered index finger lingering on the middle one. 'The Hierophant, mademoiselle. Your strong will might well be your undoing. Prudence and discernment should be practised. This card, The Two of Wands, represents riches, but also great sadness. The Four of Pentacles is another card indicating prosperity.'

Letitia nodded. 'Sadness and prosperity. Perhaps the prosperity may cancel out the sadness.'

Romain's mouth curved in a reluctant smile. 'If there is an indication of sadness, then there will be sadness. Take it as you will.'

Letitia reached out and mixed up the cards, shuffling them in a slow circular motion, her eyes fixed on the tarot reader. 'How do I know you are not a charlatan, monsieur?'

'I suppose you will know the answer to that when your future reveals itself, mademoiselle.'

❧

Duc Hugo d'Amboise had organised an elaborate fête. The performers had arrived from Versailles, their loan a favour from the king. They were to dance and sing in an opera ballet later that evening. Hugo sat and watched them from the window as they laughed in the rose garden, practising their pirouettes. He enjoyed this time of the morning, the muffled hush of his blue and grey rooms, with their draped silks and velvet, and the window seat, where he could observe all undetected.

The dancers spun amid red and pink roses, their hair flying with each rapid turn. Their supple bodies, their easy movements, reminded the duc of Letitia. The duc's eye twitched and he strummed his fingers on the windowsill, thinking of her curtain of blonde hair, fanned over his chest. Her body yielding beneath his as she let out small, rhythmic gasps. Perfect rounded breasts, bluish-white. The pink buttons of her nipples. He took a deep breath and shut his eyes hard, trying to compose himself. It just would not do to lose his head over her.

Charlotte had volleyed questions at him the previous evening, her voice shrill, her face flushed. She asked his intentions, accused him of behaving like a lovestruck boy, and reminded him of his responsibilities to her, to Estelle, to his mistresses.

Hugh wondered how to placate her. A diamond necklace, perhaps, or a visit to Versailles. Charlotte enjoyed the rigid protocol of the palace and the sumptuous fashions of the courtiers. Her close friend, Martine Foulbret, lived at Versailles and Charlotte often stayed with her for days on end, gossiping and God knew what else. Hugh had never been comfortable with these sojourns—the male courtiers were flirtatious, and the duc worried that his wife might become embroiled in an affair.

Arthur, Hugh's valet, entered, his head bowed. He wore a shirt with voluminous ruffles and his fingers were covered in sparkling rings 'Your Grace, Madame de Poitiers wishes to see you.'

The duc sighed. 'Show her in, Arthur.'

'She is upset,' Arthur warned, 'not quite herself.'

'Thank you, Arthur, it's all right.'

Céline strode in the moment Arthur opened the door to admit her, two bright daubs of clumsily applied rouge on her cheekbones.

'Céline. This will have to be brief. We must prepare for the festivities this evening. What do you want?'

'Hugo, you have not called for me in two weeks. Do I need a reason to come and see you? I have missed you terribly.' She sidled up to him, placing her hand on his waist. 'You have grown thinner, my love, without me tending to you. Come and sit with me, we must talk.'

Hugo lifted her hand, gave it a cursory pat, and removed it from his waist.

'I will call for you soon, but I'm busy at the moment. There has been the fête to organize and the duchesse has needed me.'

Céline's lips thinned. 'It's not the fête, Hugo, don't try to deceive me. It's that girl, Letitia. I'm sure such a child does not know how to please you.' She reached down, stroking him through his breeches.

Her lips curved in a smile, but her eyes were earnest, desperate. Hugo felt himself harden but looked away from her face—the intensity in her gaze bothered him. Staring out of the window, he could see Yves, the ballet master, pirouette in a blur of movement.

'Stop now, Céline.'

She gripped him with one hand, and massaged his chest with the other. Her ferocious dark eyes did not leave his face.

'I said, stop!' His deep voice erupted into the room, louder than he was expecting.

Céline recoiled. Her cheeks flooded with colour and a film of tears shone in her eyes.

'What has happened to you, Hugo?' Her voice shook. Lifting her skirts, she turned and fled from the room.

CHAPTER 3

The sky was deep blue with wisps of dark pink and mauve as the afternoon ebbed away. Beside the fountain of Zeus and Hera stood a towering castle made of marzipan, its golden turrets glimmering gold in the dying light. Double doors opened to a drawbridge, tiny balconies jutted from windows, and soldiers stood guard on the battlements. A fabled patisserie in Paris had created the confection, over which chefs had laboured for countless hours. Two hundred courtiers had arrived from Versailles and the king was due later in the evening.

The crowd conversed, their silk shoes crunched on the gravel paths as they walked around the castle, unsure if they were yet permitted to eat it. Other courtiers sat on the edge of a rectangular marble pool, a fountain at its centre. The first flowers of spring sweetened the air.

Tomas scampered through the throng and broke off a castle door, his tongue darting out to lick the confection. Several guests laughed and a servant waved a gloved hand, his white wig slipping forward on his head.

'Off with you!'

Tomas ducked nimbly behind the servant and broke off a castle balcony for Solange. Holding hands and giggling, they dashed for cover behind the hedges.

The children's audacity prompted one of the guests to reach forward and snap off a turret. Grinning, he sat on the edge of the fountain to consume it, balancing his prize on the blue velvet of his waistcoat, which strained over the ball of his stomach. In an instant the remaining nobles lurched forward, their voices raised as they pounced on the sweet turrets, doors, and walls. The structure collapsed on one side, and there was a collective intake of breath as the men and women glimpsed the miniature furnishings within—

brass beds, mirrors, and carpets, decorating tiny bedchambers and sitting rooms.

Letitia strolled alone, watching the other mistresses from the corner of her eye. The duc was occupied with greeting his guests and she did not dare approach the duchesse, or the sour one whose name she had forgotten.

White dahlias lined the pathway, illuminated by iron candelabras as tall as men. Letitia crouched and traced the petals of one, as soft as a baby's cheek. Blinking back tears, she thought of her mother bidding her goodbye, fussing with Letitia's hat, tying the silk ribbon with care and pulling her close.

Since arriving at the château, Letitia had lectured herself every day. *You are a woman now, not a child. Watch the others, see how composed they are, how regal. They do not cry or miss their families. You are mistress to one of the most powerful men in France—you could have been married to a sixty-year-old governor, living in a village you had never heard of. Head up, back straight, smile!*

Letitia's father, Comte du Massenet, owned a vast manor near Calais. It had once been graced with twenty servants and a stable full of horses. Letitia remembered the oak table piled with delicacies, and the servants who filed through the arched door of the dining room with silver platters towering with food.

She remembered the day her father announced the obliteration of their wealth. A business venture gone wrong—much of what remained was funded with borrowed money. Letitia's mother had locked herself in her rooms for days, sobs muted behind the gilt-edged doors. One by one the horses were sold, except for her father's grey mare. Their meals became silent as they ate thin onion soup, the servants sent packing, the aromas of game and baked pastries no longer emanating from the kitchens. Letitia's aunt arranged a meeting with the duc. The preparations for his arrival took many days. Money was found for almond pastries and other delicacies. Letitia's only remaining good dress was adjusted and mended. Roses were placed in vases around the manor and their one servant dusted and polished the furniture.

Letitia sat opposite the duc in the drawing room, blushing as his gaze flitted over her, from her averted blue-grey eyes, to her legs buried beneath layers of white chiffon. Later, she placed her ear to the door as her father negotiated a regular sum, to be spent on the upkeep of their manor and living expenses.

This was now in the past, and memories were of little help to her here. Turning at the sound of footsteps, she saw one of the mistresses approach, her shoulders swathed in a gauze shawl the same green as her eyes. Her reddish-brown hair was fastened high on her head, with ringlets curling around her neck. Letitia was tongue-tied as the woman astutely examined her.

'Good evening, Letitia. I'm Henriette, we met some days ago. Please, you must join us near the Apollo courtyard—the entertainments are about to start. We can walk together.'

'That's kind of you to tell me—I was in my head, thinking too much, and would have missed everything.'

'There is no such thing as thinking too much,' Henriette said as they strolled toward the château. 'Of course, men would prefer we do not think at all, merely adorn ourselves for their pleasure. I have a game for you. Watch the women tonight, and the fine courtiers. Some live only to please men and others live only to please themselves. Of course, as mistresses, we fall within the former group. It's not impossible, though, to think of ourselves.'

Letitia gave Henriette a sideways look, uncertain how to respond. 'I've not considered this,' she said, 'and have never known women who please themselves. My mother hardly instructed the servants without checking with Father. My presence here is entirely due to the bartering of men. What power could I possibly have?'

Henriette laughed. 'You see child, men are quite stupid and simple. They do not plan, devise, or see subtleties the way we do. This is our advantage. Some might say the bedroom is our advantage, too, but this is rather less dignified. It is a weapon in our arsenal, but a lesser one. The true weapon lies in the use of our minds.'

Letitia nodded, watching the way their shadows pooled over the gold light cast by the candles. Narrow beds of snowdrops lined the path on either side. 'I will observe the women and try to find others like you.' Letitia's eyes met those of her companion and the young girl smiled shyly.

On the east side of the gardens an elaborate stage had been erected, the edges painted with billowing clouds, and its ceilings festooned with glittering chandeliers. The crowd had multiplied, and servants scurried here and there, extra chairs slung over their shoulders. The duc waited at the edge of the throng, his eyes scanning the faces.

'Ah, there you are, Letitia,' he said, taking her arm. 'Come, come, there are seats for you both at the front. Have you been taking good care of her, Henriette?'

'I have. I was worried she might get lost in the gardens. Some of the paths can be confusing.'

'Thank you. Letitia needs to learn many things—negotiating the gardens is just one of them.'

Hugo took Letitia's elbow and guided her to the seats at the front. She reddened, feeling the scores of eyes upon her as a hush fell over the crowd. There were two vacant chairs next to his and the duchesse stared from her seat, her eyes hard. Next to the duchesse were eight chairs for the king and his closest attendants. The three remaining mistresses sat in the second row.

Letitia looked down at her hands. Behind her she could hear the whispers and muffled sniggers of the mistresses. She opened her fan and bit her lip, turning her attention to the delicate painting depicted in the folds—a woman in a field of blue flowers, her suitor kissing her hand. Tears stung her eyes. The babble of conversation gained volume then abruptly stopped. Letitia turned to see the arrival of the king, followed by a small retinue of courtiers and attendants.

The king appeared impatient to be seated, but stood immobile for some moments, radiating a melancholic charisma as he allowed the crowd to stand, bow, and curtsey. His cheeks sagged at the jowls beneath the long, curling hair of his rich brown wig.

The duc made a rapid approach, bowed deeply and escorted

the king to his seat. This was the cue for the entertainments to commence. Yves, the rangy ballet dancer, glided to the front of the stage on splayed feet, his eyes sparkling with delight as he paused, absorbing his moment of glory. His curling blond hair, backlit by the chandeliers, gave him the appearance of an angel slightly past his prime.

'Good evening, Your Royal Highness, Duc and Duchesse d'Amboise, *mesdames et messieurs*. My name is Yves de la Motte, and I am the ballet master for this evening's performance. I would like to introduce the director, Henri du Charlemagne.'

Fervent clapping ensued as a middle-aged, rounded man with a grey wig took to the stage. He squinted at his notes and avoided the eyes of the audience.

'Tonight I am honoured to bring you a performance of the opera ballet *Hésione*, composed by André Campra. We have many famous talents from Paris. The incomparable Fanchon Moreau is our soprano, who plays the part of Hésione, and Charles Hardouin is our baritone in the role of the Sun. I would list all of our illustrious cast, but I am sure you're impatient to be entertained. Thank you, and please enjoy tonight's performance.'

Letitia had heard about opera ballets—her parents had often attended them in Paris. Yet nothing had prepared her for the spectacle. The sweet notes of the strings and harp coalesced with the purity of the performers' voices as they soared in harmony above the crowd.

Fanchon Moreau took centre stage in a silver gown, her pale hair tumbling around her shoulders. As the troupe danced around her, her song electrified the crowd, the flawless notes ringing out in the warm air. She extended her long arms as the song climaxed, and a roar of applause broke out. The dancers leapt and pirouetted in graceful formation around the stage, their costumes shimmering in the candlelight.

After the last act, the guests congregated near the orange grove at the edge of the stone courtyard. Row after row of neatly pruned trees, not yet bearing fruit, dappled the moonlit earth in rippling shadows,

19

the soil raked in precise geometric patterns. In the adjacent courtyard, guests gathered around the central fountain. Liveried servants in blue velvet coats circulated among the crowd, handing out coupes of champagne. Joyous laughter rang out, heated conversations and the clink of glasses could be heard as toasts were made. Letitia followed the duc and duchesse and was comforted by the presence of Henriette by her side. A group of guests swarmed around the king and his attendants formed a line, trying to edge them back.

The duc and duchesse stopped under an oak tree, some distance from the guests. An attendant hovered but the duchesse waved him away, gesticulating at her husband. The duc shifted on his feet, avoiding his wife's eyes. Although Letitia could not hear what was being said, the duchesse's voice was shrill as she wrung her hands and leaned toward him.

'Come,' Henriette said, drawing Letitia away. 'I don't believe you've met Céline, Isabelle, or Héloise.'

Henriette took Letitia's elbow and guided her to the small group of women standing near the fountain of Apollo.

'Good evening, ladies, I would like to present Letitia du Massenet. Letitia, this is Madame Céline de Poitiers, Madame Isabelle Franche-Bastien, and Mademoiselle Héloise d'Aguillons.' The three women's conversation dwindled to silence as they scrutinized the newcomer. Letitia's heart hammered in her chest, but she kept her chin high and forced a smile.

'Good evening, it's a pleasure to meet you all.'

The mistresses nodded and smiled, murmuring their own welcomes as they eyed her dress of lustrous yellow silk. The duc had sent the duchesse's lady's maid to Paris to find it. A contrasting white band accentuated Letitia's small waist.

Héloise spoke first. 'I hear you're from Calais?'

'Near there. You probably wouldn't have heard of the village— Montreuil-sur-Mer.'

'No, I haven't. Well, considering you are from the provinces, you are dressed very well. Can you read?'

Céline interjected. 'Héloise, Letitia is from a noble family, and is most likely far more accomplished than you. You must mind your words.' She smiled, and Letitia noticed the clownish daubs of rouge on her cheeks. 'You must forgive Héloise, my dear. She takes a while to warm to newcomers.'

Héloise had thin lips, painted pink around the edges to make them appear bigger. She was still young, but held herself with a slight stoop. Her reddish-blonde hair was piled in braids on top of her head and she examined Letitia with large grey eyes.

'I saw *The Misanthrope* last week. Have you seen it?'

'Oh, the play by Corneille?'

'Molière. Oh my goodness, you don't know who he is, do you? I suppose there's not much opportunity for culture in…what was the name of your hamlet again?' Héloise sniggered behind her fan.

Letitia flushed. 'I do know his work, but it doesn't matter.'

'Well, we all have to learn somehow. I hope the entertainments enlightened you.'

Henriette glowered at Héloise. 'We were all new here once. It wouldn't hurt you to remember that. Come now, Letitia.'

Letitia allowed herself to be led away toward a row of orange trees, the damp earth beneath giving off a loamy smell. Henriette shook her head, her lips pursed.

'I'm sorry for the way Héloise treated you; she is easily threatened.'

'It's all right. I don't need to be friends with everyone.'

The duc strode over to join them, beaming and shifting from one foot to the other. His thinning brown hair was pulled back and tied at the nape of his neck, and his tailored grey coat fitted his frame to perfection.

'Henriette, I'm going to spirit Letitia away for a few moments. She must meet the king.'

Henriette smiled. 'Of course. I will just admire Apollo; his form is beautifully rendered.' She made her way over to the statue and sat on the fountain's edge.

Hugo led Letitia toward the king, the crowd around him parting

21

to let them through. The king was a giant with wide shoulders and a round girth. Letitia lifted her chin to gaze up at his face for a moment, before lowering into a curtsey.

'Your Majesty, I would like to present Letitia du Massenet.'

'Good evening, it is indeed a pleasure.' The words rolled out, resonant and commanding, but the king's fish-like eyes skimmed the top of her head. Either he was distracted or he deemed her not worthy of notice.

The duc gave a dry laugh and Letitia, glancing to her left, met the stony expression of the duchesse, her cheeks flushed.

'I hear Your Majesty enjoys the hunt?' Letitia attempted. 'What animal is the most challenging to find and kill?'

The king's gaze dropped and he scanned her face for the first time, his eyes dipping to her bosom, which rose and fell in her yellow silk dress.

'The hunt. Yes, it is indeed a great love of mine. The answer to your question would have to be partridges. The birds are intelligent, and adept at concealing themselves. Sometimes the hounds have great trouble in finding them.'

'Thank you, Your Majesty. It is an honour to meet you.'

'Yes, child. You are very fetching with those long fluid arms—I would have liked to see you on the stage, leaping and singing.'

The duc bowed and murmured his thanks, before turning to Letitia. 'You may go back to Henriette now.' He squeezed her hand and his eyes flashed with approval.

A servant edged into the middle of the crowd, ringing a silver bell. 'Dinner is served. Please follow me to the outdoor dining room.'

CHAPTER 4

Maman, look what I found in the orange grove! He was climbing a tree—maybe he likes oranges.' Solange held out a dun-coloured frog, its legs extended and its amphibian eyes bulging.

'Ugh, let it go, quickly! Some of the ladies might faint if they see it. Look at your dress covered in dirt already. This is a very important evening for your father and he won't be able to introduce you to anyone looking like that. Go and find Bérénice—ask her to put you in the dress with the pink rose embroidery. Honestly, that Tomas is a bad influence. You are a young lady, not a milkmaid, or a boy. *Va-t'en!'*

Henriette joined the stream of people who followed the red feather held aloft by a servant. The stone path led them through tall hedges, which opened up to a rectangular clearing. Long tables laden with linen, crystal, and white lilies filled the space, surrounded by gilded cages of exotic birds and silver tubs of tuberoses. Moorish servants stood to attention, their skin inky black and gleaming in the flickering candlelight. They wore turbans sparkling with gold thread and Arabian costumes with bright pink sashes.

The head servant beckoned Henriette over to the furthest table, where she was seated next to Letitia and Romain, the tarot reader. At the head of the table was a red velvet armchair for the king. Actors and dancers milled about, deep in excited conversation. Céline strode toward the head servant, who hovered behind Henriette, her mouth tight, her dark eyes flashing. Cornering the servant, Céline shoved her index finger under his nose. Henriette caught snatches of their conversation—'Scandalous to sit so far away from the duc... Unacceptable.' The man's face, turning a purplish hue, gestured toward a studious man in a dull coat who had been seated next to Romain. A local government official, Henriette knew. The man frowned at the servant, as if sensing bad news.

23

'I'm terribly sorry, sir,' the servant said, 'but there has been a mistake in the seating plan. I do hope you might be gallant enough to exchange places with this lady?'

'The duc promised me a seat at the king's table weeks ago,' the official protested, his voice a nasal whine. 'Where are you proposing I sit?'

The servant waved his feather into the far distance. 'Do you see that table, just near the far hedge? I am sure the king will walk around and meet his subjects—do not be concerned.'

'I am not concerned but offended. Have I upset the duc in some way, to be so unfairly demoted? I pushed the permits through for him to build his menagerie last summer. This is an outrage.'

The servant scratched his wig with one finger and let out a loud exhalation, waving his drooping feather.

Romain cleared his throat. 'May I be so rude as to interrupt? That table is occupied by the Comte de Vermandois, the Duc du Polignac, and the most fetching Marquise Françoise le Beauregard. It is fairly dripping with noble blood. Might I suggest, dear fellow, that if you were to become friendly with these esteemed members of the court, you might be granted an audience with His Majesty. So, would you be so kind as to allow this lady to rest her feet?'

The official gave a slight nod, bowed his head to Céline, and rose from the chair. 'Please, madame, you may take a seat. Good evening.'

Romain, Céline, and Henriette watched the man scuttle away, his eyes fixed on the duc. Céline turned to the tarot reader next to her, her cheeks flushing beneath her rouge.

'Bravo, Monsieur de Villiers, I am most grateful. I can't stand the Comte de Vermandois. He is so vulgar and as fat as a milking cow.'

'It's my pleasure. Your rouge is very beautiful, may I borrow some?'

Without waiting for a reply, Romain reached over and stroked her cheek with a tapered index finger. He patted his red-tipped finger over his own cheekbones and smiled in a glimmer of white teeth.

Céline laughed into her hand, a girlish chuckle. 'Well, well, you are a naughty man. Are you going to steal my lip colour too?'

Romain leaned forward, placing his hand on her lap. 'A very good question, madame. And how might you suggest I do that?'

'I think you know, monsieur. Perhaps one day I might give you the opportunity to try. Until that time, we shouldn't ignore our friends. I am sorry, Henriette, Letitia.' Céline prised Romain's hand from her lap and sat back in her chair.

❧

Henriette watched the exchange with amusement and unease. Céline, as far as Henriette was aware, had only ever flirted with the duc in public. She wondered about her intentions.

The king, duc and duchesse entered the clearing, after which the head servant clapped three times. Everyone rose and waited for the royal party to take their places. 'Your Majesty, Duc and Duchesse d'Amboise, esteemed guests. Welcome to the Château d'Amboise. Please take your seats and dinner will be served.'

Henriette then sat in silence, content to watch the scene. Letitia was drawn into reluctant conversation with an elderly count, Comte d'Auvergne, and she fidgeted, her eyes darting toward Henriette. A string quartet played a pastorale, the notes clear and sweet among the chatter of conversation and occasional burst of laughter.

As Henriette had grown older, she found that she enjoyed conversation less and often wished to be alone. Solitude was a rarity at the château. Surveying her companions, she could almost see the cogs of Romain and Céline's brains working, assessing the table for opportunities, potential dalliances, and those who could assist them. Henriette sighed, took a sip of wine, and placed her linen napkin on her lap. The scent of garlic preceded the servant arriving with her entrée—ballotine of quail, seasoned with tarragon, and served on a bed of roasted asparagus.

'Ah, Letitia, your entrée is here. Quickly, you must start before it gets cold.'

The old gentleman kept talking, unaware the conversation had long been over.

Letitia leaned over and whispered in Henriette's ear. 'The

Comte d'Auvergne was telling me all about his stomach problems. Apparently he has trouble with his digestion. It could be rather noisy after he has eaten.'

Henriette laughed into her napkin and picked up her cutlery. The quail was cooked to golden crispness, and its intense flavour halted her conversation for a moment. She was about to speak when the duc appeared behind her.

Hugo leant over Letitia's shoulder. 'Letitia, I just wanted to see how you were faring? Ah, you have your entrée, very good. And some red wine? It's from Burgundy, the best grapes of the season.' He turned to Romain, 'Monsieur de Vaillet, is it?'

'No, Your Grace. I am Monsieur de Villiers.'

'Yes, the tarot reader. I hope you are entertaining everyone with your tricks. Like a circus, but with cards, is that right?'

'Not quite, Your Grace. The tarot is a form of divination, practised by many but understood by few. I have been a student to its intricacies for many years and have become quite adept at prediction. Perhaps I might do a reading for you at some stage?'

The duc gave a humourless laugh, almost a cough. 'No, you may save your performing for the ladies of the château, and my wife. She is partial to mystical madness. Enjoy your dinner, monsieur.'

'I'll see you after the *plat principal*.' Henriette heard him whisper in Letitia's ear. His eyes were tender and he clasped Letitia's hand for a moment, circling his thumb on her palm.

Letitia blushed and nodded, eyes downcast. Henriette watched her, trying to decide if her feelings mirrored those of the duc. She decided if they did not, they soon would. Henriette felt a sense of foreboding—the duchesse was accustomed to the presence of mistresses in her home, but would not tolerate her husband developing real feelings for one of them.

Céline frowned and stabbed at her quail, the juices spattering the bodice of her dress. Romain reached over and dabbed at the specks of oil with his napkin. 'Never mind, madame, the stains are tiny and no one will notice, unless they are studying your magnificent bosom.'

'Monsieur, are you always this forward? I would hope that you found my face more intriguing than my bosom.'

'Indeed I do. You have soulful eyes.'

Henriette sighed and pushed the remainder of her quail to the side of the plate.

❧

Next to her, Letitia raised her wine glass to her lips and watched the other guests. The court ladies adorned the table, resplendent in brocades and silks, their hair powdered, twisted into intricate styles, and threaded with gemstones. Their rouged cheeks were decorated with artificial beauty spots and their throats and ears glittered with lavish diamond necklaces and earrings.

The dark faces of the Moorish servants blended into the shadows, with only the gold thread of their costumes and the whites of their eyes gleaming in the candlelight. The servants bent at the shoulder of each guest, serving the *plat principal*, veal with carrots, fennel and orange.

Letitia noticed a woman in green silk, her long white fingers fluttering at her décolletage as she reached out with her other hand to stroke the servant's tunic, laughter bubbling from her mouth, lips stained dark red with wine.

The duc's baritone travelled the length of the table as he regaled the king with a story of a recent hunt. The duchesse stared, bored, into the distance.

'Are you all right?' asked Henriette, touching Letitia's wrist. 'You seem far away. Do you not like veal?'

'I was admiring the dresses and jewels of the ladies,' Letitia said. 'I do like veal, but there is just so much to take in.'

'Eat, it's truly delicious. The tartness of the orange is perfect.' A parrot squawked behind them, and Letitia felt the draught from its wings as it flapped on its stand. The warm air carried the scent of hyacinths from another part of the garden.

'What can I expect when the duc tires of me?' Letitia whispered. 'He can't be besotted forever.'

'Perhaps not, but he will always be courteous. He is incapable of bad manners.' Henriette smiled. 'But you need not concern yourself, your beauty is pure and your heart is good—he will not tire of you for a long, long time.'

Letitia was about to reply, when she noticed the duc beckoning to her. She excused herself and made her way over.

The duc had a soufflé set before him, and had pushed the remainder of his veal to the side. The king, an empty ramekin in front of him, swilled his red wine at an alarming pace.

'His Majesty wished for soufflé and wanted me to share the experience. It is heavenly—you must try it. Vanilla.' Hugo held his spoon up to Letitia's mouth with a teasing smile. The duchesse looked on, her chin raised, her eyes glacial. The girl froze. If she were to taste the dessert, the older woman would be shamed, whereas disobeying the duc was an unthinkable affront made worse by the presence of the king. Her heart thudding, Letitia leaned forward and closed her mouth around the silver. The taste of airy vanilla bean infused her tongue. The duchesse's face flushed maroon as she flung down her napkin and fled the table.

The duc gave a short, nervous laugh and nodded to Letitia. She understood she had been dismissed.

Letitia frowned as she returned to her seat. Whispering in Henriette's ear, Letitia gestured discreetly toward the arched opening in the hedge through which the duchesse had fled. Henriette rose, picked up her skirts, and hastened away.

'So, tell me how you know the duchesse?' Céline asked Romain, her feline eyes languid as she studied him.

'We're both from Chartres. My father was an intendant and worked with Charlotte's father to curb government corruption. We spent more time together as we grew older.'

'It sounds as though you were courting her?'

Romain's lips curved in a half smile. 'She was a ravishing girl, long-limbed and of a bright nature. I was in love with her, all the boys were. And, yes, we spent hours entwined under a beech tree, talking about philosophy and art. It was then that I first became interested in the unseen, and years later, the tarot. It was a most peculiar thing,' Romain mused. 'I would hear Charlotte's thoughts before she spoke them and could discern her mood before she had even arrived at the tree. Nothing like this had ever happened to me before, and at first I was afraid.'

'What stopped you being afraid?' Céline asked.

'I realised we had a deep connection, that our minds were linked in an unusual way. She felt it too. After a while, her thoughts rushed into my head like a waterfall. There was no stopping them. While we were thrilled at this unexpected intimacy, we were young, and it was, at times, overwhelming…' Romain's voice trailed off. With a start, he came back to himself. 'Forgive me, madame, for my childish tales. You are an attentive listener.' Reaching out, he picked up her hand and brushed his lips over it.

Céline leaned forward. 'Tell me more.'

'I cannot, madame. It's a private story, between the duchesse and myself. Let me study you—you have something erotic about you, but submerged. I would like very much to bring it to the surface and let it breathe.'

CHAPTER 5

Céline sidled up behind the duc as he bent over his mahogany dressing table, splashing water on his face. She wrapped her arms around his waist, her breath brushing his ear.

'Céline, you startled me. You have the footsteps of a cat. I would appreciate your knocking.' He dried his face with a linen towel.

'You ignored me last night.' Céline ran a hand over his chest, tucking her fingers beneath his shirt.

'The king required my attention. You're being childish.'

'Not just the king,' Céline pouted. 'Your little concubine, too.' Her hand trailed to his breeches and she brushed her lips over the nape of his neck. 'I miss you so much.'

A flicker of irritation crossed Hugo's face as he unhooked the back of her dress and yanked it down, ripping the delicate seams. He dismantled her stays with expert hands, his gaze resting beyond her shoulder as he unbuttoned his breeches, sat on the bed and drew her to him. Fondling her breast with one hand, he gripped her waist with the other, and plunged into her, his eyes still averted. He rammed with a grimace, his fingernails digging into the flesh of her hips, before shuddering with a low groan. Placing his hands on her waist, he lifted her upright and dismissed her.

'You may go.'

❧

The dirt road leading to Blois was potholed in places and Céline stepped with care, wobbling slightly in her heeled boots.

Thibault, the coachman, had been brushing a horse when she poked her head around the door of the stables earlier that afternoon, looking for a ride into the town.

'Not until four o'clock,' he said, glancing up at her, his arm moving in circular motions across the horse's gleaming rump.

She frowned. 'Where is Raoul? Or Bénédict? Why is only one of you on duty? This is unacceptable.'

'They have gone into the town to see their families and attend mass. It is Sunday, madame,' he replied.

'And why, may I ask, are you not able to take me?'

'The master has instructed me to groom the horses. He said no one would need to go anywhere today.'

Céline rolled her eyes and left, cursing the coachman under her breath.

It had taken her almost an hour to reach Blois by foot. Peering out from under the brim of her straw hat, Céline sighed with relief when she saw the church spires on the horizon. Several farmers passed on a horse-drawn cart, shouting bawdy greetings, the wheels of the cart sending clouds of dust into her path.

The sky was a brittle blue and the sun scorched her back as she hobbled into the town, her cheeks flushed and perspiring, her legs aching and her heels blistered.

Céline made her way to a stone house at the edge of town, next to the tannery. Its door had not seen paint for years and the grime-smeared windows were closed to prevent fumes from invading interior rooms. A number of the terracotta roof tiles were either broken or missing, and open gutters in front ran with the dun-coloured liquids used to soften the leather. The stench was overpowering and Céline held her handkerchief up to her nose as she rapped on the door.

The door opened a crack and the bloodshot grey eyes of Arnaud de Poitiers stared through the gap, widening when he recognized his wife. 'It's you. Have you got some money for me?' he demanded in a wheezy croak.

'Are you planning on letting me in?' Céline asked. 'I can hardly breathe out here.'

Arnaud waved her inside, appraising her fashionable dress and pearl-drop earrings. They sat opposite each other in front of the fire, on threadbare armchairs.

31

'I have debts as you know,' Arnaud began. 'You must do something to help me. Sell your earrings.'

Céline cringed, her hand fluttering upwards to touch the tear-shaped drops—a gift from the duc when she had still been favoured.

'I will see what I can do.'

'Would you like some brandy?' Arnaud retrieved a chipped decanter and two cloudy glasses from the sideboard.

The room looked much as Céline remembered it. A layer of dust covered the stone floor tiles, and the walls were dotted with white squares where oil paintings had once hung. Glancing toward the bedroom, she saw a flimsy canvas cot. Their carved oak four-poster was long gone, sold after an early loss at faro. Curlicues of smoke drifted through a dim shaft of light from the window.

Her husband sat, hunched over his clay pipe, his face sunken and haggard, etched in grimy lines. A tangle of grey hair reached his shoulders. The shadows under his cheekbones deepened as he inhaled.

'Yes, I would like some brandy,' Céline replied. 'It's been a long walk.'

With a shaking hand, Arnaud poured a glass for each of them and passed her one, sloshing brandy on her boot.

Céline took a sip and felt the liquid warmth burn her throat. 'I see you've sold my Chinese chest. It was the only piece of furniture I had left from my mother.'

'It was a useless object. We didn't need it. I had people bashing on the door, day and night. Couldn't sleep. What could I do? You've lost touch, Céline, living in a château. You no longer understand what it is to be poor.'

'I loved that chest, Arnaud. *You* are the thing that is useless. As for poverty—once experienced, it is never forgotten. There are some objects that have meaning and memory. You have no sentiment left in your heart. All you care about is filling your mouth with drink, gaming, and throwing away money.'

'That's not true. I care about you, Céline. I care about the fact that my wife prostitutes herself for money. When I walk in the streets, people whisper behind their hands. In the tavern, the men call me a cuckold. How do you think I feel, as a man, to have lost the respect of my neighbors?'

Céline drained her glass, her chest tight. 'A prostitute, am I?' she spat. 'And how do you think you can afford to live such a dissolute life? Do you think God pays for it? It is the patronage of the duc, you fool. You can forget about your money. I'm going.' She rose, slammed her glass on the sideboard, and made for the door, her skirts rustling.

Arnaud leapt to his feet, his eyes wild. 'I'm sorry, dear one. That was a terrible thing to say. You are a gift from God, a blessing in my wretched life. Forgive me,' he pleaded, kneeling before her with a bowed head, clutching at her skirts. His other hand crept beneath her dress and made a tentative journey up her calf. 'You are still beautiful, Céline. And you smell like a goddess.' He gazed up at her, his voice plaintive. His hand felt calloused and rough against her skin.

Céline's face was expressionless as she stared down at him. Beneath the deep lines and dirt on his face, she saw glimpses of the younger man who had scaled trees to pick her apples and undone her bodice with gentle fingers. She remembered impassioned words whispered in her ear and his polite diffidence on meeting her father. It was difficult to believe the dishevelled, skeletal figure before her was the same man.

'I was not a beautiful girl, and I am not a beautiful woman. Save your lies and remove your hand. You don't deserve it, but I will try to find the money. Understand that you are my husband in name only and I find you pathetic. Good day.'

Céline's heels were bloody by the time she reached the stone gateposts at the edge of the town. Removing her boots, she leaned against a fencepost. The sound of horses' hooves and the creak of wheels caused her to glance up.

An old man with grey teeth smiled at her as he tightened the reins on his mare, her coat the same shade as his smile. 'You look like you need a ride, madame.'

'Yes, thank you,' Céline replied, rising to her feet. 'I am going to the Château d'Amboise.'

He shifted over to make space for her, a sparkle in his rheumy eyes. 'Please, take a seat.'

Céline's thoughts drifted as the cart clattered away. She was preoccupied with the fate of Sabine Rousseau-Cologne, the duc's ex-mistress, now disgraced and banished, without any means of support.

No one except the duc knew the precise reason for Sabine's dismissal, but there had been talk of items pilfered from the duchesse's rooms. Rumours had filtered back to the château, of Sabine's descent into the pleasure halls of Toulouse, servicing soldiers from a back room. Céline shuddered, glad of the sunlight warming her back, and grateful that while she was out of favour, she had, at least, a roof over her head and coins in her pocket.

With sudden alarm, Céline realised they were headed toward the château's main entrance. 'Please, turn left here.' She pointed in the direction of the side gate, near the stables.

Thanking the driver, she waved him off and he tipped his cap. Céline glanced around to see if anyone had witnessed her ignominious arrival—only the horses, snorting in their stalls.

The château halls were quiet, scented with roses. A maid, atop a ladder, polished an immense gilt mirror. The Persian carpets muffled Céline's footsteps as she limped toward the doors of her small rooms. Passing a side passage, she heard a snuffling noise and jumped at the sight of Letitia, sitting against the wall. She hugged her legs and wept in near silence.

Céline crouched before her. 'Letitia? Are you all right?'

The girl started and looked up. Despite her swollen eyes she was radiant. Her skin glowed with health and her cheeks were flushed pale pink. A smooth lock of hair curled on one creamy shoulder.

Céline was speechless for a moment, absorbed in a gaze so wide and pure she understood the duc's obsession. Pain knifed through her heart and for a moment she could not breathe.

'Whatever is wrong, child? Surely it can't be so very bad?'

'You don't need to concern yourself. I'm sure you have your own worries,' Letitia said as she wiped her nose with a lace handkerchief.

'We all do, my dear, but it means we can better understand the problems of others. Unburden yourself—it will take the weight from your heart.'

Letitia hesitated, before confiding in a half-sob. 'I miss my mother terribly. And my home, too. My maid, Françoise, and my horse. There are so many rules here. I don't understand them,' she hiccuped, her eyes awash with a film of tears.

'There, there,' purred Céline, patting Letitia's hand as she lowered herself to the floor next to the girl. 'I can teach you everything you need to know, don't fret. It's not as difficult as you might imagine. Just be yourself and follow my guidance. At least you have the duc's favour, although that, too, can be fleeting.'

'What do you mean, fleeting?'

'When someone has so much power, their attention span can be limited. They can flutter away to something new, just as you are becoming accustomed to their attention. But don't you worry, with your beauty you should be able to hold his attention for quite some time.'

CHAPTER 6

'Ten, nine, eight, seven...'

Solange could hear Tomas counting in the hallway. Exhilarated by the thought of finding a secret hiding place, she darted down a passage and into a neglected bedroom, unoccupied since its previous mistress had been banished years ago. The air was thick with dust and she coughed as the motes tickled her throat. An enormous four-poster bed, with festooned curtains of green embroidered silk, dominated the room. Solange ducked behind the lustrous fabric and spluttered again as a cloud of dust billowed.

Footsteps could be heard outside the door, followed by muffled voices. Solange stood rigid, her breath shallow as the door creaked open. The voices were clear now, and impassioned. Through a small gap in the curtain, she saw Duchesse Charlotte and Romain de Villiers, the tarot reader, enter and close the door behind them. Solange's heart thudded in her chest and she swallowed the tickle in her throat.

'I wish to know him better,' said Romain.

'What right do you have? There is no need to confuse him.'

Romain's hand caressed the curve of the duchesse's breast and lingered there. He ran a finger down her jaw with the other hand and pressed his lips hard against hers. The only sound was a low murmur from the duchesse as she yielded to his kiss. He drew her closer, clasping her around the waist. Solange's eyes widened and she held her breath.

The duchesse pulled away, struggling for breath. 'You mustn't do that, Romain. I am a married woman.'

'You are so beautiful, Charlotte, I cannot help myself. But it is not just you that draws me here. I wish to know Tomas. Will the duc object to my presence?'

'Hugo cannot object. He denies me attention and loves the child he calls his new mistress. If I wish it, then you may stay.'

'I know you still love me, Charlotte. I can see it in your eyes.'

The duchesse smiled and took his hand, placing a tender kiss on each finger, her gaze fixed upon his face. 'You have beautiful fingers, Romain. And you are the naughtiest man I've ever known. Love? Let's not speak of it. Love is the cause of all my troubles. We must go back. You take the stairs.'

Solange watched as they crept out, Romain's palm pressed against the small of the duchesse's back.

&

The live mistresses sat together as the maids served them breakfast. Letitia shifted in her seat, the stiff upholstery digging into her back. The only sound was the tinkling of silver against china.

Letitia sipped her hot chocolate and toyed with the triangles of buttered toast on her plate. Her stomach roiled as she took a small bite, aware of the suspicious eyes of Céline and the penetrating stare of Héloise. A wave of nausea rushed through her and she pushed herself upright, holding the edge of the table.

'Excuse me, I will be back shortly,' Letitia said in a clipped voice. She made for the door, maintaining a regal pace.

As soon as she was out of sight, Letitia dashed to the washroom at the foot of the stairs, which housed a chamber pot. She crouched, retching violently into the pot, holding onto the wall as the room spun around her. Wiping her mouth with the towel, Letitia rose to her feet and tried to compose herself.

A soft rapping sounded on the door. Checking her dress for vomit, Letitia opened the door and edged out. She shut the door behind her, aware of the sour smell in the washroom. Céline faced her, a furrow of concern between her brows.

'Are you all right, dear? You're looking decidedly pale.'

'Yes. It's kind of you to be worried. I'm just not feeling hungry this morning, and didn't get enough sleep.'

'Well perhaps you'll need a nap this afternoon. I do it all the time. Sleeping during the day leaves one feeling very refreshed. Now, I'll just slip past you to use the washroom—'

Letitia grasped Céline's hand and gave a terse smile. 'I wouldn't go in there if I were you. I was just about to call for a maid—someone has left an unsavoury deposit.'

'Goodness, that sounds awful. But fortunately nothing shocks me. If you would just let me pass'

'No, Céline, I almost vomited it was so terrible. You really must wait.'

'That's the trouble, child. At my age, there is no such thing as waiting and the other washroom is quite far.'

At that moment a young maid was passing with a duster. Letitia waved her over. 'Would you please clean the chamber pot? Immediately.'

The girl curtsied and went inside.

Céline eyed her. 'Letitia, you look positively green. You can tell me. I know you're not feeling well.'

'I'm perfectly fine, thank you. I thought you needed the washroom? You had better go to the other one, before it's too late. This one isn't ready.'

Céline nodded and smiled, her eyes glinting as the maid reappeared, a towel draped over the chamber pot in her hands. The girl's footsteps clicked on the parquetry and she headed for the servants' quarters, the unmistakable odour of vomit trailing in her wake.

Céline's nose twitched. 'You're right. I'd best find it now.'

Henriette watched Céline return to the table with a flickering smile. Céline shook out her napkin and sat straight-backed in her chair, her thoughts passing over her face like wisps of cloud chased by the wind. Henriette mused idly that it must be exhausting to be Céline, with her constant schemes and calculated moves.

Charlotte arrived moments later and Céline spoke to her in a low voice before handing her a note. The duchesse tucked it into her sleeve and sat down.

'Where is Letitia?' Henriette asked.

'How should I know?' Céline muttered through a mouthful of boiled egg.

Henriette rose, excused herself, and strode toward the door. The corridor was empty and a sour smell lingered in the air. A maid rounded the corner.

'Have you seen Mademoiselle du Massenet?'

'Yes, she went outside, toward the fountain of Apollo. She seemed a little unwell, madame.'

'Thank you.'

Letitia sat hunched on the edge of a fountain, her hair coming loose from its pins and obscuring her face.

'Letitia, whatever is wrong?'

The girl looked up, shading her eyes from the sun. Her skin had a greyish cast and her eyes were lined with dark circles.

'Good day, Henriette. Thank you for your concern, but you should have just finished your breakfast.'

'Was Céline bothering you?'

'Oh, she just likes to know everything.'

'I must ask you, when did you last bleed?'

Letitia clutched her stomach and winced. 'I'm not sure, maybe six weeks ago.'

'Do you understand what a late bleed means?'

The girl shook her head. She dipped her hands in the water of the fountain, patted her cheeks with dampened fingers, and took several deep breaths.

'You could be with child. When a woman is with child, it can be near impossible to eat—at first, anyway.'

Letitia met Henriette's gaze, her eyes wide. 'It cannot be true. I don't feel old enough to be a mother.'

'If your bleeding doesn't start soon, then you must accept that you are with child, which is always a blessing. You'll see. Come to my rooms, I have a special herbal tea that might calm your stomach.'

❧

It seemed to Letitia that wherever she went in the château, Céline lay in wait. Her words flowed over her—cajoling, charming, educating. Céline never stopped talking, and sometimes the girl felt overwhelmed by the older woman's intensity. Being with Céline felt like being trapped in a whirlpool, her destination chaotic and unknown. The elder mistress left little notes outside her door, inviting her to walk in the rose garden. Cups of tea and books of ponderous prayers were often delivered by Céline's servant. Céline had a purpose, Letitia was sure of it, but she had yet to discover what it was.

Letitia was strolling in the garden one morning, admiring the pink and red peonies planted in neat rows on either side of the path. She tried not to think about the possibility of something growing inside her—the inexorable formation of tiny fingers and toes, rosebud mouth, and spindly legs. Letitia feared motherhood—there was so much she didn't know and understand. How could she hope to guide a small person, be responsible for him, when she had so much to learn herself? Letitia wanted her own mother near her, not to become one herself. Yet, she knew a baby made her position in this hostile place more secure. She heard Céline's approach before she saw her. After being pursued with such fervor, she recognized her shuffling footsteps and her habitual clearing of her throat.

'Hello, Letitia. I have a favour to ask—I'd like to go riding this morning. Last time I went, I had a terrible fall, was bruised all over, and injured my arm. I want to gain confidence again. It's…' Céline's eyes filmed over with tears and she dabbed at them with a handkerchief, averting her gaze. 'It's been very hard to work up the courage. I'm told you're an excellent rider. Please tell me you'll come with me.'

'I'm not an expert.'

'Perhaps. But at least you'll be safe on your mount and able to help me if I tumble. Please.'

Céline's face was flushed and desperate beneath her twin spots of rouge. The girl's stomach flipped at the thought of a lurching horse, stirring up the nausea she struggled to keep at bay.

'I suppose so. When did you want to go?'

'How about now? I could quickly change and meet you at the stables.'

'Yes, I'll meet you there.'

☙

At the stables, Céline tapped her foot on the dusty ground and watched the path from the château. The stableboy had saddled the horses—a grey mare and a young stallion with a gleaming black coat. She had chosen the mare, Béatrice, for herself, familiar with her gentle ways. The black horse, Hochert, was new to the stables and pawed the ground with jerky movements, snorting in wild gusts of breath.

'Hochert's not been ridden much,' the stable boy warned her. 'He does like to jump over logs and he's keen to get going. You know what these younger ones are like, more energy than sense. My mother says the same about me,' he said with a grin.

Hearing footsteps they both turned as Letitia approached in the distance.

'Which horse did you want for the young lady, madame?'

'Hochert will be perfect, thank you.'

'I'm not sure that's a good idea, madame. He needs a firm and experienced hand.'

'As I said, he will be perfect. Find him a saddle,' Céline told the boy, her gaze cold and imperious. 'Are you ready, Letitia?' she said brightly as the girl drew alongside. 'I have selected the most beautiful horse in the stable for your ride. This is Hochert. Isn't he gorgeous?'

Hochert pawed the ground, sending up billows of dust beneath his hooves. His eyes had a crazed glint and he bared his teeth with a snort.

'Yes, I haven't seen him before. Is he new to the stables?'

'I don't believe so. I think he's just been hiding in the back, eating all the time. Look at his fat stomach!'

Letitia frowned. The horse was svelte and muscular.

'Let's go.'

The boy approached and helped Letitia into the saddle, handing her the reins, before doing the same with Céline. He waved them off, reminding both women to stay on the forest trails.

Céline and Letitia set off across the field, the sun dappling the yellow stalks of grass that grew on either side. The forest was a blue and grey mass of cedar trees in the distance, impenetrable and gloomy. Letitia held fast to the reins, adjusting to the erratic pace of her mount. Hochert refused to respond to her pull on the reins, or to the nudge of her foot to his flank. Instead, he pranced sideways, ignoring Letitia's attempts to direct him. Jostled on his back, Letitia's stomach roiled and the nausea rose sweet and heavy in the back of her throat.

Céline smiled at her, holding Béatrice to a steady gallop.

'Turn him toward the forest, I want to go on the trails.'

'I'm trying,' Letitia called, 'but he seems to have a mind of his own.'

'Kick his flanks—hard.'

Letitia gave Hochert a firm kick, her hands maintaining a white-knuckled grip on the reins. The horse nickered and galloped faster, the landscape a greenish blur in her peripheral vision. The wind ripped through her hair and her hat whirled away into the distance. Too late, Letitia glimpsed a rock concealed in the grass. Hochert stumbled, let out a deafening whinny and lurched forward, sending Letitia flying over his head and crumpling to the ground with a sickening thump.

Céline pulled Béatrice to a stop and dismounted, surveying the scene with cool detachment. Letitia lay still, her eyes closed, a trickle of blood at the side of her mouth, her face ashen. Céline took Letitia's wrist, felt for a pulse, then rose and mounted her horse.

CHAPTER 7

Henriette placed a wet cloth on Letitia's forehead. The girl's face was white and she had barely spoken in the days following the accident.

The duc's physician, Doctor Mouret, had frowned at Letitia's broken ankle and strapped it with bandages. 'She was very lucky to have only broken her ankle and bruised her ribs. She will recover, but it may take some weeks.'

After the doctor's examination Henriette confided, in hushed tones, of Letitia's possible pregnancy. 'She has not bled in two months and has suffered nausea and dizziness.'

The doctor nodded. 'There would be bleeding, if there were a miscarriage. We can only hope this does not happen in the next few days. Keep a close eye, and let me know.'

The following day, the duc burst through the doors of Letitia's room, his shirt ties undone, his eyes bloodshot. The Duchesse Charlotte, it appeared, had kept news of Letitia's accident from him.

'How is she?' he asked Henriette. 'My poor darling girl.' He sat on the bed and stroked Letitia's hair, taking her hand in his.

Letitia's lips turned up in a wan smile. 'Hello, Hugo. I'm all right, really.'

'Don't be silly. Of course you're not all right. The doctor told me about the possibility of a baby?'

Henriette curtsied and withdrew from the room, closing the doors gently behind her.

Céline lay in wait at the bottom of the stairs, a stricken expression on her face.

'How is the dear girl? Oh, I feel terrible, Henriette. I shouldn't have let her ride so fast.'

'Letitia will be fine, although confined to bed for a few weeks, I imagine. Her ankle is broken and she has bruised her ribs. Which horse was she riding?'

'Oh, I forget his name. A spirited one, though, to be sure.'

Henriette raised an eyebrow. 'Spirited? Wild, more like. I suppose your mount was more docile?'

'Indeed she was. I thought Letitia's horse looked quite calm, but once he sped up, there was no stopping him.'

Henriette sighed. 'I see. She really shouldn't have been riding in the first place. Good day, Céline.'

Charlotte was accustomed to hearing the murmurs and chatter of the women in the drawing room. She knew all their moods from the tone of their voices—from gossip, to bickering, to mirth. Out of habit, she paused at the door to listen; she liked to gather information, to know if they were keeping anything from her. Today the women sounded different. Something was amiss. Ear pressed to the door, Charlotte could make out gasps of surprise and rapid interjections, each tumbling out faster than the one before. Sighing, she pushed the door open and entered.

Héloise, Céline, Henriette, and Isabelle rose to their feet and each dropped into a curtsey.

'Good afternoon, ladies. Please, relax and keep talking. I am just looking for my embroidery hoop. Has anyone seen it?'

The women shook their heads and returned to their seats, except Héloise, who remained standing. 'No, Your Grace, I have not seen it. Perhaps the maids have tidied it away. Come and sit with us.'

Charlotte suppressed a wave of irritation—she did not want to be drawn into their conversation, she just wanted to know what they had been talking about with such fervor.

'Summertime is here,' Héloise said as she settled her skirts around her chair. 'I was walking in the fields near the town and the ewes were in season, the cows, too. Lots of little calves and lambs have been born. I just adore this time of the year, don't you? Of course, it's not just the animals that are multiplying. Summer is a busy time for people, too. '

Charlotte was familiar with Héloise's tendency to skirt around gossip, to tease it out for maximum enjoyment. She found it tedious and her eyes darted to the door. Specific questions needed to be asked and answered, by her and the other mistresses. Her patience left her.

'Héloise, summer is indeed a lovely time of the year. I enjoy the orange and pink roses in the garden. Yet the multiplication of farm animals has never really held my attention. Did you perhaps grow up on a farm, to be so fascinated with the base habits of these creatures?'

The women giggled behind their hands and Héloise's cheeks flamed red. 'No,' she replied stiffly. 'I grew up in a convent, Your Grace. St Francis de Baumiere, near Arles. Perhaps you are prudish about God's creatures, but I am not. They do reflect our human impulses.'

Charlotte watched the blotches of pink spread from Héloise's face to her neck and décolletage.

'Héloise, I am going to the garden to gather some flowers for my rooms, so if you could get to the point, I would appreciate it.'

Héloise pursed her lips and false empathy flooded her features, like a curtain being drawn across a stage. 'It is Letitia, Your Grace. She is with child.' The news imparted, Héloise sat back with a triumphant air.

The duchesse straightened her back, holding Héloise's gaze as a sharp pain seized her chest. She clasped her hands together to stop them trembling. 'Well, that is lovely news for her. I'm sure she will make a very sweet maman. Now, I will go and collect the flowers before they wilt in the afternoon sun. Good day.'

Shutting the door behind her, Charlotte stumbled to her rooms, her breath coming fast in her throat, her heart thudding in her chest. Leaning against the column of her four-poster, she felt a warm trickle edge down her thigh, and lifted her skirt. Her linens, fastened with a belt around her waist, were drenched in vivid blood.

She let her skirt drop and stared absently at the trail of blood dotted and glistening on the parquetry. Then the tears came. She sobbed and hit the bedpost with her palm.

The doors flung open and Yolande, the duchesse's head maid, hurried in. Her rounded face paled as her gaze fell to the floor. 'Your Grace, oh dear me! Your bloods have arrived. Please, give the linens to me and I'll fetch new ones.'

Charlotte removed the linens from beneath her skirt, and flung them at the girl's feet. 'Take them. Take them!' she wailed, beating her fists on her stomach.

Charlotte collapsed on her bed, her body shaking with sobs.

'I will be right back, Your Grace.'

The duchesse's voice was muffled beneath her hands. 'I don't care if you come back. What does it matter? I cannot make more life. I am wasted on this earth. I am nothing.'

Charlotte was almost asleep when Céline crept up beside her and stroked her hair. 'Charlotte, being Letitia's friend is not going to work,' she whispered. 'This baby changes everything, do you see? It is a battle now—it is war.'

The duchesse took Céline's hand in her own and gave a small nod.

The stables were quiet, other than the snuffling and pawing of horses as Henriette entered. Thibault was alone, arranging bridles on hooks along the wall.

'I need to speak with you.'

'Yes, madame. How can I help?'

'The other day, when Madame de Poitiers and Mademoiselle du Massenet came to ride. Who was on duty?'

'Young Benoît.'

'Where is he now? I need to ask him about what happened.'

'I'm afraid that's not possible, madame. I let the boy go, yesterday, on the instruction of the duc.'

'Why is that?'

Thibault hesitated, his eyes downcast.

'Please, Thibault. Mademoiselle du Massenet could have been killed. You need to tell me why the boy was let go.'

'It's not right, Madame, for me to tell you. So keep this to yourself.'

She nodded in assent.

'The horse was half wild, barely fit to be ridden. We were going to train him more. Benoît was intimidated by the lady and allowed it. So the duc was angry and insisted I let him go.'

'Thank you, Thibault. You've been most helpful.'

Henriette turned and strode through the gardens, her mind jostling with thoughts as she seethed.

The duc hung his head as he approached his wife's rooms. He gave a limp knock on the door, before edging it open. Charlotte's slumped form twitched at the sound of his voice and she buried her head in the pillow.

'Go away.'

He sighed, lowered himself onto the mattress and reached out to touch her hair. She flinched and pulled away.

'Shouldn't you be attending to your little concubine? She needs special care now she is carrying your child.'

'Charlotte.'

'I told you to go, I want to be alone.'

'We can keep trying. You're still young.'

'Don't patronize me, Hugo. That would mean sharing my bed and we both know you no longer wish to do that. I don't want to be a duty. Leave me.'

Her pale hair covered part of her face and the sliver he could see was reddened and shone with tears.

'Pull yourself together, Charlotte. The servants will gossip, and their words go straight to the town. You are a duchesse and you must show strength.'

A manic sound emerged from the shaking figure under the bedclothes—halfway between a sob and a laugh.

The duc rose and retreated from the room.

❧

1690

The grass was as high as Charlotte's waist, tickling her arms as she parted the long stems. Hugo slowed his stride to match hers, his gaze catching hers as he reached for her hand. His brown hair reached his shoulders, curling over his forehead, and his eyes were a deep fathomless blue.

'Where are we going?' he asked.

She laughed. 'I thought you were leading me?'

'It's your father's land. Show it to me.'

'All right. Follow me.'

With a laugh, Charlotte broke into a run, her fair hair fanning out behind. She heard the swish of the grass as Hugo chased her. At the far end of the field the grasses gave way to a stately row of oaks, with a forest path winding between them.

Charlotte had spent hours traipsing this path in her childhood, picking wildflowers and observing squirrels and woodpeckers. As far as she was aware, no one ventured in this forest, other than the woodcutter who supplied her father's enormous fireplaces. As she darted toward the path Hugo caught her and spun her around.

'You're meant to be following me, not catching me!'

'Your waist was demanding to be caught.' He ran a finger along the blue ribbon encircling her waist and she could see the sun reflected in his eyes, gold amid blue.

Charlotte took his hand and led him along the shaded path edged with wildflowers. 'Come. I have something else to show you.'

Sunlight poured in shifting patterns through the canopy above, casting the shadows of trees onto the grass beneath.

A giant beech tree dominated a small clearing, its branches extending outward from an immense knotted trunk, twisted toward the sky.

'My tree,' Charlotte said, tracing the bark with her finger. 'I bring picnics here, or my embroidery. Sometimes I climb it,' she grinned. 'Which makes Mother very cross.'

Moss grew thick at the base of the trunk. Hugo sat, and taking her hand, drew her down next to him. 'So, mademoiselle, do you want to tell me why a girl like you is still unmarried at the age of twenty?'

'Mother says I'm choosy. Father says I'm willful. Take your pick. Perhaps I don't care enough.'

Hugo smiled, leaning closer to kiss her mouth. Despite the pleasure of his kiss, Charlotte felt a pang of guilt. While the beech was her tree, it also belonged to Romain. As Hugo's hand fluttered over her breasts, she wondered where he was and what he was doing.

Several chairs clattered to the ground as the mistresses jumped to their feet. Charlotte watched the frog leap over the teapot, the platter of pastries, and the central flower arrangement. The women squealed and darted away, climbing onto chairs and cringing in the corner. Solange and Tomas raced around the room, clamouring to catch the creature. Tomas managed to seize it by one leg and jam it into a jar. Both children stood with eyes downcast as Charlotte approached them.

'Well? Who let the frog out? We were attempting to have our breakfast.'

'Your Grace, he jumped out...' Solange piped up.

'Solange, there are always mishaps with you. You need to start acting like a lady. Ladies don't keep frogs.'

'It was me,' Tomas admitted as he screwed on the lid.

'Why do you always favour Tomas?' Solange demanded of Charlotte, eyes flashing. 'It's as if you think he's a saint.'

'I'm no saint,' Tomas muttered.

The duchesse tucked her fingers under Tomas's chin. 'No, you're certainly not a saint, young Tomas, but you have potential. Make sure you keep frogs behind glass, unless you're outside, and let Solange play with dolls some of the time.' She patted the boy's head. 'Now Tomas, you must sit down and eat your breakfast. Solange, take the frog back to the nursery.'

'I need you to help me, Romain.'

Charlotte paced the room, a deserted suite tucked away in a forgotten corner of the château. Cobwebs hung like silver lace from the bedposts, and muted light filtered through gauze curtains.

'She is harmless and with child. I can't do it,' Romain said.

Charlotte stifled a sneeze. 'She has stolen my husband.'

'You expect *me* to care about that? I still have feelings for you.'

'Precisely. Which is why you must help me. It won't be difficult to make her situation insecure. You must talk to Céline. She knows how this sort of thing should be done.'

Romain frowned. 'Was Céline behind the accident with the horse?'

'I do not know.'

'My feelings for you are strong, Charlotte. However, you are asking too much. I have my career and Tomas to consider. I want to provide him with an annuity. What of my reputation if my role in this should come to light?'

'Assist me in her fall from grace, and I will ensure Tomas is provided for and that your reputation is secure.'

'How much?'

She leant over, and whispered in his ear. He raised an eyebrow, and his lips turned up slightly. 'That will be sufficient.'

Henriette sat opposite Romain, as he spread the cards on the surface of the table. Her expression was impassive, her mouth pursed. There was something held in and he wondered if she ever gave in to passion. The only part of her that yielded was her eyes, their expression astute but gentle.

'The Ace of Cups, the Lovers, and the Hanged Man. You will embark on a new relationship and it will have the potential, if nurtured, to be a great love. This spread also demonstrates a need to give up small concerns for the greater good, to be selfless. You will be of great benefit to another.'

'I don't believe a word of it.' Henriette dismissed him with a wave of her hand. 'Do you just wait and see what inspiration strikes? Perhaps you would have been better as a playwright.'

Romain frowned and picked up the cards. 'Are you quite knowledgeable about mystical practices? I have studied the art of the tarot for ten years and have many satisfied customers who would vouch for my accuracy.'

Henriette shrugged. 'I'm a pragmatist. What I see and feel is what I believe. Other than God, that is—I do have faith.'

'Is that not a contradiction? You cannot see God, yet you believe in Him. How is the tarot any different from blind faith? At least people witness my predictions come true. What proof do you have of God's existence?'

'I feel Him when I am in the chapel and I see the candles flickering; I feel Him when I hear the mass and the singing of the altar boys. I also feel Him near me when I walk in the forest.'

'And when you make love, madame, do you feel Him?'

She flushed and ignored the question. 'Do you believe in any kind of God?'

'Sometimes. In happier moments, yes; in times of melancholy, less so.'

'Ah, I see. So when you are bedding every woman who is willing, you feel your God. Yet, when someone has the audacity to refuse you, you revert to the state of a despondent disbeliever? I wish you good day.' Henriette rose from her chair and turned, with a swish of her taffeta skirts, to the door. Romain swallowed, shifting in his seat as he shuffled the cards. He had glimpsed heaven as Henriette rose. Perhaps there was a God. Her dress had gaped open at the top of her bodice, revealing the fullness of powdery white bosom.

CHAPTER 8

The carriage was stifling as it lurched along the uneven road to Onzain. The duchesse, seated next to Henriette and Isabelle, fanned herself furiously while Letitia, Céline and Héloïse jostled against one another on the opposite seat. The women sweltered beneath their tight bodices and heavy skirts, perspiration shining on their cheeks and foreheads as they swished their fans back and forth. Charlotte refused to look Letitia in the eye, but her gaze fell often to the younger woman's stomach. Letitia shifted in her seat, placing a protective hand over her belly.

Letitia had recovered well from the accident, and her face was radiant, flushed with good health. It had been Isabelle's idea to have a picnic and enthusiastic preparations had taken place amongst the women. On instructions from the duchesse, the cook and her assistants had spent the previous few days making foie gras, baking bread, and curing meats. Salmon, sponge cake, and other provisions were bought from the town. Isabelle had enlisted Henriette to persuade the duchesse to join them. She had been in hiding for some weeks and had emerged drawn and thin, with dark hollows beneath her cheekbones. Her eyes widened when Thibault brought the carriage around. 'Thibault, where is the other carriage?'

'I am cleaning the others, Your Grace. And the duc has taken one to visit a friend.'

Her face darkened. 'This is outrageous. I gave instructions yesterday for the carriages to be readied for our excursion. Six of us in one carriage in such sweltering weather? Explain yourself.'

'I'm terribly sorry, Your Grace. If you're able to wait an hour I can have a second one ready.'

'If we leave later it will be much too hot,' she snapped. 'Just help me inside.'

'Yes, Your Grace.'

'Henriette, you may sit next to me.' Charlotte patted the leather seat beside her.

As the temperature in the carriage rose, Isabelle beamed, seemingly oblivious to the thick wall of tension. 'Goodness, I'm terribly hungry. I hope Imogene packed the extra ham. I sent her into town this morning to fetch it.' She folded her arms and sighed. 'Such a beautiful day. Letitia, I hope you'll be comfortable enough. There are some extra cushions for you if the ground is too hard.'

'Thank you, Isabelle. I'm perfectly fine.'

Isabelle had Italian ancestry, evident in her limpid brown eyes and glossy dark hair, piled in curls on her head. Always quick with a kind word or entertaining story, she often erupted into gales of laughter. Her warmth was a welcome contrast to the duchesse's chill, Letitia reflected, relieved that Isabelle was accompanying them.

'Oh look, there's the Château de Mirabeau! We must be close now.' Isabelle craned her neck as they passed the enormous turreted estate.

An expansive field dotted with oak trees came into view as the carriage jolted to a stop. The ladies stepped out and smoothed their dresses, shading their eyes as they surveyed the field. Charlotte pointed to a tree near the middle, instructing the servants to set up the carpets beneath it. The two coachmen carried the picnic supplies over the field. Yolande, who had ridden on the back of the carriage, descended from her high perch, red-cheeked and windswept, her dress coated in dust from the road.

Cicada song pulsated around the women as they ambled toward the giant tree, stepping with care to avoid rocks and thistles. The grass came up to their calves in places, tickling them beneath their skirts.

Henriette took Letitia's arm. 'How are you feeling, my dear?'

'Not bad. I still can't eat very much though.'

'I remember how that was. I lived on melon for three months when I was expecting Solange.'

'Can I sit with you, under the tree?'

'Of course.'

'I worried that you might get into trouble with the duchesse.'

'Perhaps, but it wouldn't be the first time.'

By the time they reached the tree, large velvet cushions in lilac and grey had been scattered over several Persian rugs. The servants waited to the side, hands folded.

The duchesse arranged herself on a large cushion, shaded by the canopy above. She sat with her legs folded to the side and flipped out her fan.

'Sit here, Henriette.' Charlotte pointed to a neighbouring cushion. Henriette obliged and the rest of the women found their seats. Céline pushed past Isabelle to secure the other cushion next to the duchesse, and Letitia sat next to Henriette, ignoring glares from the duchesse. The women donned their sunhats as beams of light penetrated the foliage. Letitia picked a wildflower and twirled it between her fingers as the grass rustled in the breeze.

Yolande and the other servants unpacked the picnic entrée, covering each dish with netting. Céline launched into a discussion with the duchesse about dresses and town gossip. A comtesse had seduced her manservant behind the changing curtain at the tailor's whilst her dress was being pinned. Céline's voice lowered to a near-whisper so that only the duchesse could hear. Charlotte let out a shriek of laughter, turning her back to Henriette and Letitia.

'We can't hear you, Céline,' Henriette said. 'Can you please speak up? The rest of us may have something to contribute.'

'We're discussing the financial ruin of the Comte Perrault,' Céline said peevishly. 'He is about to lose his farm and his land. You may know more, but I very much doubt Letitia will have anything useful to add. She's not even from these parts.'

The duchesse turned her cool gaze on Letitia. 'Perhaps you're right, Céline. Yet, I do believe Letitia knows quite a lot about financial ruin—her father lost everything, after all. Well, not *everything*. He managed to save some of his fortune by selling off his only daughter. What love and affection!'

The two women raised their fans, their shoulders quaking with laughter. Henriette stiffened and opened her mouth to speak when Letitia squeezed her fingers and shook her head.

'My father made the error of trusting a long-time friend with the investment of his money. People make mistakes. Whether a woman is a mistress or a wife, both unions resemble an exchange of sorts. I am sure the duc would have benefitted from your dowry, if not from the joy of your presence?'

A collective intake of breath followed Letitia's remark. The hum of the cicadas and the drone of the bees accentuated the sudden silence. The duchesse lifted the netting from a platter, and withdrew a cylinder of ham. She took a small bite and chewed, as if lost in thought. The ice of her gaze swung to Letitia and the girl sucked in her breath.

'Interesting idea. The sanctity of marriage compared to the life of a mistress. Ladies, you have a certain position at the château and are respected and appreciated. You all know this. But do you truly consider your position to be equivalent to marriage?'

Isabelle winced, cutting herself a generous slice of chocolate cake. She bit into it and her cheeks bulged as she ate, her eyes wide, darting left and right.

'We all dream of having a position like yours, Charlotte,' Céline said in a gentle voice. 'However, there are, lamentably, only a limited number of ducs. To be married is to have a deeper relationship and stronger commitment. It is far more significant than the mercenary alliance of a man with his mistress. The relationships are not the same, and to suggest such a thing is to denigrate your illustrious title. Apologize, Letitia.'

Letitia's mouth formed a hard line as she met the duchesse's eye. 'I'm sorry if my observations upset you.'

'It might be a good idea to keep your observations to yourself. You would do well to remember your position; otherwise, there are always vacancies in the kitchen.'

Letitia forced a smile. 'Goodness, if I were to help out down there, you might all be poisoned. I haven't a clue about food preparation.'

'You would just have to learn.'

Henriette sighed. 'Come, Charlotte. A girl of Letitia's station can't possibly work as a servant. I think it's time for the main dishes. Yolande, Raoul, can you please assist?' Charlotte flushed, her lips pressed together. Héloise and Isabelle stared at Henriette open-mouthed.

There was a flurry of movement as the servants uncovered the dishes and placed extra platters of cold meats, fruit, salmon, and other delicacies on the rug. They served the luncheon on china plates and distributed them among the women. Isabelle devoured her food in haste, as if worried tension might erupt once more to disturb her digestion. The duchesse gossiped with Héloise and Céline, her hands fluttering as she told a story.

Yolande hovered, ready to pass platters and wave away bees. The sun rose higher in the sky, and the heat shimmered over the grass.

'Bravo, Letitia,' Henriette whispered. 'You were brave, but be careful. It's a fine line between defending yourself and landing in trouble. Charlotte places people in one of two camps—you are either an ally to be trusted, or an enemy to be defeated. There is no way to earn favour in a situation like this; just ignore her rudeness. If there is something to be said, let me say it. She is cross with me now, but I know how to placate her.'

'She is a bully. You know, in my village the priest was a bully. Those who didn't attend mass were cornered by him in the street. He had a shrill voice, and he would lecture them about eternal damnation and the devil's fire pits. The flames were higher for those who never received the sacrament. If they had sinned, then there was no hope.'

Henriette smiled. 'Were you one of his targets?'

'I was. I spent too many Sundays climbing trees, picking lavender, or riding my horse. I wasn't very interested in the salvation of my soul. So, I told him that I didn't have a soul, that I was a vampire.'

'Good heavens. What happened?'

'As the priest attempted to ruin my reputation by preaching about my evil ways, my father searched for somewhere to send me—be it a man or a convent. Then my father lost his fortune. My poor parents.' Letitia fidgeted, plucking the petals from a daisy as she caught her friend's eye. 'I hope you still think well of me?'

'Of course. It might be a good idea to at least pretend to be demure and humble, though. Do you think you can manage it?'

'I will try.'

❧

'Ninety-nine, one hundred.' The man squinted at Romain and nodded, his heavy jowls bulging beneath his chin as he counted the notes and louis d'or, which clattered in a golden heap on the wood tabletop. 'It's all there. Better late than never, I suppose.' Romain had forgotten his name—Henri perhaps, or Hervé. He was squat and solid, with the crooked nose of a pugilist. Greasy black hair flopped over his low forehead.

The tavern was half empty, and Romain drained his glass of ale before pushing himself from the table. 'Well, if that's all then, I'd best be going.'

'Wait.' Hervé's fat fingers clasped Romain's forearm. 'If you are late with your next payment, I may not be so kind.'

'Understood. The black eye your thug gave me last month took a long time to fade.'

'You were lucky it was just the eye. Georges has been known to cripple debtors, and others, well, they just disappear,' Hervé sneered.

'I'll keep that in mind,' Romain nodded, placing his velvet purse in his pocket. He muttered farewell and made for the door.

In the street the wind sent spirals of dust and grit into Romain's eyes and mouth. Covering his mouth with a handkerchief, he ambled in the direction of Madame Rochas's establishment, hidden away near the church of Saint-Vincent-de-Paul. The white stucco-and-red-roofed house was at the top of a steep road; water stains crept up the walls like veins and the blue shutters were tightly closed.

The only sign of life was the presence of a young girl, leg bent as she leaned against the wall, her skirt hitched up to reveal a freckled calf. Under her breath she sang a folk song, her eyes half closed.

'Hello, Marjolene. That's a very pretty song.'

Marjolene gave him a languid stare, her painted lips turning up in a smile. 'I am singing, monsieur, because when I sing, I am home again.'

'Is Giselle here?'

'Last I saw. She has been waiting for you, monsieur.'

'Thank you, Marjolene. And keep singing, your voice is lovely.'

'You flatter me.'

As he entered the reception room, Madame Rochas dashed toward him, the ribbons of her bonnet flying out behind her. She clasped his forearms, her plump cheeks flushed. 'Welcome back, Monsieur de Villiers. If you will excuse me, I will tell Giselle to prepare her toilette for you.' The room was furnished with overstuffed brocade sofas and made dim by the red velvet curtains drawn across the windows. The cloying smell of decaying flowers mingled with Madame Rochas's strong patchouli perfume.

'Ah, you are too kind, madame, but that won't be necessary. I enjoy Giselle in her most natural state, without the artifice of fragrance or paint.'

'As you wish, monsieur. I will inform her of your arrival.'

'I would prefer to surprise her, madame.'

'You are a romantic, monsieur,' Madame Rochas exclaimed, her cheeks creasing in girlish dimples. 'It's no wonder Giselle looks forward to your visits.'

Romain extricated himself from Madame Rochas's grasp and climbed the stairs to the second floor. In the dim hallway he stared at the row of doors, trying to recall which was Giselle's. The muffled sound of a woman's high-pitched laugh sounded from one room, and Romain nudged open the door. He retreated at the sight of an obese man pinioning a girl on the edge of the bed, his hirsute torso engulfing her slender form. Romain shut the door with quiet care.

He knocked on the next door. 'Giselle? It's Romain.'

He heard hurried footsteps and the door swung open to reveal

Giselle in her stays and a transparent lavender robe. Her black hair curled around her heart-shaped face and her smile was wide. 'Romain! I've been waiting for you. Come here, you devil.'

Giselle seized him by his cravat and led him to a velvet daybed beneath the window. A shaft of feeble grey light illuminated them as she peeled off his shirt and breeches. Romain unlaced her stays, revealing one breast and then the other, before cupping them in his hands and tracing his tongue around her nipples. Giselle helped him with the stays until she stood before him, her skin so pale he could see faint tracings of blue veins interlaced beneath her skin. With a light shove, she positioned him on the daybed and straddled him.

Céline intercepted Romain as he walked along the gravel path toward the side entrance of the château. His pockets were considerably lighter and his limbs ached.

'Monsieur de Villiers, we need to talk. Would you please walk with me?'

'Can we sit down somewhere?'

'Of course. Let's go to the fountain of Apollo.'

The head gardener was digging in the rose garden and tipped his hat as they passed. The air was full with the scent of rain and Romain saw a bank of storm clouds gathering over Mont Pinçon.

Romain motioned for her to sit, then lowered himself next to her. 'So, Madame de Poitiers, I think I know what this is about.'

Céline smoothed her skirt and gave him an inquisitive look. 'Have you been consulting the tarot?'

'No,' he said with a dry laugh, 'The duchesse instructed me to talk with you, just yesterday, in fact.'

'That's good—you won't be shocked with what I'm about to tell you. Her Grace is most bothered by Letitia, as I'm sure you know. We need to arrange a few...er...disturbances. Baby or not, Her Grace is determined to propel Letitia back to her father's house.'

'What would you like me to do?'

'I need you to obtain the key for the housekeeping closet from Yolande. You must pilfer a bottle of lye.'

'Am I to do some cleaning?' he raised an eyebrow.

'I will put some in her stays.'

Romain blanched. 'The duchesse mentioned it. Asked if I'd carry it out. What will it do to her?'

'Oh, nothing much,' Céline said airily. 'Just make her a little uncomfortable. It will amuse the duchesse.'

❧

At noon, Yolande knocked on the door to Henriette's rooms.

'Her Grace wishes to see you, madame.'

Henriette felt a small lurch in her stomach and placed her book on a side table. Her maid, Clementine, had only just finished Henriette's toilette and was plumping embroidered cushions on the chaise longue. Solange sat on a gilded chair, swinging her legs, her eyes darting from her mother to the ormolu clock on the mantle.

'Go on. I'm sure Tomas is just as impatient to start playing this morning. I might see you later on, when I go for my stroll.'

'Maman?'

'Yes, my love?'

'Why are you frowning?'

'Oh, no reason. Perhaps I didn't have enough sleep.'

Solange shrugged and jumped to her feet. 'Tomas said we'd try to catch some frogs from the stream today. After we might race our paper boats. Maman, could I perhaps keep a frog in a glass jar?'

'Darling, that would be terribly cruel. Imagine if you were an energetic young frog bouncing around a stream, before being caught in a jar. Do you think that would be a good life for a frog?'

'No, Maman. I suppose you're right. I might see you later.'

'Yes, off you go.'

Henriette made her way to the duchesse's rooms at the other side of the château. Life-sized portraits of the duc's ancestors stared down at her from the walls and the scent of cut flowers filled the air. As she approached the five spacious rooms that formed the duchesse's personal chambers, several liveried servants passed in the opposite direction. Yolande, among them, shot her a sympathetic look, her arms straining under an enormous silver platter with porcelain and a teapot.

Henriette greeted Hercules, who stood to attention at the door and held out his palm, indicating she should wait. His curled grey wig was immaculate, his swarthy skin powdered white with a faux beauty spot. He stared down at her with piercing black eyes.

'Just a moment. I will see if Her Grace is ready to see you.'

Five long minutes passed and Henriette tapped her foot on the Persian runner, glancing idly around the hallway at the precious china and oriental vases balanced on ornate side tables.

'You may come in,' announced Hercules, waving her inside.

The room smelt of delphiniums and tuberose, the duchesse's favourite flowers. The drapes were flung wide, and Henriette was momentarily blinded as she entered from the dim hallway into the bright spill of sunshine.

The duchesse sat in a straight-backed armchair, her legs folded to the side underneath lilac satin skirts. The tight bodice of her gown revealed the bones of her ribcage, and rouge on her cheeks did little to disguise her pallor. Her hands formed a white-knuckled grip in her lap.

'Please sit,' Charlotte said, her eyes downcast.

'Good morning, Charlotte.'

'You will call me Your Grace.'

Henriette felt a knot form in her stomach. 'Is there something wrong, Your Grace? You don't look at all well.'

'What could possibly be wrong?' Charlotte's voice was shrill, her thin torso heaved. 'If you are determined to feign innocence, I shall explain it to you—disloyalty, forming plots against me, befriending Letitia. I thought we were close, Henriette. You are nothing but a pretender.'

Henriette drew herself up. 'Char...Your Grace, I *am* your friend.

Letitia is no threat to you; she is just an innocent girl. Is it her fault His Grace is taken with her? Doubtless, he will tire of her soon enough, but what do you expect her to do in the meantime? Wear rags to try and dissuade him?'

The duchesse raised her head, her eyes blazing. 'No threat to me? She is carrying my husband's child and he has fallen in love with her. He no longer loves me. Have you suddenly lost all intelligence? I have always respected you, Henriette, and thought you would support me in this. I warn you, abandon that girl, or I will make sure you do not receive any more privileges. You will be on the same level as Céline.'

'Oh, that's good. Céline seems to have become an ally of yours—my place is assured.'

'How dare you be so insolent! Céline will take your place, and you hers, if you continue to be obstinate. You must work out your priorities. The position of lowest-ranking mistress is a pitiful one. Last to be served, the smallest rooms, the least expensive tailor and only one personal servant. Not to mention the scorn of the others. It's grim, but I think you'll cope. '

'Your Grace, Letitia doesn't have anyone else. I will ask her to apologize for her rudeness the other day. If I abandon her, Céline and Héloïse will make her life very difficult. You have power. What does she have?'

'She has youth, beauty, and a baby to come. She has my husband's affection. She has everything. Me? I have lost the things that matter most. Your friendship was once important to me. But no more. Now leave me.'

'Your Grace,' Henriette murmured from the depths of her curtsey. 'I'm sorry to have caused tension between us. I hope in time you will understand my motivations.'

The duchesse turned her face to the window, staring out at the line of orange trees that graced the courtyard below.

CHAPTER 9

'Tomas,' Letitia called. 'You may as well come out. I can see your shirt, you goose.'

The moist soil surrounding the orange trees was criss-crossed with blue shadows and smelled of citrus and sunshine. The sun warmed Letitia's head as she stood, arms folded across her chest, the trees in endless rows around her.

Tomas emerged from behind a tree trunk with a grin, tucking the muddied hem of his shirt into his breeches.

'I was sure you wouldn't see me. I bet Solange is hiding underneath the old cart again. She is so predictable. Come on, I'll show you.'

'You're not exactly full of new ideas yourself—I'm sure last time we played you always hid behind trees.'

'Perhaps. And you tend to favour bushes.'

The rotting cart, pitted with holes from boring insects, stood against the wall next to the kitchen door. A shadow beneath announced the presence of Solange.

'Solange, we can see you.' Tomas said.

Solange scrambled out, her skirts hitched up on one side and her hair askew. 'Ah, you two have me figured out. But next time you will see how ingenious I am. I have a plan, you see.'

Tomas smirked. 'Will it involve hiding behind the cart rather than underneath it? Pure genius.'

'Shut your mouth. You will be surprised and impressed.'

'Well, you two, what's our next game?' Letitia asked.

Solange pondered for a moment, her finger on her chin. 'We could play our favourite, but you may not be comfortable....'

'And why not?' said Letitia, 'What is it?'

'Spying. We play it more than hide and seek. One day we might tell

63

you everyone's secrets. We wander around the château, looking for things we're not meant to see or hear. It's fun.'

'Do you have a favourite person to spy on?'

'Madame de Poitiers,' Tomas replied with a grin. 'She is often up to something, even if it's just spying like us. Let's go then.'

Tomas and Solange barrelled through the kitchens, pressing their palms into a mound of flour as they passed. Letitia giggled as she tried to keep pace with them. Up the back stairs they raced until they approached Madame de Poitiers's rooms, their steps now muffled by the thick carpets underfoot. Hearing someone approach, the three ducked into an alcove and crouched in its shadowed recesses.

'It's her, Madame de Poitiers,' whispered Tomas. 'She shuffles, and clears her throat a lot.'

Tomas, Solange, and Letitia watched, barely breathing, as Madame de Poitiers passed, her red silk skirts rustling. She cradled a white bottle in her hands and wore gloves, thick and unwieldy, like the ones worn by the gardeners.

Solange's eyes glimmered. 'I'm going to follow her. Tomas, you can spy on the rest of this floor. Letitia, the downstairs rooms. Let's meet back here in half an hour.'

Solange followed some distance behind Madame de Poitiers, the thin leather soles of her shoes soundless on the carpet. The upstairs hallway was lined with marble busts on pedestals—soldiers with Roman helmets, serene goddesses, and philosophers. Solange recognized Plato from the illustrated plate of a book her mother was reading. Céline walked with slow but deliberate purpose and stopped in front of Letitia's door. Ducking behind a bust, the young girl frowned and watched her glance around, once, twice, before turning the gold handle and entering Letitia's room.

What could Madame de Poitiers be doing in Letitia's room? Solange wondered, crouched behind the classical bust of a Roman warrior. She felt pressure in her bladder. To distract herself, she traced the aquiline nose of the warrior, admiring his sensuous lips. She had traced his profile many times before Céline emerged, a strange flush creeping up her neck and flowering over her cheeks. The bottle she held was half empty. Solange felt her breath quicken in her throat.

When the sound of Madame de Poitier's footsteps faded to silence, Solange crept to the door of Letitia's room and opened it. A faint scent, astringent and somewhat familiar, filled the air. The top drawer of the dresser was slightly open, the gap as wide as two fingers, but Solange had played the spying game enough to notice the smallest things. As Solange approached the drawer, the odour intensified. Within, she saw neatly folded rows of undergarments, with three pairs of stays on the top. The third pair of stays, brought to her nose, made her gag as strong fumes emanated from the stiff fabric.

'Put it back,' a sharp voice sounded. Solange swung around to see Madame de Poitiers, standing behind her.

'Why did you come in here? What have you done to Letitia's stays?' Solange demanded.

'This doesn't concern you, and if you say a word to Letitia, or anyone else, about what you've seen, your mother will pay the price. It's not the first time I've caught you following me. Go on, get out of here!'

Solange dashed out of the room into the hallway. She could hear the rapid beat of her heart in her ears and the lingering smell had become a sour taste in her mouth.

Letitia was slow to rise. Her maid, Adele, drew the curtains, and she shut her eyes tightly against the glare flooding the room.

'It's a lovely morning, miss. Your hot chocolate is here. I'll help you up.'

Adele held out her hand and Letitia allowed herself to be coaxed out of bed. Adele brushed Letitia's hair until it was gleaming, and sponged her body with floral scented water before patting it dry.

'I had to spray your stays with rosewater,' Adele remarked as she lifted Letitia's undergarments from the drawer. 'They had such a strange scent. Have you been playing with the cats again?' Letitia sleepily shook her head as Adele arranged the stays over her shoulders and tightened the laces at her back. 'Very soon you won't be able to wear stays at all, miss,' Adele said. 'And won't that be a joy, indeed.'

Letitia grimaced. 'It itches.'

Adele nodded, pulling the laces and tying a bow at the top. 'My maman said none of her clothes felt right when she was with child. She was never comfortable. It will be better when you can just wear a silk undergarment instead of these stays.'

At breakfast, Letitia shifted in her seat. The itch in her stays had intensified to a burning sensation that spread across her stomach. Unable to eat, she sipped orange juice and tried in vain to hide her discomfort.

'Whatever is the matter?' asked Céline, buttering some bread. 'You are wriggling around like a child.'

The other mistresses stared at Letitia, who rose to her feet, then bent forward, her cheeks flaming red, her hands gripping her ribs. She let out a low, guttural moan. 'It hurts…it hurts so. Excuse me I…' Her eyes rolled back and she crumpled to the floor.

'Fetch the physician, now!' Henriette told a servant. The parquetry floor echoed with the sound of rapid footsteps. Three servants carried Letitia to her rooms and another was sent to find Doctor Mouret.

Adele burst into the room as they laid Letitia on the bed, her eyes wide. She rushed to her mistress's side, placing a wet cloth on her forehead. Letitia drifted in and out of consciousness. In the brief moments she was awake, she moaned and writhed, her hands moving spasmodically over her chest. There was a rap on the door and Henriette entered with Doctor Mouret, who cast an exacting eye over the patient. Henriette ushered the male servants out of the room.

'Get her clothes off,' he ordered, as he flipped open his leather case, full of vials and ointments. Together, Adele and Henriette turned Letitia on her side and unlaced her stays. A pungent smell escaped from Letitia's undergarments as they removed them. 'Hurry,' urged the doctor, before pushing between the women and helping them. Adele gasped as Letitia's blistered, raw skin was revealed—her chest and back were covered in angry lesions. The exposure to air seemed to increase her pain and Letitia let out a high, keening sound, her body shaking.

'I need wet towels,' Doctor Mouret said. Adele dashed out to retrieve them while Henriette held Letitia's hand. She watched in growing alarm as Letitia's face turned a deeper shade of red, her body twisted in agony.

'What is wrong with her, Doctor Mouret? Can you not do something for her pain?' Henriette cried.

Adele returned with a pile of sodden towels, which the doctor wound with care around Letitia's torso. She moaned, her back arching, perspiration beading on her forehead. There was a rap on the door and Céline entered.

Henriette glared. 'What do you want?'

'Oh, mother of God, whatever is wrong with her? Is there anything I can do to help?' Céline asked, wringing her hands.

'The doctor is attempting to treat her, as you can see. We don't yet know the cause of her suffering. It would be best if you leave—she needs calm.'

'Can I perhaps fetch some more towels for her?'

'We have enough,' said Henriette, waving her hand at Céline. 'Please just go.'

'Of course,' Céline murmured. 'Please tell me if there is anything I can do.' She closed the door behind her.

Doctor Mouret withdrew a set of ceramic cups from his bag. 'We must start the cupping, her fever is too high.' He turned to Henriette. 'She needs water. Even if she just takes a sip, it will be better than nothing.'

Henriette nodded and rushed out of the room.

The bleeding started two days later. Adele and Henriette were helping Letitia to a sitting position when they noticed the deep red stain spreading across the sheets. Doctor Mouret was called in, and he shook his head as he placed rolled-up fabric between Letitia's legs.

He spoke to Henriette in a low voice, rubbing his temples. 'It is likely that the bleeding will continue for a day or two, maybe more. It seems her body, and the baby, were not able to tolerate the shock of her injuries.'

Approaching the bed, Doctor Mouret touched Letitia's shoulder. 'I'm very sorry. You are no longer with child.'

Letitia gave a slight nod, her eyes enormous in the pallor of her face. 'And my body, the wounds,' she whispered, 'what of those?'

'There may be some scarring, but your body will heal. I have given your maid some ointment, which must be applied twice a day. Your fever has abated, at least. Try to rest.'

Letitia's voice was faint and caught in her throat as she spoke. The light from the window bathed her face, as white as bone. 'Someone has done this terrible thing.'

Three days later, the Dowager Duchesse Oriette d'Amboise arrived in a gold and cream-coloured carriage. Every servant in the château lined up on either side of the entrance stairs, hands folded before them, eyes on their feet. A liveried footman guided the dowager down the carriage steps. As her silk-encased feet reached the gravel, the entourage of servants bowed and curtsied.

The dowager stood and surveyed them, her back ramrod straight, her grey eyes stern. She wore a pale green dress with a black velvet insert in the bodice, her silver-grey hair neatly wound in an immaculate chignon.

'Where is my son?' Her commanding voice was a stark contrast to her bird-like frame.

The head butler stepped forward, his head bowed, his body resembling a question mark. 'He is coming presently, Duchesse.'

The double doors swung open and the duc strode out, combing

his fingers through his hair. 'Mother, do forgive me for not being here to greet you. I was caught up in the stables.'

The dowager glared at him and tapped her closed fan on her wrist, holding out her elbow. 'Take me to the drawing room, Hugo. Where is your wife?'

'She will be back from town soon. Apologies, but you did not send word of your arrival.'

'Why?' she demanded. 'Am I not welcome? Must I send word to my own son? I should be able to be spontaneous, to visit at any time.'

'Of course, Mother.' Hugo led her through the grand entrance, with its domed ceiling, gold banisters, and frescoes of fawns and angels.

The duc and the dowager duchesse were trailed by several servants, including the butler, Thierry. Having received the duc's mother on many occasions, they were well accustomed to her preferences. She drank only warm water with lemon; ate only steamed perch, caught fresh; and had an extreme dislike of loud noise. As the dowager was deaf in one ear, difficulties arose when people wishing to engage in conversation could not remember which ear was impaired. Victims of her displeasure were cut down with a single lacerating look.

Hugo guided her to a padded armchair and perched next to her on the chaise.

'May I fetch you some refreshment, Duchesse?' Thierry asked. 'Warm water with lemon?'

The dowager nodded and flicked her long fingers at him. 'Yes.'

Her eyes locked on her son. 'Tell me, Hugo. How are Charlotte and Estelle?'

'Charlotte is fine, thank you. Estelle I haven't seen in several days. She spends a lot of time with her governess—learning Latin, I believe.'

'I've heard alarming reports regarding Charlotte. Blois is rife with rumours of her desperate unhappiness and weight loss. As for Estelle—what an apathetic attitude to have toward your only daughter. Do you not wish to be involved in her life? She needs your guidance.'

'Mother, please settle down. You asked how they were. Charlotte has been somewhat withdrawn—'

'I have heard she is near breaking point. She is your wife, and you would do well to take care of her. We both know what the problem is here, Hugo.'

'And what might that be, Mother?'

'Your new little mistress. Lavinia, is it?'

'Letitia.'

'Thinking with your breeches rather than your head. You always were selfish, and some things, it seems, never change. And what about a grandson? How are you to present me with one if you barely speak to your wife?' The dowager sighed. 'Charlotte has never been emotionally stable. You know this. Promise me you will pay her more attention. We do not need our family name tarnished by gossip.'

'Mother, Charlotte shuts herself away in her rooms or seeks to avoid me by visiting friends. Of course I want a son, but what do you expect me to do?'

'Try harder. I'm sure she just feels rejected, with you fawning all over that girl.'

Thierry returned with a silver tray. He handed the dowager her water with a white-gloved hand and poured tea for the duc.

'The duchesse has arrived, Your Grace.'

Hugo nodded and sipped his tea, waiting for the butler to leave.

'There you are, Mother. You can ask Charlotte yourself. I'm sure you'll find her in good spirits.'

The duchesse's clipped footsteps sounded out on the parquetry as she approached the drawing room. Hugo placed his teacup on a side table and stood as his wife entered the room. 'Good day, Charlotte.'

Charlotte nodded at her husband, allowing him to lean over and kiss her cheek. As his lips were about to make contact, she pulled away, so he kissed the air.

'Good morning, Duchesse. Ah, you have your water. Would you care for something to eat?'

'Thank you, Charlotte, but I'm quite happy with my water. I trust you're well?'

'Yes, thank you. How about you?'

'Thank you, as well as can be expected. Although my hands do ache from time to time. I have had to forgo cutting flowers for the moment. You are looking too thin. Hot chocolate of a morning would fill you out.'

'Perhaps. I'm not trying to be thin. The body sometimes reflects our inner state.' She gave her husband a pointed stare, before turning back to her mother-in-law. 'And how are your roses, duchesse? I do remember some spectacular orange and yellow ones the last time I visited. They were simply enormous.'

'They're still blooming and I have begun cultivating a purplish red variety that I'm most fond of.'

'I look forward to seeing them again. Your son used to bring me roses every day. Did you know that?'

Hugo flushed. 'Now, my dear. You have so many in your rooms, you don't need me to bring them for you.'

His mother's eyes glinted as she rose to her feet. 'Hugo, I do believe I need some time alone with your wife. We shall go for a stroll. Come, Charlotte, show me your garden. I hope my cuttings are thriving.'

'Yes, Mother,' said Hugo. 'I will speak to you afterwards.'

The two women walked along the path, breathing in the scent of the roses. They were in full bloom, their petals downy in shades of vermillion and pink. The dowager stopped several times to admire particular blooms, bending to sniff them.

'I see the gardeners have been taking excellent care of my cuttings. They've grown remarkably from the tiny shoots I gave you. Glorious. And what a fine day it is to view them.'

'It is indeed.'

'Charlotte. I do hope you feel you can confide in me. The tension between you and my son disturbs me. Now, what has brought about this change in your relations, do you think? Is it this new mistress I've heard about?'

'Yes. He has brought a schoolgirl into this house, one whom he loves above all others, including Estelle. Thankfully, she is no longer with child.'

'I see. Unfortunately this is what we must endure as women, Charlotte. You must make an effort to spend time with my son, and he with you. A young girl won't be able to converse with him as you can.'

'I don't think it's her conversation he's interested in.'

'Quite. But he still enjoys conversing, and seduction takes place in the mind as well as in the body. Now, don't look so shocked. I may be old, but I was once a young woman. Marriage wasn't meant to be easy. And marriage to a duc is even more difficult. He is inclined to assert his power and take whomever he wishes into his bed. And this is his right, Charlotte.'

'Yes, duchesse. I shall try and entice him back to me.'

'Good. You're clever. Sometimes too clever.'

CHAPTER 10

The duchesse refused to share a carriage with Henriette and Letitia, so the two women found themselves in a cramped carriage with grimy seats attached to two sleepy mares.

Estelle accompanied Henriette and Letitia and sat opposite, her eyes fixed on a book. Her pale hair fell in loose ringlets, with two blue satin bows on either side. She had a face that was almost pretty, except for a decidedly weak chin.

Henriette whispered in Letitia's ear, 'The duc was unhappy about your coming. He's worried your innocence will be tainted by the courtiers with their ribald jokes and flirtatious innuendoes. I told him there were rumours you were dim-witted or lame, and it seemed odd you were being sequestered away like some kind of rare bird. I said the trip to Versailles would cheer you up after all your recent trials.'

Letitia smiled. 'Well, it's worked, and now we are on our way. I can scarcely believe it. My mother had a friend who was a courtier at Versailles, and she told stories of all the intrigues and debaucheries.'

'We have enough of that at the château,' Henriette sighed. 'It tires me so. There are two types of courtiers—those who partake in the machinations and those who rise above them. Which would you like to be introduced to?'

'Both.' Letitia said. 'I need to learn about machinations, as I seem to be part of them whether I like it or not.'

'In any case, I'm sure you'll enjoy your visit. I've been only once before. The Hall of Mirrors is quite extraordinary.'

Estelle raised her head from her book. 'Maman says I'm to meet the Marquis d'Urveilles, the handsomest man at court. Do you know him, Madame d'Augustin?'

'I do. He is most refined and indeed handsome. Good grief, is your mother trying to set you up already? A child bride?'

The girl laughed; her teeth were small and even. 'No, not yet. But if he meets me now, then I might remain in his mind for the future. I'm already twelve, you know.'

'Twelve is a long way from being a woman. Besides, I thought you were more interested in your books?'

'Perhaps, but Maman says I must think of my future. She wants me to take more dance lessons, and extra singing too. I keep telling her I can't sing, but she ignores me. What do you think, Madame d'Augustin? Can a terrible singing voice improve with lessons?'

'I think not, my dear. I would speak with your mother, but I don't think she'd listen.'

The gilded gates of Versailles shimmered in the afternoon sun, flanked by rows of Swiss Guards. The duchesse's carriage was waved through, and there was a small jolt as their own carriage slowed and followed.

Groups of courtiers strolled on either side of their carriage as they crossed into palace grounds and some peered inside, curious about the newcomers.

Letitia examined the fine silks of the courtiers' dresses and their elaborate wigs, returning their stares.

The duchesse, Isabelle, Héloïse, and Céline were escorted from their carriage by a team of servants in white wigs, dressed in blue velvet coats. One approached the second carriage, his face impassive. He opened the door, his gloved hand extended for each of the three women.

A statuesque woman emerged from the yellow doors of the palace and embraced the duchesse. Henriette recognised her as Charlotte's friend, Madame Foulbret. Her dress was embroidered in white dahlias on a green background, her cheeks bright with rouge. 'Estelle, come!' Charlotte called imperiously, before turning toward the palace. Estelle scurried toward her mother, casting an apologetic glance at Henriette and Letitia, who stood together under a threatening sky.

The two mistresses, alone on the cobblestones of the Versailles courtyard, watched as the palace doors closed heavily behind the retreating figure of the duchesse.

As they stood, shifting from foot to foot in their uncomfortable heels, a light drizzle began. Henriette approached the door and knocked. It was opened by one of the servants, whose eyes settled on her forehead.

'May I help you, madame?'

'Yes. We are with the party who just entered. For some reason, we've not been admitted with the duchesse.'

'Ah, I see. Just a moment please.' The door clicked back into place. The bewigged servant returned some minutes later, opening the door.

'Madame Foulbret advised me that you will be collected shortly.' He attempted to shut the door but Letitia wedged it open with her foot. She smiled and forced him to meet her eyes.

'We are going to be quite wet, monsieur, if we stay out here in the rain. Can we please come inside?'

The man blushed beneath his mask of powder and motioned them inside. 'You may wait here. I'm sure it won't be long.'

He bustled away, his footsteps echoing on the parquetry. Letitia stood with her mouth agape, drinking in their surroundings. The walls were lined in pink marble, the vaulted ceilings painted with delicate frescoes and hanging with glittering chandeliers. A series of gilt-edged doors lined one wall. Statues jutted out from alcoves above the doors—fluid goddesses and plump cherubs.

'Why must we wait?' Letitia asked.

'We are receiving further punishment. The duchesse wants us to know that we don't deserve to be here.'

The novelty of the room soon dissipated and the two women stared at the doors, willing one of them to open.

'My legs are starting to hurt.'

'Mine too. And not a chair in sight. Lean on me if you like,' Henriette offered.

Letitia sighed, the deep pink of her painted lips a startling contrast to her pale face.

'This is my fault, Henriette. I have cursed you.'

'Not at all. You are a true friend. Now please, take my arm. I'm sure it won't be much longer.'

The middle door opened and they stood up straighter. An usher emerged, clasping his gloved hands.

'*Mesdames*, please follow me.'

He led them through one magnificent hallway after another. Beyond the vaulted windows that overlooked the gardens, the rain stopped and the sun appeared, accentuating the vivid colours of the frescoes and reflecting on the polished wood floors.

Letitia glimpsed her pallid face in a mirror. She pinched her cheeks and smoothed the sides of her hair. The servant strode without pause, at a rapid pace. He did not glance back to see if they followed.

Entering the vast Salon de la Paix, they noticed clusters of courtiers seated on embroidered silk sofas and armchairs. The hum of conversation dwindled as the two women were led before Madame Martine Foulbret, who rose from her ornately carved chair to greet them. Her powdered grey hair was piled high and decorated with mother-of-pearl combs and feathers.

'Good morning. Madame d'Augustin, is it? And you must be Mademoiselle du Massenet? Please, come and sit with us.' She gestured to an empty sofa near the duchesse and Estelle, who sat amid a cluster of women—Isabelle, Céline, and Héloise among them, as well as several ladies from the court.

Letitia squinted at the light streaming through the windows and glanced at the frescoes above her head. The sun played against the golden mouldings and mirrors that lined the walls, and lit the floor to a polished brilliance. She sat in silent awe, her eyes drawn from the room itself to the sumptuous fabrics of the ladies' dresses. Their cuffs were of Spanish lace, their skirts of the finest brocade and silk. Above her, a fresco depicted a crowned woman with a shield seated in a dove-drawn chariot, flanked by cherubim and other heroic-looking women.

'*Mesdames*,' the duchesse said curtly.

Martine turned to the duchesse. 'We've been consumed with a story these past few days. Two ladies, the Duchesse de la Motte and the Comtesse de Reynaud were having a dispute. The comtesse, standing behind the duchesse as they were waiting to be presented to the king, smeared dog *merde* on the other's dress. She was called, the king remarked on the dreadful smell, and we haven't seen her since. I have heard she returned to her family's estate in Burgundy and has permanently taken to her bed.'

The duchesse's eyes widened. 'And what did the Duchesse de la Motte do, to warrant such humiliation?'

'It seems she outwitted the Comtesse de Reynaud in a game of words. One pun after another.'

'Oh, I see,' the duchesse remarked airily. 'Mademoiselle du Massenet'—Charlotte waved one hand in Letitia's direction—'is a natural talent with games like that, aren't you, my dear?'

'No, Your Grace,' Letitia replied. 'I am from the provinces and directness of speech is highly valued there.'

'Ah, but you are too modest, child. She banters and jousts with words all day long,' the duchesse declared. 'Who is the best at court?' she asked Martine. 'I should like to see them spar together.'

Martine scanned the room. 'The Marquis d'Urveilles is the most accomplished. There he is, I shall go and fetch him. What fun.'

Letitia's stomach churned and her palms were damp with perspiration. She cast an imploring glance toward Henriette, who appeared pained but was unable to intervene. Marquis d'Urveilles, a man with an angular face, framed by neatly tied brown hair, returned with Martine. A gold-threaded waistcoat glimmered beneath his green silk coat. Martine made introductions and the marquis bowed before taking a seat next to Letitia.

'Well? Are you not going to begin?' demanded Martine, tapping her foot beneath her skirts.

'Madame,' the marquis smiled, 'verbal sparring should happen spontaneously. Let me acquaint myself with this lovely girl first and then we shall see.'

The colour drained from the duchesse's face as the marquis turned away, crossing his muscular legs as he leaned toward Letitia.

'What brings you to Versailles?'

'I am a mistress of the Duc d'Amboise. I've come with Her Grace and my companions; we're visiting together as a party.'

'I know the duc. His father knew my father, in fact.'

'Oh, really? I shall tell him I had the privilege of making your acquaintance.'

The marquis turned to his audience and dismissed them all with a wave of his hand. 'You may continue your conversations. There will be no display of wit today.'

Letitia smiled, her tension dissipating. 'Thank you. I'm afraid I haven't played that game before. I would need some tutoring before a public show.'

'I surmised that,' the marquis said, his voice low, his face close to hers. 'May I ask you a personal question?'

Letitia nodded.

'Why are you a mistress?'

'My father lost his fortune. It seemed the most prudent choice at the time.'

'I see. Well, you could do worse than the Duc d'Amboise. He is a good man, if a little self-absorbed, as indeed most ducs tend to be.'

Letitia ventured a question of her own. 'You seem calm and straightforward in your manner. What do you make of Versailles, with its intrigues and manoeuvring?'

The marquis laughed softly. 'It's hellish. The women are conniving and shallow. The men jostle day and night to be close to the king. They would sell their families and their souls for a royal appointment. I have been here for six months and it seems six years. I am attempting to obtain funds to rebuild a village near my family's estate in Chartres which was razed after an uprising. If it weren't for this cause, you would not be conversing with me. This court is a den of rats, mademoiselle.'

Letitia's eyes twinkled. 'I am also from a den of rats; smaller, but no less unpleasant. Speaking of which, I'll be in grave trouble if I continue to speak with you. The duchesse wishes for you to meet her daughter.' She gave him a conspiratorial smile and he smiled back, his eyes warm and teasing. 'Estelle,' Letitia murmured, rising to her feet, 'let me swap places with you. The marquis would like to make your acquaintance.'

The young girl blushed and shuffled awkwardly toward the marquis, her posture bent forward and her eyes on her shoes.

The marquis spoke in a gentle voice with the girl, his manner gracious. Before long, Estelle was tossing her ringlets and babbling about her book. The marquis was polite and made thoughtful comments at the appropriate moments, but it was clear he thought her a child.

Martine waved over a servant. 'Tea, please. Seven cups. Some cold water on the side and some almond pastries. You may run to the kitchens—I am thirsty.'

Letitia felt Martine's eyes on her as the older woman twisted a fan in her long fingers, her expression one of weary melancholy. 'Mademoiselle du Massenet, the marquis was kind enough to excuse you from word games. I can see intelligence in your face and I would like to converse with you in the manner of the court. Follow my lead.'

Letitia sighed inwardly. She wished only to observe the glorious room and its occupants without being the focus of attention.

'Of course, Madame Foulbret. Please begin.'

'Your dress gives me distress as it needs a press.'

Letitia raised an eyebrow. 'Did you not know? Crinkles are the fashion, as they intensify passion.'

Martine's eyes sparkled. '*La mode?* Or is it to be put away in your *commode?* Ah, but *la mode* is different in the country. Clothing must be practical and functional. Feeding the pigs, the chickens, and riding horses. Not meeting *chevaliers*, but *chevaux*. Not eating *foie gras*, but *gras de porc.*'

'But madame, I have met many nobles as fine as yourself in the country. The peasants have a nobility of spirit. Their clothes are crinkled but their spirit is as free as an angel on a cloud. *L'esprit de noblesse, comme une comtesse. Sans détresse.'*

Martine smiled into her fan—laughter was frowned upon at court.

'Bravo, you have played well for a first timer. Charlotte, what do you think of mademoiselle's wit?'

'Acceptable, if a little coarse.' The duchesse accepted a small teacup from a hovering attendant. 'Wit is but one musket in an arsenal. Yet without rank, what use is it?'

Henriette frowned. 'It is my belief, Your Grace, that rank should be used to assist those less fortunate, not to deride them.'

'Always the moralist, Henriette. I was merely making an observation, not being derisive.'

Henriette glowered but did not respond. The court ladies leaned forward on their chairs, eager to catch Henriette's retort. Letitia understood, in her friend's resigned expression, that she would not so entertain them.

At that moment Romain de Villiers swept into the room, tossing his hat to a nearby servant and scanning the room for familiar faces. He seemed relaxed, as if visiting the palace of the king was something he did every day. Spotting the ladies of the d'Amboise household, he came over and sat down.

Martine greeted him with a coquettish tone. 'Monsieur de Villiers, how charming to see you. The Comtesse de Vaubert was asking after you just yesterday. She said you gave an intriguing reading the last time you visited. Now, who have you not met here...?'

The three court ladies had not made his acquaintance and extended their hands for him to kiss. Letitia watched as he stood and flirted with them all before taking his seat.

❧

Henriette resisted rolling her eyes as she watched Romain's languid performance. Women, it seemed, were often susceptible to his charm. Even the duchesse, who was reserved with men, softened her expression and sat straighter when he was near. Romain seemed to sense this and positioned himself next to her. On his other side, the court ladies did everything but prod him with their fans to gain his attention, pestering him for readings. He smiled and gave vague promises of fitting them in, accepting a cup of tea from Martine.

'You'd never guess who I saw on my way here.' He waited until all eyes rested on him. 'Do you remember Gilbert Franchet, the singer? Just a year ago he was in this very room, enchanting us with Italian arias. Well, I saw him on the back of a farmer's cart, sitting on a bale of hay with a pitchfork. I waved at him, but he pretended not to know me. Shame, really. I suppose he could sing as he herded sheep.'

Laughter almost breached the sanctity of the Salon de la Paix. The women's tightly bound torsos shook with half-suppressed amusement as they imagined the fallen singer. They hid their smiles behind their fans.

Henriette spoke, shaking her head. 'I remember Monsieur Franchet well. He is a good family man and a wonderful talent. His fall was the result of generosity to his swindler of a cousin, Monsieur Vaumeil. Monsieur Franchet paid the legal fees so Vaumeil could avoid prison. His ignominy is no laughing matter. Ill fortune can beset anyone.'

The duchesse let out a loud exhalation. 'There she goes again, Saint Henriette. Do you even have a sense of humour?'

'I do. Perhaps I would laugh if it were you herding sheep, Your Grace. What a splendid sight that would be.'

The duchesse smiled, but her eyes were like splinters of blue glass.

'I cannot imagine you herding sheep, Your Grace,' Romain interjected. 'However, Madame d'Augustin is right about the singer. I have read the tarot for a number of years and all too frequently those in exalted positions have the most spectacular falls. To mock such a descent is to encourage fate to similarly smite us. I shouldn't have told that story. We are fortunate to sit here, among human Gods, drinking the most delectable tea and feasting our eyes upon the delights of this salon.'

'Hear, hear,' said Céline, earning a look of rebuke from the duchesse. The others raised their cups and Henriette smiled at Romain.

❧

On the way back to the château, Henriette saw Romain beside them on his horse, the red feather in his hat waving jauntily. As the carriage approached a bend in the road, Romain urged his horse into a gallop and disappeared around the corner.

Letitia's voice broke into Henriette's thoughts. 'When will we return to Versailles, do you think?'

'I'm not sure. That will be the duc's decision.' Henriette glanced over at Estelle, intent on her book, her lips pressed together in concentration.

'I know why you want to go back,' Henriette whispered in Letitia's ear. 'The marquis is a very handsome man.'

Letitia blushed. 'There are many handsome men at court,' she replied in a low voice. 'I'm sure the duchesse will tell them I'm simple, or lame, or both. Yet I suppose the fact that I'm a mistress of her husband is off-putting enough.'

'If you flirt, do it away from her eyes. She is looking for any reason to discredit you.'

'Yes, I know. The duc has been kind to me, and I do not wish to betray his trust. You can flirt and I will enjoy watching.'

'My flirting days are over, child. I'm content to observe others' intrigues and games.' Henriette smiled. 'Oh dear, did you see Héloise when the duchesse introduced her to the Comtesse de Vaubert? She almost tripped over her skirts in her eagerness, and then told the comtesse an interminable story about farm animals!'

Letitia laughed. 'Yes, and then we had to hear all about her childhood in the convent too. I'm surprised she didn't give the comtesse a Bible reading.'

The two women giggled, tucking their arms one through the other, as they watched fields of wildflowers through the carriage window, the shadows of clouds flitting across them. The sun was high in the sky; they would return in time for luncheon.

CHAPTER 11

Romain watched Tomas, his lanky frame silhouetted by the sun as he leaned over the side of the fountain, adjusting the sail of his toy boat. Romain approached tentatively—it was rare to observe the boy unnoticed and he wished to prolong the moment.

'Hello there,' Romain said, hands behind his back.

'Good day, Monsieur de Villiers.'

'Good day, Tomas. You may call me Romain. That's a fine boat you have there. Teak, is it?'

'I'm not sure, sir. Do you think so?'

'Looks like it to me. Here, I had this made for you.'

Romain withdrew the boat he had concealed behind his back, its wood gleaming in the afternoon light, the cotton sails translucent. The flag of the French navy hung from the top of the mast. The boy gasped with pleasure, then gave Romain an uncertain glance. 'It's magnificent, truly. May I hold it?'

Romain grinned. 'Well, it's yours, so of course you must. I'd like to race you, with your other boat. There is no wind, so we'd need to push them.'

'That boat belongs to Solange. She likes boy's things, so I gave it to her. I was having my last turn with it. Your gift has come at the right time. Thank you.'

'Good to hear. Are you ready?'

'Yes.'

Romain grinned. 'Excellent. Hold yours evenly next to mine. All right, starting now.'

Romain allowed the boy to gain a strong lead as they guided their boats around the fountain. The water cleaved at the bows of the vessels and splashed their breeches as they laughed and jostled each other. After numerous circles around the fountain, Romain declared Tomas the winner.

'You must have the superior vessel,' Romain said, attempting to regain his breath.

'No,' Tomas said with a smile. 'You're just old. I can run faster. But it is a wonderful boat.' The boy dried the hull of the new vessel with the tail of his shirt.

They sat on the edge of the stone basin and placed the boats back in the water.

'How is Isabelle...I mean, your mother?'

'Maman is well, thank you. She keeps trying to fatten me up with pastries. Says I'm like a scarecrow.'

'I think you're looking very healthy. How is your learning progressing with your tutor?'

Tomas wrinkled his nose. 'He is a bore. All he does is drill me in Latin and sometimes mathematics. I want to work with horses; maybe I could run a farm. I watch my mother, the other mistresses, and all the people who visit here. They only seem to care about pleasing others. Yet the duc just pleases himself. I want to be like that, but I don't care at all about châteaux, fine clothing, or power.'

Several ducks, their wings stippled deep blue and green, landed on the edge of the fountain and dipped their beaks in the water.

'You have integrity, and at such a young age,' Romain said. 'I was like you when I was young, but I am afraid the world has corrupted me. The duchesse allows me to stay here, living in splendour, and in return I must entertain her ladies with readings. When positive predictions come true, they might slip me small pieces of jewellery or a gold louis or two. The negative predictions—well, no such luck for those.' He gave the boy a wry grin.

'But monsieur, do you not need an income in addition to these small handouts?'

'You're quite right, young man. My profession is tarot reading and the court is the most lucrative position for a tarot reader. The duchesse promised to help me with further introductions at

Versailles. Although I do have some connections there myself. I'm not completely useless.'

&

Tomas examined Romain's face, noticing the shape of his nose and the colour of his eyes. Like Tomas, he flicked his hair out of his eyes with a quick jerk of his head, and Monsieur de Villiers laughed with his whole body, touching his hand to his chest as if he were trying to hold his mirth in. Solange had often teased Tomas for laughing in the same way.

'You look like me,' Tomas said.

'I do, a little. There were many tribes in France, thousands of years ago. Perhaps our ancestors came from the same tribe?'

'Perhaps. Do you know anyone else who looks as much like you as me?'

'No, but let me tell you,' Romain said, crouching down to look the boy in the eye, 'if you look like me when you're older, you'll be fighting back the ladies. Do you like girls?'

'Ugh, no. They are so annoying, other than Solange, of course. She's as much fun as any boy.'

'But surely you appreciate their beauty, delicacy, and grace?' Romain smiled.

'Huh? I haven't really thought about it.'

'You should, Tomas. You know when the sun sets and you watch the colours change from pink to dark orange, and then deep blue? Well, women are like that—utterly mesmerising.'

&

The duchesse paced before her chamber window. She could see Romain and Tomas sitting on the edge of the fountain, deep in conversation, and felt a stab of envy. The boy had grown so tall, his limbs angular. She spoke to him sometimes, when they passed in the halls. He was polite and deferential but never at ease with her. Charlotte's chest ached. She placed a forefinger on the glass—from her perspective, it appeared as if her finger caressed the boy's head.

Behind her, Céline sat on the sofa and embroidered a small circle of fabric in a frame. The duchesse's Bichons napped on the Persian carpet, blue ribbons around their necks. Charlotte's thoughts turned again to her enemy.

'The cheek of that girl, monopolizing the Marquis d'Urveilles at court. Estelle was able to converse with him for only a few minutes before he took his leave. Letitia presumes to think she is an aristocrat, as high born as the courtiers. What are we to do, Céline?'

'A flirtation might be useful,' Céline mused with a sly smile, putting aside her embroidery and lifting a dog into her lap.

'Useful? How do you mean?'

'If Letitia were to have an illicit dalliance and the duc found out…' Céline smiled as she stroked the pink underside of the dog's ear.

'A marvellously wicked idea, Céline. We must dissuade Henriette from helping Letitia. Henriette is inclined, at the moment, to do the opposite of what I instruct and support the girl at all costs. To think we were once such good friends.'

'Henriette's self-righteousness is indeed a bore. She talks as if she were a devout Catholic, when everyone knows her late husband was a Huguenot who was tortured to death in the king's dungeons.'

'Heavens,' Charlotte said. 'I had heard he was a religious traitor, but I didn't realize the dramatic nature of his demise. Perhaps her piety serves as penance for his crimes.'

'Perhaps. She never speaks of him, have you noticed? It's as if he never existed.'

'Henriette did mention her husband to me once. She said he had…integrity. That's the word she used. She said it was his integrity that undermined him. I didn't dare ask how at the time. She was near tears, so I changed the subject.'

'Your husband hasn't even touched her hand in years,' Céline smirked. 'I think her piety makes her a cold companion in the boudoir.'

'I would prefer not to dwell upon the bedroom relations between my husband and his mistresses. I think if I consider it too much, I will need to banish you all.'

'Oh dear.' Céline laughed. 'I will desist then, as I am much in need of a home.'

꙲

Henriette sat on the same pew as Céline, but as far from the other woman as possible. A faint odour of straw and manure drifted through the open window from the adjacent stables. Streams of vivid-coloured light fell on the marble floor from stained-glass panels above the altar.

The priest, tall and emaciated in his black habit, resembled a scrawny crow with his consumptive face and sharp brown eyes. Leaning forward over his pulpit, his sermon filled the chapel with ecclesiastical menace.

'And I ask you, who of us has sinned and not felt the burning shame and desire to confess? It is only through confession and a sincere desire to repent that our sins can be cleansed in the eyes of God. May we avoid the fires of damnation and be carried through our travails, the breath of God behind, beside, and ahead of us.'

Henriette fingered the gold lettering on her Bible and avoided Céline's eyes, which she felt at intervals during the sermon. It was often just the two of them at chapel, and she always made sure to slip out before the other woman could engage her in conversation.

The priest gave his final blessing and nodded to them before retreating to the small anteroom at the rear of the chapel. Henriette walked outside and Céline hastened behind. The autumn air was cooler each morning, but the sun still radiated warmth on Henriette's upturned face. She watched the gardeners at work amid the damask roses, their petals bright pink. Despite her rapid stride, Céline kept pace until she was alongside her fellow mistress.

'Good day, Henriette. Isn't the garden looking splendid?'

'Indeed, Céline. This is a lovely time of year.'

'My mother used to love roses, bless her soul. Tended them for hours, as if they were babies. The duchesse, as I am sure you are aware, is obsessed with them too.'

'Now that you and the duchesse are such close friends, you might need to accompany her and learn about roses yourself,' Henriette remarked. 'Just be careful you don't get pricked by the thorns.'

Céline laughed, her eyes narrowing. 'I'll wear gloves, don't worry.'

'I'm not worried. What is it you want, Céline?'

'Your little charge, Letitia.'

'What of her?'

'She was flirting with the Marquis d'Urveilles. The duchesse wishes for him to get to know Estelle. You mustn't encourage this flirtation.'

'Is this an order, or a request?' Henriette came to a halt and folded her arms. 'How am I to control such a thing? If Letitia wants to flirt and the duc responds, what am I to do about it?'

'It is merely a request from Her Grace. Perhaps you can just guide Letitia toward proper behaviour and encourage in her a sense of loyalty to the duc.'

'I'm sorry, Céline. I don't believe I have as much influence with Letitia as you might imagine. In any case, she wouldn't do anything improper—she is grateful for her position here and faithful to His Grace.'

'Perhaps you're right. Just be aware, Letitia's behaviour is being scrutinized.'

'Thank you for keeping me informed. Now I must return to my rooms—Solange and I are going into town. Good day.'

Henriette stalked through the garden, her face flushed with anger. *How dare they*, she thought. *I won't be a puppet to either of them.*

Thirteen years before, Henriette's life had been quite different. She had lived with her husband, a printer of chapbooks and pamphlets, in a small stone cottage in Rennes. She'd spent her days traipsing through the woods with her daughter, teaching her songs and collecting mushrooms and roots that would form the basis for her *bourguignon* and other dishes. Money was often scarce, so she took in sewing to help meet the rent. Her husband's occupation was a perpetual worry. Léonard was an ardent advocate of the Huguenot cause and spent many nights making illicit pamphlets in their attic. Henriette knew he was discreet, but in Rennes word of traitors spread quickly. Anyone, from the baker who sold them bread to Madame Desroches, their watchful neighbour, could have denounced him. The week before he was taken into custody, he sent them away.

'Just to ensure you are both safe,' Léonard told Henriette, taking her hand in his. 'One day there will be religious tolerance in this country, Henriette. Perhaps in Amalia's lifetime.'

'Léonard, you must come with us.' She grasped his hand and kissed it fervently.

'I will feel better to have you both away from here, and St. Malo will be safe. If the king's guards come for me, you must go to my aunt's house in Beaune. She has a stack of gold bars for you underneath her floorboards, enough to keep you very comfortable. The coach is here. Quickly now! Where is that cheeky girl?'

'Here, Papa.' Amalia peeked out from beneath the tablecloth.

'Come here, my poppet. Give Papa a cuddle.'

All three embraced and Henriette kept her tears locked in her chest, unwilling to upset the child.

'I don't want to go, Papa. I can't take all my dolls. And St. Malo is deathly dull.'

Henriette took Amalia by her shoulders and swivelled her toward the door. 'You've never been, my sweet. The sea is so beautiful there. You know, I think there is a fair with a view of the water. Come now.'

The little girl broke free and ran to her father, wrapping her arms around his leg. Henriette coaxed her away, tears now streaming down her face.

In St. Malo, they waited weeks for news that it was safe to return, but in vain. By the time a courier delivered word of her husband's imprisonment, Henriette had started to sell her jewellery. Her wedding band secured them travel to Beaune. On discovering her husband's aunt no longer resided at the address she had been given, Henriette went from door to door, asking after Madame Rochard's whereabouts.

These enquiries led her, one early morning in October, to an Italianate mansion at the top of a hill, surrounded by grand stone walls. Fog blanketed the grounds, obscuring everything but the trees and the imposing lines of the mansion. A groundsman held back two growling wolfhounds and ushered her up the entrance road, lined with towering oaks. A manservant answered, with white gloves and an imperious gaze.

'I'm here to see Madame Rochard.'

'She is not here at present.'

'I'm her nephew's wife. I know she's here.'

The manservant retreated and there were muffled words from inside. Léonard's aunt appeared and stared through the gap in the door, her face pinched and scowling, her wiry hair pulled back tightly from her face.

'What do you want?'

'I am Léonard's wife. You must be Madame Rochard. Your nephew has been captured and he told me to find you. You have something of his, I believe?'

'I have his blood and that is all.'

'I beg you, madame. My husband told me to find you. We need help and you do have something for us.'

'I do not. Good day to you.'

Henriette wedged her foot in the door as the woman attempted to shut it. 'I refer to the gold bars Léonard gave you, the gold you keep hidden beneath your floorboards.'

Madame Rochard gave a mirthless laugh. 'You see before you a fine example of reverse alchemy, madame, the miraculous transformation of gold into stone and mortar. Now leave, before I set the dogs on you.'

'The gold was meant to support us if Léonard was imprisoned. What do you expect me to do? Sell myself on the street? You say you carry Léonard's blood. So does this innocent child. If you won't help me, please help my Amalia.' The little girl looked up at the older woman, her grimy face pleading.

Madame Rochard sighed. She fished a small drawstring bag from the folds of her skirt, and pressed a handful of louis into Henriette's palm. 'This should cover your travel to Blois. Saint Bernard de Thiron is a convent where you can leave the girl. Mention my name to the abbess, she knows me well. Wait here.' She turned and disappeared into an adjoining room.

Henriette's heart hammered in her chest and she gripped Amalia's hand, her mouth dry.

Madame Rochard returned with a small piece of paper. 'This is the address of my friend, Madame Tavel. She has connections at the Château d'Amboise. They are often looking for servants there. Good day.'

Before Henriette had a chance to reply the door had clicked shut and she was left standing with Amalia, watching the fog lift on the gridded gardens.

The maid had placed the brown paper package on her dresser. Charlotte ripped it open and withdrew five glass vials, unmarked and containing a liquid the colour of pond scum. *Thank you, Martine*, Charlotte thought, as she placed them in her concealed drawer. In her letter, Martine had described the liquid's capacity to cast a growing lassitude on a love affair, to bring forth feelings of restlessness and boredom. Martine swore to its efficacy. Charlotte burned the letter and sat to compose a reply, asking for as many bottles as Madame Foulbret could spare.

Charlotte had seen little of Hugo since his mother's visit. Her husband was surly in her company and her attempts at conversation were met with brusque monosyllables. One night Charlotte was jolted awake by the weight of Hugo's body as he slid into her bed, and the insistence of his fingers as he massaged her inner thighs. Before she could object he pushed himself hard into her. He placed one hand over her mouth and pinched her nipple with the other, his hips frenzied. Only months before, their coupling had been preceded by tender words and embraces. The following day, it was as if nothing had happened. Hugo nodded to her as they passed in the hallway. Later that day she saw him with Letitia, headed toward the stables. He was whispering something in her ear and she gave a coy smile in response.

Charlotte bit her lip, blood rushed to her face. She strode to her rooms and sat at her dresser. In the mirror, she noticed that the blotches that appeared on her chest and neck when she was upset had blossomed. Unlocking the drawer, she took out a vial of Madame Foulbret's liquid. Her letter had advised the application of two drops in food. She and Hugo were to dine together the following night. On the menu was pea soup, her husband's favourite.

'I've heard you're an excellent horsewoman.' Hugo draped his arm around Letitia as they stood at the entrance to the stables, inhaling the smell of old straw and dung.

'I'm not sure about that, but I've ridden horses since the age of five. I had my own stallion but he was sold to pay my father's debts.'

The horses snorted and whinnied in their stalls as Thibault approached, doffing his cap and bowing.

'Your Grace, Mademoiselle du Massenet, good day. How may I help you?'

'Good day, Thibault. Please prepare Tabour.'

'Yes, Your Grace. A perfect mount for the lady.'

Hugo walked ahead to find the stall of his horse, Zephyr.

'Ah, here you are,' he said, and pulled a carrot from his pocket. 'The king of horses. Come and see him, Letitia.'

She peered over the top of the stall. 'Goodness, he even eats elegantly. You're right, he is a beauty.' The horse snuffled in his food trough, his honey coat glossy.

'He's an Arabian. They're known for their intelligence and are bred for royalty. Look at the pride in his bearing. His queen is the black mare next door, Tabour,' Hugo said, gesturing toward the neighbouring stall.

Thibault readied the horses and Hugo and Letitia set out for the forest. Tabour was responsive and placid, and Letitia could feel the sun warming her back as they cantered toward the rear of the château, where it met the vast meadows and forests of the estate. Glancing up at the château as they passed, Letitia could make out the unmistakable silhouette of the duchesse at the window. She could not see her expression, yet dread filled her chest and dried her mouth.

Hugo urged Zephyr into a gallop and bellowed, 'Race you to the trees!'

Letitia tightened her grip on the reins and kicked Tabour's flanks, and the mare quickened her pace across the meadow, closing the gap between the two horses. The wind roared past her ears and Tabour's mane tickled her hands as she overtook the duc, the towering trunks of the forest looming closer. Letita flashed him a grin over her shoulder as she urged Tabour toward victory. As she approached the trees, she pulled hard on the reins and Tabour reared up, neighing in protest.

Hugo slowed Zephyr to a trot, then swung himself to the ground, his face gleaming with perspiration.

'You're quite mad,' he smiled, shading his eyes from the sun. 'You could have run that mare into a tree.'

'I could have, but I didn't.' Letitia slid to the grass below and smiled back. 'I know what I'm doing. I'm an excellent horsewoman, remember?'

Hugo reached over and brushed a lock of hair from her face. 'Cheeky. You will be punished. Come.'

Letitia was familiar with the look he gave her, both imperious and suggestive, and allowed him to lead her by the hand through the trees into the dappled light of the forest. The birds trilled above them and groups of red mushrooms and clusters of white cyclamen nestled between the rocks. The air was cool beneath the canopy, the shadows blue and undulating on the forest floor. The two reached a moss-covered clearing and Hugo spread his cape out upon the ground.

'Lie down,' he commanded. As soon as she was comfortable, he reclined next to her and clasped her to him, hiking up her skirts and petticoat. He spread her legs with one hand and kissed her mouth hungrily. Removing his breeches, he straddled her and was soon deep inside, pinioning her to the ground. She gasped and raised her hips to meet his. They rolled over the moss, tiny flowers and small twigs collecting in their hair, panting and groaning.

When it was over, she lay absorbed in her thoughts, twisting a piece of grass in her fingers. Hugo's arm was flung across her waist and he was half asleep. His physical attentions made her feel beautiful and womanly. Yet she knew in many ways, she was still just a girl.

Outside Madame Pauline Rolain's atelier well-dressed people strolled past the window and glanced at the finished gowns on display. Fresh lilies were placed around the room in crystal vases. Solange squirmed as the dressmaker finished a row of pins under her arm. She hung her head and glared at her mother.

'I thought we were having a *chocolat chaud* at Café Victoire. You promised. After, I wanted to go looking for frogs with Tomas.'

'We will, my dear. And when we return home, I'm sure Tomas will be waiting for you. But you also need a new dress, and for it to fit well, it must be pinned.'

'Ouch!' Solange winced, and Madame Rolain gave her a sharp look. She was a slender woman in middle age, with observant blue eyes and brown hair in a tight bun. Her movements were quick and capable, and she gave the impression of thinking more than she spoke.

'Mademoiselle, you must stop fidgeting. It won't be long now.' She frowned and tried to still the girl with her other hand. Pauline's atelier was situated in the most fashionable part of Blois, near the Café Victoire and the église Saint-Nicolas.

Henriette had declined Pauline's offer of tea and was regretting her decision. The stool she sat on grew harder each minute and her back ached. Glancing out the window, she caught sight of Romain sauntering down rue Saint-Laumer. His eyes locked with hers through the window and she felt heat rise in her cheeks.

'Excuse me, Madame Rolain. There is a gentleman I must say hello to outside.'

'Of course, madame.'

'Maman, you're leaving me here?' Solange whined.

'Only for a minute, my darling. Stand up straight, or the dress won't sit right. Shoulders back. Good girl.'

A bell tinkled as Henriette opened the door and she stepped outside, enjoying the crisp air on her cheeks. Romain smiled broadly as he removed his hat. Grasping her outstretched hand, he kissed it.

'What a lovely surprise. Good day, Henriette. I was just ordering a new pin at the jewellers. What brings you to town?'

'Solange needed a new dress. Any excuse, really, to get away from the château.' She flushed. 'I mean, er—'

Romain laughed. 'It's all right, I understand exactly what you mean and I admire your frankness. It is a little stifling there at times.'

'I don't know how you stand it,' Henriette confided, relieved at the opportunity to speak candidly. 'I've been there for such a long time and am accustomed to the mistresses' petty games. For others, from the world beyond the château, it all must seem very tedious.'

'The world beyond can be a chaotic and dangerous place,' Romain replied. 'For all the games, the château can also be a safe haven for those within its walls.'

Henriette twisted her hands, glancing at her daughter through the glass. 'There's something else I wanted to ask you. I would like a private tarot reading.'

He grinned. 'Madame, you amuse me. I thought you were a sceptic? You were quite the non-believer last time. What's happened since to change your mind?'

'A friend has convinced me that perhaps there is more to the tarot than I had realized. So, can you do it?'

'I will meet you in the library at nine o'clock tonight. Do you promise not to insult me this time?'

She smiled. 'I swear on the Bible.'

❧

The candelabra cast snaking patterns on the walls and the silver glinted in the low light of the dining room. The duc and duchesse sat at opposite ends, the mistresses and Romain on either side, and liveried servants took their places along each wall. The guest of honour, seated next to the duchesse, was Madame Martine Foulbret, who was dressed in a white gown with silver thread, with a phalanx of diamonds circling her throat.

'This pea soup is quite delicious,' Madame Foulbret pronounced. 'It is a balm to see you, my dear, as always. Your Grace, your wife has such splendid taste. She advised me on redecorating my rooms at Versailles.'

The duc tilted his head, as if trying to make sense of a foreign language. 'Yes, redecoration. Cushions, drapes, oriental vases and rugs. I seem to remember an endless process here, several years ago, and the exponential bill that followed. Fortunately you have the king's coffers behind you. I must forage for money in the air.'

'What a strange idea,' Madame Foulbret smiled. 'Good grief. Perhaps if you are foraging in the air, God might provide.'

'And that He does, madame. We are not at the poorhouse yet and may take pleasure in our comforts.'

The duc swirled the wine in his glass. 'Madame, my household visited the court recently. It was kind of you to look to their entertainment.'

'Yes, they all made quite an impression. Mademoiselle du Massenet, in particular, demonstrated her skill at word games.'

Letitia flushed with pleasure.

Charlotte glared at Madame Foulbret. 'Beginner's luck, I imagine. I would recommend another game, but I hear Letitia's too busy traipsing around the countryside like some peasant girl to be interested in court.'

'Letitia does like fresh air and riding. Exercise makes her even more beautiful,' the duc scowled at his wife. 'I don't believe these interests stop anyone from enjoying court.' Charlotte frowned, her husband's meaning as subtle as an executioner's axe—she was to desist or he would insult her, a humiliating outcome in the present company.

Charlotte glanced at Romain, seated next to Henriette. They appeared to be sharing a joke and she gripped her napkin in her lap, vowing to speak to him. She felt sealed off from them all, as if enclosed in a silent bell jar. She could not reach out, nor could anyone reach in.

❧

Henriette tapped her foot on the rug as she read a passage of Molière's *Tartuffe*— the words made little sense. She read them again, her mind scattered. The shelves of books reached the ceiling, their spines in reds and blues with gold lettering. Voluminous lilac drapes were drawn across the windows and she gave a furtive glance to the open doors.

Romain hesitated at the entrance and looked behind him before entering. 'I hope you don't mind if I read without my costume and candles—I couldn't smuggle it all here without drawing attention to myself.'

'Not at all. Please, come and sit down.'

Romain dragged an oriental table in front of Henriette's chair and moved another into position for himself. With a flourish, he drew the tarot cards from his inside coat pocket and shuffled them. 'So, what is it you would like to know?'

'My fate here at the château,' Henriette said.

Romain spread the cards face down on the table. 'Pick five cards. Select them carefully, madame. Choose ones you feel particularly drawn to.'

Henriette turned over five cards. The Hermit, the Tower, the Lovers, the Ace of Pentacles and the Four of Wands.

Romain examined the cards for a moment, touching each one. 'There will be great upheaval in your life, and a conflict which you cannot control. You will be forced to make a choice. The Ace of

Pentacles suggests a new start. You will feel at home with this person, a sense of fulfilment. This is indicated by the Four of Wands. The Lovers, of course, shows romantic love. You have been alone in your life, often feeling like an outsider looking in. This phase will end. The Hermit represents your past, and the Four of Wands a prophecy of your future, which suggests a partnership, of sharing in the bounty of life with another and celebration. Harmony and new beginnings. Henriette, I don't feel your future entails life at this château. Although there are trials ahead for you, the outcome will be positive. However, as with all prophecy, the outcome is still dependent on human choice, which cannot be foretold with certainty.'

Henriette traced the outline of the Lovers card with her index finger, where Cupid aimed his arrow at the pair from a cloud above. 'Thank you. Things are complicated already, you know.'

Romain placed a warm hand over hers, his thumb stroking the inside of her wrist. 'Yet if our lives were devoid of complications, how dull they would be.'

Henriette withdrew her hand slowly, her eyes level with his. Her breath was shallow and her mind raced. *I can't do this,* she thought. Being with him made her feel both pleasure and uncertainty.

'I must say goodnight to Solange. Thank you for the reading.' Henriette rose abruptly to her feet.

'There's no need to go. Stay. Have a brandy with me.'

'I cannot. Perhaps another time. Good evening.'

'How long will it take to work?' Charlotte asked Martine as they strolled along the garden path surrounding the orange grove. 'Hugo barely looked at me last night. I don't have much time, Martine.'

A fine mist gathered at the tops of the trees, and Charlotte gathered her shawl around her shoulders against the morning chill, her skirts sweeping out behind her.

'Slow down, Charlotte,' Martine protested, one hand over her heaving chest. 'My legs are stiff from sleeping. You will need to administer the potion over the course of three days before it will take effect. Although, I must warn you, it is not infallible.'

'And if it doesn't work? What then?'

Martine gave Charlotte a long look, as if measuring her words. 'There are other methods. We can look at directing powers against the girl instead, such as a Black Mass. Have you heard of this?'

'Yes,' Charlotte stood still, her brow furrowed. 'People have been imprisoned for performing the Black Mass, even for mentioning it in letters. Martine, what do you know about it?'

'The consecration can be charged with intent. You would need to participate in the ritual, however, and it can be dangerous.'

'What does it entail?'

'The sacrifice of an animal, the drawing of pentacles on the soles of the feet, ritual singing, the cloak of darkness, and utmost secrecy. You would need to be unclothed. If we were caught we would be imprisoned, possibly excommunicated. Would you consider it?'

Charlotte shuddered, imagining devil's horns and blood. Worse, being shut out from her faith, her church. 'I'm not sure. Let's see what transpires with the potion first.'

CHAPTER 12

Henriette studied the letter from the dressmaker. She read it, and reread it again, unable to believe its contents. Pauline's invoice to the duchesse for Henriette's last order had been unpaid. Henriette resolved to speak to the duc about the bill, before folding it and putting it away in the drawer of her bureau. She was sure he would not want his daughter or her to dress in worn clothing. *What might Charlotte inflict on me next?* Henriette thought. *Deny me meals in the dining room? Make me sleep in the hallway?*

Solange, twisting her hair around a finger, watched her mother as she stared pensively out the window. The sun was obscured behind a bank of thick cloud, and their rooms were dark. The firelight flickered, casting rippling shadows across the brocade drapes and plush Turkish rugs.

'Where are you going, Maman?' Solange asked as her mother slipped into her woollen coat.

'I have some business to attend to in town. I won't be too long. Why don't you go and do some reading in the library? You spend too much time with that ruffian Tomas—he is turning you into a boy. I'll have to hide my scissors lest you cut off all your hair.'

Solange grinned. 'No, Maman, I would never do that. I might start wearing breeches though. Watch out.'

Henriette smiled back. 'I will pray for you.' She tied the ribbons on her hat and hastened from the room.

Following the path to the stables she tried to distract herself from her worries. The duchesse had ceased to acknowledge her, and Henriette was sure she was speaking derisively about her to others. The other mistresses shifted away from Henriette during conversations, and sometimes even ignored her questions. The door of the stables creaked as Henriette pushed them open. Thibault was occupied brushing the duc's horse. In the adjacent coach house, an open *calèche* seemed the only carriage available.

'I'm sorry, madame,' Thibault said. 'I can give you a blanket, which should make you quite comfortable.'

'Thank you, Thibault. I'm sure it will be fine.'

Thibault helped Henriette into the carriage as Raoul, the driver, clambered into the front seat, a pipe between his teeth.

'Where are we going, madame?' he asked, the blue-tinged smoke from his pipe spiralling into the air.

'Saint Bernard de Thiron, Raoul.'

The wind picked up as they exited the towering iron gates, and the ochre leaves of the plane trees shivered. A weak sun emerged from the clouds, and shafts of light filtered through the foliage.

As they passed the fields, Henriette observed meandering sheep and farmers stacking hay bales.

They travelled through the town, pausing as children darted across the narrow streets, trailing after a farmer guiding his sheep to market. The glittering Loire came into view and the carriage traversed the arched bridge before veering onto a tree-lined boulevard. The horses cantered around the curve of road and the gates of the convent of Saint Bernard de Thiron came into view. Once grand, with ornate curlicues decorating a gleaming black surface, the gates had now fallen into disrepair and rust bloomed like flowers in the crevices.

Raoul pulled the reins and leapt out of the carriage to open the gates, wincing at their weight as he pushed them aside. Clambering back into his seat, he guided the carriage down the wide gravelled path to the convent's entrance, which was surrounded by a pillared portico. A bell tower with terracotta tiles crowned the building, a copper cross at its apex.

Henriette climbed the marble staircase to the front door.

A stooped housemaid, her grey hair covered with a white lace cap, opened the door to Henriette's knock.

'Good day, Madame d'Augustin. I will fetch Amalia for you and inform the abbess of your arrival.'

'Thank you, Béatrice.'

Henriette waited in the dim entrance hall. Coloured light streamed through the stained glass windows at the top of the grand staircase. The cold penetrated her boots through the tiled floor and she shivered. A grandfather clock ticked loudly against a wall and a faint chorus of laughing girls reached her ears. She jumped as a frigid hand covered her eyes then abruptly withdrew.

'Good morning, Maman.' Amalia was dressed in a simple blue serge dress, her dark hair plaited and wrapped around her head. Her face was freshly scrubbed and her blue eyes mischievous. Henriette felt her shoulders relax—Amalia was in a good mood.

'Amalia, you frightened me,' Henriette said. 'I'm glad to see you.'

'Let's go outside, Maman.' Amalia skipped toward the door. 'We can go for a walk before tea.'

Henriette handed her a package wrapped in brown paper. 'Open this first.'

Her daughter beamed and ripped the package open. She held out a white silk dress with a lace collar and and examined it before holding the fabric to her cheek. Its pearl buttons were lustrous.

'Thank you, Maman. It's lovely.' Tucking it under her arm, she led Henriette through a hallway to the back doors which opened up to the convent grounds.

The gardens were planted with oak and sycamore trees, which were dotted around winding paths. An elderly man dragged a rake over fallen leaves as they passed.

Henriette stole glances at her daughter's scarred wrists. The abbess had ordered the dormitory to be searched on several occasions, but Amalia's knife could not be found. Henriette suspected that Amalia pilfered blades from the kitchen and returned them after use.

'How is your Bible study? Are you still on the Corinthians?'

'Yes. When can I come to the château? The abbess says I may visit, that I only have to ask.'

'It's not possible, Amalia. I've told you that. I can visit you here.'

'I want to meet my sister. To see your rooms. To meet the duc.'

Henriette sighed and placed a hand on Amalia's shoulder. 'The duc does not know about you. If he did, I wouldn't be able to live at the château. If I didn't live at the château, you wouldn't be able to live here. I've told you this before.'

Amalia shrugged off her mother's hand, her eyes distant. 'I can come next week. I'll wear my best dress and you won't be ashamed of me.'

Henriette felt tears prick her eyes and stopped to put her hands on Amalia's upper arms, turning to face her. 'I'm not ashamed of you, Amalia. But you need to try and understand. My position, and your survival, depend upon your not coming to the château.'

Amalia pulled away, her lip curling, her eyes sharp points of fury. 'You're selfish and mean. I'll tell them all about you, you whore! You have the devil in you. I'll tell the priest to exorcise you. Everyone knows you manipulate me.'

'I'm not manipulating you, Amalia. Please calm down. We could visit another town perhaps. Would you like that?'

Henriette watched the furious rise and fall of her daughter's chest. Her arms and legs were rigid, and her eye twitched. 'Maybe. But I want tea now. I want to sit down.'

'Tea. What a lovely idea. Come now.' Henriette took Amalia's hand and led her toward the convent. At that moment, the abbess emerged from the shadows of the colonnade that ran along the side of the building.

'Good morning, Madame d'Augustin.' The abbess's robust form was clad in a long black habit, the only adornment a pearl and onyx crucifix hanging from her neck. Astute grey eyes were deep-set in her round face, unblemished and as pale as the moon. She wore a white headdress of starched linen.

'Good morning, Abbess de la Fontaine. Amalia and I were just about to ask for some tea. Would you like to join us?'

'I've already asked Béatrice to fetch it. Thank you, I'd like to sit for a while; my hip is troubling me.'

They sat in white cane chairs under the dappled shade of the colonnade. Groups of chattering girls passed, released from their morning prayers. The sun peeked from behind the clouds and Henriette listened to the rhythmic swish of the scythe as the gardener cut the grass.

Amalia sat perched on the edge of her chair, as if ready to dart away. As Béatrice placed the tray of tea on the table before them, Amalia submitted to the abbess's gentle instruction.

'Tell your mother about your recitation the other day. You spoke clearly and even made some eye contact with the girls.'

Amalia stared at the abbess, as if recognizing her for the first time.

'It was from the book of Job. He is like me. I have no one and God punishes me.'

The abbess gave a nervous laugh. 'Now, child, that is not true. Is this not your mother sitting before you?'

'She is ashamed of me.'

Henriette frowned. 'Amalia, I'm *not* ashamed of you.'

Her daughter ignored her. 'Job's wife says "Curse God and die." I want to do that. I want to curse him and I want to die. You are kind to me, Abbess, but only because your beliefs command you to be.'

'We must never curse God, child. He giveth and taketh away. To curse Him is to invite the latter. My kindness to you is that of a mother or an affectionate aunt. I've watched you grow from a child into a young woman. I assure you, my care for you is much more than just duty.'

'Why didn't you believe me then?'

'Believe what?'

'What I told you about Brother Deniel.'

'You know about her flights of fancy, madame,' the abbess spoke quietly to Henriette. 'Amalia's wild accusations are unceasing. How am I to know what is real and what is the elaborate construction of an unstable mind?'

'Now, dearest, apologize to the abbess,' Henriette insisted.

Amalia folded her arms. 'I will not. The disgusting man still comes here, you know. He has little stumps on his head, like the devil himself, and his feet don't touch the ground. I'm not the only one who knows this. Ask Françoise, or Isolde.'

Henriette sighed and placed her cup back in its saucer. 'Amalia, if you cannot show respect to the abbess, then perhaps the word of God might humble you. You may return to your dormitory to read your Bible.'

'But Maman—'

'Go.'

The girl lingered for several moments, sniffling, her eyes darting from the abbess to her mother, before she slunk back to the convent and disappeared through its doors.

'Normal discipline, madame, is for normal children.' The abbess's voice was just above a whisper, her eyes downcast. 'The girl will be silent, probably for days.'

'Perhaps I was a little harsh,' Henriette sighed. 'It's just...I come here and each time there is a part of me that expects things to be different, for us to have a conversation that is like a still pool, rather than a pitching ocean. I don't know how to talk to her.'

The abbess raised her chin, her gaze steady. 'Why don't you just let her talk to you?'

'You're right, of course. I'm too quick to react.'

The slam of a shutter caused Henriette to look up—a white object tumbled from the window, half engulfed with snaking flames. It landed a few yards from their table, and Henriette ran to it, stamping out the flames with her shoe. All that remained was a charred fragment of white lace and silk, two pearl buttons still attached.

The abbess dragged Amalia to the storeroom as soon as her mother left. A tiny window allowed a shaft of light to penetrate. Amalia hugged her knees as she sank into the corner, humming to herself. There was a leak in the roof and a steady drip sounded on the floor. Buckets, brooms, bottles of vinegar, and cloth dusters were stacked upon the shelves—all the necessary items for cleaning, sweeping, and scouring the endless halls of the convent. A thick layer of dust impregnated the airless space with a stale odour.

Amalia rose and peered through the lock. The garden was empty, and the wind tossed the branches of the trees to and fro. She tried the handle again but the lock held firm.

Through the keyhole Amalia could see flashes of orange between the branches: the sun was fading and supper was being prepared. She salivated at the thought of the stew and potatoes as she returned to her spot on the floor.

Amalia knew every crevice of the storeroom, even the location of the dead mouse the maids skirted around. Amalia could sense when she was about to be locked up. The abbess's anger would build over several days, increasingly apparent in a twitch around her mouth, a tremble in her hand, and the hard edge in her voice.

Footsteps sounded outside and the door creaked open. Brielle, a maidservant, stood with a crust of bread and a bowl of stew. 'Is a good dinner. You hungry, Amalia?'

Amalia nodded and took the bowl, scooping the food to her lips and muttering her thanks. Brielle's smile was bright against her inky skin. 'What you do this time, child?'

Amalia swallowed. 'Burnt a dress. Jumped on the beds without my clothes on.'

Brielle stifled a laugh. 'You full of the devil. Abbess will beat you soon if you not behave.'

Much later, when moonlight filtered through the high window, the abbess let Amalia out and guided her back to the dormitory.

'Make a list of your sins for the confession. It's been a bad week. Try to do better tomorrow.'

'Yes, Abbess. I'm sorry.'

❧

Amalia lay on her back, the sheets stretched over her body and tucked tightly beneath the mattress. Moonlight fell on the line of beds, giving them the appearance of graves in a cemetery. She listened to Isolde, who lay in the neighboring bed, talking under her breath to Renée. 'Clémence told me. It's true. Brother Deniel touched her, then she killed herself by jumping from the dormitory roof.'

'I've seen her,' whispered Amalia.

'She's dead, Amalia, how could you possibly have seen her? And fairies, have you seen them as well?' Isolde sniggered.

Amalia rolled on to her side. She had glimpsed the girl in her long white nightgown standing in the dormitory, staring out the window. Sometimes Amalia couldn't see her but felt her presence, knew that she was there. Amalia, too, felt like a ghost, barely seen by the other girls, drifting from bed to garden to prayers, as transparent and unnoticed as a cloud.

Romain weaved around a procession of servants carrying silver-domed platters, from which wafted tantalizing aromas of suckling pig and onion soup. Madame Foulbret had invited him to Versailles, suggesting he read the cards for the Vicomtesse de Chambord. Word of his talent had reached her ears, and most likely whispers of his other abilities. Charlotte also wished him to facilitate communication between Letitia and the Marquis Antoine d'Urveilles. He knew the marquis well, having grown up in his family's château, as the son of their head maid. They had been out of touch for some years, and met again at the tavern as young men. In those days, the marquis had not yet found favour at court, and had been drinking to excess after a recent gambling loss.

In the Salon de la Paix, Romain spotted the marquis near the window, ignoring the chatter of three women clustered about him. Antoine stared at his pocket watch with a glum expression.

'Good day, Antoine. Why the sad face? All these flowers are blooming around you.'

The marquis looked sideways, as if noticing the women for the first time. 'Ladies, my friend and I need to speak alone. Why don't you go for a stroll?'

The three women rose and glided away, their displeasure evident.

'You're staying at the Château d'Amboise, is that right?'

Romain nodded, taking the seat next to Antoine. 'Yes. The duchesse is an old friend of mine.'

'Come now, Romain. Everyone knows that's a euphemism for an old lover. Do you still bed her?'

'If she'd let me. She's too focussed on intrigues and reining in her husband. Still, there's much to keep me entertained there. Why do you ask?'

'The young girl, Letitia. She haunts my every moment. Will she be visiting here again, do you think?'

'Perhaps. You know, I see her most days. If you wished to write to her, I would be happy to pass on your letters to her, and hers to you. Discreetly, of course.'

'Do you think she'd like to correspond? We've only met once—'

'I saw how she looked at you, Antoine. I have no doubt.'

'If there were any chance of the letters being intercepted… Romain, I've heard of the duc's skill with a sword. I don't fancy a duel.'

'I would guard them with my life, I promise.'

'All right. I'm in Blois once a fortnight; my aunt lives there. We could meet at the tavern?'

'Yes, I'm there once a week, to visit a friend.'

'A friend? Do you mean your *putain* at Madame Rochas's?'

'Giselle is very refined in her way. She looks after me, and I look after her. Loyalty. I'd wager you don't find much of that among your high-born paramours?'

'They're loyal to their hairdressers and dressmakers. Forgive my cynicism, my friend; it would be refreshing indeed to meet a woman of pure intentions, if such a one exists.'

Romain looked around the room. The women dressed in shimmering silks reclined or circulated with perfect grace, resembling elegant birds, flaunting their plumage. 'I have found such a one,' he mused. 'She lives at the château. And your Letitia, she is the same.'

❧

At dawn, dressed in a wool riding coat and breeches, Letitia tiptoed down the stairs and went to the stables. It felt strange to walk in breeches and she strode out, relishing the sensation.

Thibault had not yet arrived from his quarters, and she saddled the honey-coloured mare, Fidela. Climbing on the horse's back, she sat astride and guided the mare to the field behind the château. Coaxing the horse into a trot, Letitia leaned forward, the icy wind rushing past her cheeks. The fog cleared and the sun outlined a bank of clouds with gold.

Letitia had much on her mind and the crispness of the morning air helped clear her thoughts. She had received a letter from her mother, seeking details of her new life. Letitia wanted to reply, but did not know what to say. Would she admit she had only one friend? Or that the duc rarely asked about her thoughts and feelings? In truth, Letitia felt like a pampered doll, displayed on a shelf and taken down for amusement. The duc enjoyed her body, but only seemed interested in her words if she kept them light and trivial. No mention was made of the miscarriage, or the incident that had caused it.

As was often the case when Letitia rode, she thought about her sister, Madeleine. Ten years old forever, her rounded cheeks dimpled and pink, her hair like their father's, dark and wavy. Her riotous laugh, Letitia recalled, had carried through the halls of the manor.

She remembered the day of the accident, her sister's hair streaming behind her and her head turning with a wide smile as she galloped ahead on her mare. Letitia saw the log blocking the path, but her shout of warning came too late. She screamed as her sister was thrown over the horse's head, landing face down on the ground. She still recalled the horror of Madeleine's head, twisted at an odd angle, and her wide open eyes, now sightless. Letitia gathered her sister's still-warm body to her chest, the words of the catechism tumbling from her lips. It was hours before the groom found them. Two additional groomsmen were required to remove Letitia, eyes wild and unfocussed, from her sister.

After the funeral, her father threw himself into his new business venture with his friend Pierre and her mother consoled herself with countless dresses and shoes from Paris. Financial ruin came when her father discovered that Pierre had overestimated the returns on their investment. There were whispers of a ship sinking—somehow, Letitia understood this was connected to the investment. Combined with the debt of her mother's Parisian fashions, the family found themselves in dire financial straits. While her parents argued, their shrill, angry voices echoing through the rooms of the manor, Letitia spent more time walking the grounds and hiding in the forest. She stole food scraps for the squirrels, picked wildflowers, and wrote poems in a leatherbound journal. It was only a matter of weeks before she realized her parents' plan to avoid debtors' prison.

Letitia's legs were beginning to tire. She rode Fidela back to the château, enjoying the sound of the grass swishing against the animal's legs as they neared the end of the field.

Handing the reins to Thibault, she noticed his eyes flicker to the breeches. He looked her in the eye. 'Fine morning for a ride, mademoiselle.'

'Yes, it was lovely when the sun came out,' she said breathlessly. 'Thank you, Thibault.'

The sofa in the nursery was covered in dolls and toys of all sizes. Letitia reclined and crossed her legs. Solange appeared in the doorway and grinned when she saw Letitia. 'Did you sleep here? And why are you wearing breeches?'

'Good morning. They're good for riding. No, I didn't sleep here. Where's Tomas? I'm in the mood for a game.'

'Spying or hide and seek?'

'Spying, definitely.'

Solange sidled up to Letitia on the sofa, taking her hand. 'Can I play with your hair again? It's so pretty. I want to braid it. Tomas is coming; he's just caught up a little. One of his frogs died.'

Letitia turned her back to Solange, removed her combs and

allowed her hair to cascade down her back. 'It's all yours. Shame about the frog. Was it Gonzo or Prince Longlegs?'

'Prince Longlegs. He got his leg caught in a fence.'

'Oh, dear. Ouch—stop pulling so hard!'

'Sorry.' Solange relaxed her grip and hesitated before asking, 'How is your stomach?'

'It's getting better, slowly. I have to rise carefully from sitting, but otherwise not too bad. Why do you ask?'

'Before you were injured I saw Madame de Poitiers rummaging through your drawers.'

'She must have put something on my stays,' Letitia exclaimed. 'The witch. There are people in the world, Solange, whose only intention is to harm others. Be careful, won't you? If she knows you suspect her, she might harm you too.'

Solange picked up a silver hairbrush and ran it through Letitia's hair. 'Nobody will find out. Everyone thinks I'm sweet and innocent. I'll keep hiding and finding out what everyone is up to. I have silent shoes—look.'

She held out her feet, clad in ballet slippers, for Letitia to examine.

Letitia nodded. 'Ah, so that's your secret. You are cunning. I hope you don't spy on me, too?'

'No, silly. I don't spy on my friends. There you are, Tomas. What are we playing today?'

'Child, come here! You must get dressed!' Abbess de la Fontaine winced as she followed the scampering girl through the halls of the convent, her sore legs preventing her from anything more than a pained, shuffling walk.

The maid, Brielle, ran ahead, her white cap falling to the ground as she grasped Amalia's wrist. The girl shook her off with a laugh, dancing like a heathen, her naked torso writhing and jerking in all directions, her hair an impenetrable knot of matted clumps.

'Leave me alone!' Amalia shouted, breaking into a run once more.

Abbess de la Fontaine leaned against a nearby bannister.

'Catch her, Brielle,' the abbess urged the maid. 'Catch her and clothe her.'

'What I do then, Abbess?' Brielle's mahogany skin shone with perspiration.

'Strap her to a chair outside the dormitory, where all the girls can see her.'

Brielle bounded down the staircase after the fleeing girl.

The duchesse was bent over the last of the autumn roses, secateurs in hand. Isabelle approached, her footsteps crunching on the gravel path.

'Good morning, Charlotte. Those roses are looking a little sad.'

The duchesse turned her head, squinting at Isabelle through the glare of the bright morning sun as she dropped clippings into a straw basket.

'Good morning, Isabelle. Yes, their time is over. Happens in nature and in life. How are you? That boy of yours is a scoundrel, running all over the place.'

Isabelle smiled. 'He is no more a scoundrel than any other boy. You wouldn't understand, having a daughter. Boys have too much energy for their bodies. They need to let it out. A bit like those Bichon dogs of yours.'

Charlotte pressed her lips together. 'Thank you for reminding me of my lack of a son.'

'Sorry. There is still time, and, of course, Tomas is your son, just not in a way anyone can know about. Listen, I need to talk with you. Can we stroll together?'

'Certainly. Please, don't speak of my relationship to Tomas aloud. You never know who might be listening.'

'Yes, of course. Sorry.'

Charlotte pulled off her leather gloves and dropped them in the basket, before taking Isabelle's arm. 'What's troubling you?'

'I'm perplexed, Charlotte, and worried by your alliance with

Madame de Poitiers. I do not believe she can be trusted. Why do you confide in such a devious creature? We used to talk more often, you and I.'

The women pulled their shawls closer against the chill. The sun was weakening and the days were becoming shorter. In Blois, the winters came quickly, blanketing the mountains in snow. Above them, the skies were gunmetal with impending rain.

'She is devious. I have plans and her calculating mind has been useful to me. But you are right; we must spend more time together.'

Her words did not erase the knot on Isabelle's forehead. 'It isn't just Madame de Poitiers that concerns me. It's not unnatural for your husband to take a mistress, and Letitia really is quite a lovely girl, if you only took the time to get to know her.'

The duchesse stopped walking and looked at Isabelle as if she were mentally deficient. 'Lovely? I couldn't care less if she were Mary Magdalene herself. She has claimed the full attention of my husband. This is a situation that threatens not only myself, as his wife, but you, Isabelle, and the other mistresses. What do you think will happen when he tires of us all?'

'I understand, Charlotte, but I think the novelty will wane. Rather than undermining Letitia, which only angers your husband, why not seduce him, talk to him? If you're seen to be acting against her, he will draw further away from you, and I hate to see you so tortured, so unhappy.'

'My husband has never been so besotted as he is with that tiresome girl. Isabelle, you have a special place in my heart. Don't disappoint me by helping that little *putain*, will you?'

Isabelle sighed and looked away, her eyes filling with tears. 'No, Charlotte. Of course not.'

Charlotte patted Isabelle's gloved hand. 'Why don't you go back inside? It's almost time for tea. I will be in shortly.'

&

1692

Charlotte inhaled the yeasty scent of the little boy's head, and watched his mouth open in a yawn, his face flushed red. Her mother waited, arms outstretched.

'Come now, Charlotte, hand him over. We must be gone.'

A maid stepped forward. 'Madame la Comtesse, let me help you.'

'No. I shall do it.'

Charlotte ignored her mother, enjoying the weight of her son, the feel of his tiny hand clutching her nightgown. Long eyelashes dusted his cheeks and his lower body was swaddled in white linen. The gold light of dawn seeped in through a gap in the curtains.

Her mother leaned forward and tried to wrest the infant from her daughter's arms.

'No, Maman, you can't have him,' Charlotte protested, cradling the babe to her chest.

'You're to be married, Charlotte. The child must go to Aunt Louisa in the convent. Six months away in Antibes—you're lucky the duc didn't throw you over for another fiancée close to home.'

'There has to be a way, Mother. He is mine, don't you see?' Charlotte implored, eyes wide. 'Please, Mother, he is my son!' The boy made a popping sound with his mouth and his dark blue eyes stared into her own, filling her with guilt. Her vision blurred with tears as her mother took the baby and she watched his plump little hand separate from her collar. A keening sound erupted from Charlotte's throat and her body shook uncontrollably. She reached out for her wailing baby as he was whisked away. Hours later, his screams still reverberated in her head.

In the days that followed, Charlotte lay listlessly in her bed, unable to eat or rise. Her breasts leaked milk just as her eyes flowed with tears, both drenching her nightgown. A servant wrapped her breasts in fabric and changed her nightgown, whispering soothing words.

Isabelle visited and, stroking her hair, murmured, 'I have an idea. What if I were to come to the château with you? Do you think perhaps the duc might accept me as a mistress? With an illegitimate child—your child? Could you ask him, as a favour in light of your marriage? That he might help your unfortunate friend in her predicament?'

Charlotte turned to Isabelle, a spark in her eyes. 'Isabelle, yes. The duc desires my comfort, after all, and I shall tell him I cannot settle without my childhood friend. Oh, Issy, would you really cast such a shadow upon your reputation for me?'

'Yes, dearest. You know I adore you. I'll be a good mother to him.'

Charlotte wrapped her arms around her friend, hope blossoming within her. Isabelle—more of a younger sister to Charlotte than the daughter of her governess—had long imitated Charlotte's manner of dress and way of speaking, often accepting the blame for her idol's girlish misdemeanours.

The Comte and Comtesse de Rennes were like strangers to their daughter. Charlotte's mother spent her days at the court gambling tables or in consultation with her dressmaker. There were rumours of affairs with both high- and low-born men. Her father locked himself in the library with a crystal decanter of brandy, his approach preceded by a sour waft of alcohol. Charlotte's upbringing had been entrusted to Isabelle's mother, Juliette, and an ever-changing retinue of servants and tutors.

The comtesse sat on an armchair in the drawing room, covering her mouth with her hand to stifle a yawn. Charlotte had arranged the meeting and forced herself out of bed to meet her mother. Her brow throbbed with a headache and her legs were weak.

'And how are you feeling, dear?'

'A little better, thank you, Mother. I have decided on a name for the baby.'

'And why might that be?'

'Because I have found a way to take him to my new home. Isabelle will pretend to be the poor mother of this illegitimate child. A friend from whom I'm inseparable.'

'Are you sure Isabelle understands what she is undertaking? Never to be married and taking on another woman's child?'

'Yes, it was Isabelle's idea.'

'Dear, you are terribly naïve. I simply cannot allow it, you might be found out.'

'Yes, and what if Father found out about all your dalliances, Mother? How might he react, do you think?'

'I shall speak to your father and see what I can do.'

'Thank you, Mother.'

On the day the duc arrived to meet with the comte, the comtesse hid the brandy, but her husband found the wine. He hiccupped through the meeting, yet managed to attain agreement from the duc.

'Charlotte's desires are mine, as long as the girl is comely. Let me view her,' the duc said, watching disconcerted as his future father-in-law broke into song—a raucous sea shanty, complete with lyrics about women's anatomy. The comte bowed after the final verse and the duc stared, before giving a limp-handed clap.

'A celebratory song, dear boy. You are to be my new son! Can I get you a brandy?'

The duc shook his head. 'No, thank you. I must be on my way. Could I perhaps see Charlotte and her friend before I depart?'

'Ah no, she is in town with her mother. Throwing away money, that's womenfolk for you. But Isabelle, yes, that can be arranged.'

The duc approved of Isabelle's curvaceous Italian looks, and two months later, following a lavish wedding, the two girls and the infant went to live at the Château d'Amboise.

CHAPTER 13

Why do you not visit me more often?' Giselle murmured in Romain's ear, her fingers massaging the taut muscles in his shoulders. 'Every spare moment I have, I sit on my windowsill and watch the road.'

Romain sighed, inhaling the scent of another man's sweat on the sheets. An image flashed into his mind—Henriette staring at the cards, a tendril of hair falling over her shoulder as she looked up at him, her lips parted, her skin porcelain white. He blinked the image away and Giselle's hands stilled.

'Romain? Did you hear me?'

'I have had to give many readings, Giselle. I can't live on good looks alone; I must earn my keep.'

'Does the duchesse want to bed you, Romain?'

'Charlotte is too busy trying to discredit her husband's new mistress to think of the pleasures of the flesh.'

'I don't believe it. You know, I have a theory about you.'

'And what is that?' he asked.

'You're a bad man with noble intentions. You will be good, you just don't know it yet.'

Romain ran his hand over the length of her, before parting her legs and stroking her inner thighs.

'You think too highly of me, Giselle. I am nothing more than an entertainer saddled with debt. Nothing admirable about that.'

Giselle panted, guiding his hand higher. 'Maybe you're right. But to me, you are a saint and a gentleman hiding behind the appearance of a rogue. Ah...keep going...'

Romain pinned her hands behind her head and guided himself into her.

ॐ

Romain's aunt lived on the edge of town in a two-room house, the wooden boards patched with canvas sacking. She had four children, all under the age of eight. Romain approached the door carrying a crate of vegetables, a baguette in the crook of his arm.

'Anyone home?' he called. The door creaked open slightly, and a blue eye stared out from a face streaked with dirt. 'Is that you, Carmine?'

The door swung open and the child flung herself at Romain's leg, burying her face in his breeches. He ruffled her white-blonde hair, looking down at the bony knobs of her spine at the base of her neck. 'Where is your maman?'

'Maman is sick.'

The remaining three children stampeded toward the door and volleyed a barrage of questions at him. The eldest boy took the crate as his sister tugged Romain inside. The children were thin, hollow-eyed, and clad in ragged and stained clothing. Romain cursed himself silently for being unable to do more for his cousins.

'Have you seen the king?'

'Do you drink hot chocolate at the château?'

'Have you a lady there?'

Romain laughed, holding up his hand to silence them. 'No lady, I'm afraid. They are too good for the likes of me. Now, show me your maman.'

Carmine led Romain to a dim, airless room. Thin mattresses, pungent with damp, were laid out at varying angles on the floor. In the corner one of the mattresses was covered in a mound of blankets, his aunt's small frame cocooned beneath.

'Is that you, Romain?' she said feebly, clasping the edge of the blankets with a thin hand.

'Marianne, what is it? What ails you?' Romain asked, approaching her. He was shocked at the sight of his aunt, who had seemed robust on his last visit. The contours of her face were sharply delineated, the hollows of her cheeks sunken. A film coated her brown eyes as she winced and tried to smile.

'Romain, so kind of you to come. I'm weak, and I haven't been able to rouse myself from here since yesterday.'

He took her hand and frowned—it felt as chilled as a corpse. 'I will fetch the physician.'

'I have not a sou, Romain.'

'Don't concern yourself. I will arrange everything.'

'Francois, run and find Doctor Juret. Do you remember where he lives?'

The boy gave a solemn nod, before scampering from the room.

Marianne was helped into a rush-backed chair and Doctor Juret examined her, his forefingers held to her wrist. The children milled around, one of them sneaking a glimpse inside the physician's black leather bag of instruments. 'Your pulse is weak, and you have a fever. You are suffering from grippe, and need bed rest. Is there anyone who can help with the children for a little while?'

'There is no one,' Marianne said, 'and my youngest is barely walking.' Her chest rose and fell as she gulped in air, and tears ran in rivulets down her cheeks.

Romain clasped Marianne's hands in his own. 'What about Madame Barras, next door? Could she take the younger ones?'

'Perhaps, but I have to work, Romain.'

He pulled a wad of livres from his pocket and pressed them into her hand. 'Not for the next few weeks, you don't. This will keep you from the debtors until you're better.'

'Thirty livres?' she stared wide eyed at the notes in her hand. 'Romain, this is too much. You will need some of this, surely?'

'There are always more readings, Marianne. Take it. I'll speak to Madame Barras.' He turned to the doctor. 'Does she need medicine?'

The doctor withdrew a brown bottle from the bag. 'Yes, here is a tincture. She must take a spoonful twice a day.'

'Thank you, Doctor Juret. How much for your time?'

'It is *gratuit*, monsieur.'

'You're very kind, God bless you.'

'*Ce n'est rien.*' The doctor clicked his bag shut and placed his hat on his head. He nodded to them, and made for the door.

Romain bantered with Madame Barras, offering to give her a reading if she took care of the two youngest children. She chuckled into her apron and waved the grubby toddlers inside. 'You are a scallywag, monsieur. I need to find out if my husband has another woman. Come back next week with your cards.'

'I look forward to it, madame. Carmine, keep an eye on Edouard, make sure he doesn't put the wrong things in his mouth.'

Carmine grinned. 'Yes, Tati de Vill, I'll be a perfect little maman.'

Romain stopped at the tavern, his remaining livres in his pocket. A fug of acrid smoke hung in the air and the room smelt of spilt ale and sweat. Light filtered through the small windows, illuminating swirls of smoke and dust. He approached the gaming table in the corner, his heart thudding as the men whooped and jostled. A scowling man flung down a handful of coins and slunk away, shoulders hunched.

'New game?' Romain asked. His gambling nemesis, Jean Buvelot, watched him with wary eyes, a pipe clamped between his lips. He wore a gaudy embroidered waistcoat, and his stomach drooped over his breeches. His face was as hirsute as a bear, with the glazed stare of a heavy drinker.

'Ah, feel like a thrashing, do you, de Villiers?'

'Quite the contrary, good man,' Romain said. 'I'm here to obtain every note and coin from your pockets.' He dropped his crumpled notes on the table and drew up a chair.

Romain shook the leather cup with a flourish and let the dice tumble with a clatter to the wooden surface. Two sixes.

Jean scowled. 'That is the last of your luck,' he growled. 'Don't count on it continuing.' Seizing the cup from Romain, he rattled the container and rolled the dice, a two and a three.

Romain smiled as Jean sipped brandy from his glass, wiped his mouth on his sleeve, and moved a checker along the board. Romain maintained his lead, rolling fives or sixes each time. Jean took larger gulps from his glass, eyes unfocussed, his large frame rocking in the chair. The spectators exchanged knowing glances—they could see the outcome in advance and passed wagers under the table. One of them, a wayward priest who had left the seminary, clapped Romain on the back. 'God is with you today, son. You'll have to attend Mass this week, to pay your respects.'

Romain laughed. 'God abandoned me a long time ago, Laurent. He watched me putting frogs in the teacher's pocket and handed me over to the Devil.'

'Nonsense. He forgives everyone, even Jean here.'

Jean turned and smashed his glass on the table top, sending several checkers careening to the floor. 'You needling me, Laurent? What sort of religious man are you, anyway? You drink, gamble, and, by all accounts, fornicate. Why don't you shut your mouth?'

Laurent held up both hands in a gesture of peace. 'Now, now, Buvelot. Steady on. I was only having a joke.'

'Jokes are funny. You're about as funny as the Pope having a clyster.'

The men burst into laughter, and Jean's face reddened under his coarse nest of hair.

'Let's finish the game, all right?' said Romain. 'I have a feeling you've some sixes to roll.' Not long after, Romain scooped up the rest of his checkers, deposited them on the table, and beamed at the surrounding men. Jean withdrew a stash of notes from his pocket and slammed them down.

'Those of you who wagered on me can have a share of my winnings. Jean, terribly sorry. It might be an idea to drink water next time, hmm?'

Jean pushed himself to his feet, swayed, and flailed at Romain, his large fist swinging toward the younger man's head. Romain ducked and Jean lost his balance, rotated like a spinning top, and toppled to the floor with a thud.

Laurent, with the help of an onlooker, picked Jean up by the armpits and manoeuvred him into a sitting position. 'Cheating scoundrel, let me at him...' Jean slurred.

Romain bowed to the men, adjusted his wad of notes into a perfect rectangle, and buttoned up his coat. 'Gentlemen, good day to you.' He flung some livres onto the table. 'Have some ale on me.'

A chorus of goodbyes resonated as he grinned and took his leave.

❧

Charlotte sat at a window seat, reading a passage in her book over and over again. She tapped her foot on the parquetry and glanced at the door. The potion in the soup had had little effect on Hugo, and Madame Foulbret, upon being pressed, admitted that some people were immune. If anything, her husband seemed even more indifferent to her than before.

One of the double doors creaked open and Romain entered, the door clicking shut behind him. A fire blazed in the grate and the room was stifling. He leaned down and kissed her hand.

She sniffed. 'You've been in bed with someone.'

'No, Charlotte.' He ran his index finger up her arm and neck, letting it rest on her jawline. She took his hand and turned it over, stroking his palm.

'Have you some letters from the marquis?'

'I have two.'

'Are they ardent?'

'Very.'

'You've done well. Thank you. Keep one, and compose a suitable reply. Here is a note she gave my husband—her handwriting looks easy to replicate. I shall keep the other. Tell the marquis he mustn't discuss the letters with her, as she would feel uncomfortable given the danger of correspondence.'

'And the boy, Romain? Have you talked with him?' she asked.

'Yes. Tomas is a fine young man, as I expected.'

'He is intimidated by me,' Charlotte twined her fingers through his as she pulled him down to sit beside her. 'I try to speak with him and he won't make eye contact. I watch him play outside. There is a good view of the fountains from here, where he likes to sail his boat. Such a scamp, just like his father.'

122

Romain leaned toward her, brushing her neck with his lips. 'Let me kiss you.'

'How many others, Romain?'

'Don't concern yourself,' Romain whispered, his breath hot in her ear. 'I have no claim on you and you have no claim on me. But there are feelings and urges. Do you still know my thoughts? I know yours. You're neglecting yourself and are enveloped in sadness.'

Charlotte kissed him, raking her fingers through his hair. 'I am no sadder than I've always been,' she murmured between kisses. 'Do you know what it's like to be alone all your life?'

Romain whispered, his eyes half-closed and his breath ragged. 'You're not alone. You have me. Always.'

'Unhook my bodice,' Charlotte demanded. 'I want to feel your hands on my skin. I do know your thoughts. You want Henriette, don't you? Don't waste your time, she is too pious for you. Would she do this?' Charlotte gripped his crotch. He moaned and turned her around, his fingers fumbling at the hooks.

Romain pinioned her from behind, the bodice of her dress hanging down and the skirts hiked up. Her palms were flat on the glass, and their breath fogged the surface. It was quiet, save for the rustle of taffeta, a muffled whimper from Charlotte's throat, and the squeak of skin against glass as her hands moved.

In the rose garden below, Letitia stared up, her mouth open in astonishment.

CHAPTER 14

Sheets of rain hammered the roof of the carriage as Henriette and Letitia arrived at Versailles. They had escaped the confines of the château on the pretext of an excursion into town. Romain had promised to meet them in the reception room before taking them to the Salon de la Paix.

The footman hunched at their carriage door, holding an umbrella over their heads as they stepped down to the wet cobblestones.

'Oh, this is awful,' said Henriette, shivering. 'The silk of this dress is entirely too thin. I hope they have the fires stoked.'

They stepped with care to avoid puddles, yet the hems of their dresses were soon wet. A roll of thunder drummed the air as they hurried inside.

Romain leaned against a pillar, his posture relaxed. He wore a navy velvet coat and grey breeches, his hair tied back neatly. Henriette mused that she had never seen him look dishevelled. He approached them and kissed their hands, his eyes lingering on Henriette. 'Ladies, good day to you both. The marquis is waiting in the salon. He has just returned from hunting with the king.'

They followed him, Letitia craning her neck to absorb the frescoes that covered the ceiling in vivid colour.

Henriette smiled and nudged her. 'Perhaps save your art appreciation for the salon; you might run into something, or someone.'

The younger woman poked her in the waist, whispering into her ear. 'Is it not better than you, staring at the monsieur's back as if you wished to climb all over him?'

Henriette blushed. 'What nonsense, I'm just ensuring we do not lose him.'

'Of course. My mistake.' Letitia smiled knowingly and took Henriette's hand. 'I'm desperate for some *chocolat chaud*.'

The two women could hear the murmur of voices as they neared the double doors of the salon. Two bewigged servants stood on either side of the entrance, their faces inscrutable.

Romain nodded at one of them. 'We are here to see the Marquis d'Urveilles.' One of the manservants acknowledged them with a slight bow and opened the door.

Several heads turned as they entered and Henriette felt eyes on every part of her, from her elaborate coiffure, slightly dishevelled, to her satin shoes, damp from the rain, and her dress, fashionable the previous season. Since her estrangement from the duchesse, funds for the seamstress had ceased. *Never mind*, Henriette thought, forcing a determined smile. *I'm only here for Letitia anyway.* Her friend had often mentioned the marquis in private, and when Henriette had questioned Romain, he had been quick to offer his assistance.

The Marquis d'Urveilles sat in a corner, a small goblet of brandy resting in his tapered hand. Spotting the two women, the marquis's face brightened and he stood. 'Mademoiselle, madame, how lovely you both look this afternoon,' he murmured with a bow. He motioned to the empty armchair next to him and Letitia perched on the edge, her eyes darting around the room. Henriette sat next to Romain, on an overstuffed *fauteuil*, just large enough for two.

Madame Foulbret gliding past, paused to greet them.

'Good day, Madame d'Augustin, Mademoiselle du Massenet, Monsieur de Villiers. Is the duchesse not well today? Or have you misplaced her?'

'The duchesse is otherwise occupied, madame,' Romain answered with a smile. 'She sends her good wishes. In fact, I have a note from her.' He passed Madame Foulbret a folded square of parchment, sealed with a neat circle of red-stamped wax.

'Ah, thank you, monsieur. She does like to receive regular dispatches from me, and I am happy to oblige her. Do send my regards.'

'Certainly, madame.'

The marquis clicked his fingers and a servant took their orders for tea, *chocolat chaud*, and brandy. Henriette watched Romain from the corner of her eye. Their gaze met and she looked away, her mind devoid of conversation.

'You have a becoming flush to your cheeks today,' Romain said, a smile playing around his mouth. 'It's as if you have just returned from a walk in the forest, communing with the squirrels and birds.'

'It's the cold. I have fair skin. Tell me, how do you know the duc?'

'We grew up together. My mother worked as a maid at his estate.'

'So that is where your fine manners come from and your way of speaking.'

'Yes, that's right. I'm a *faux* noble. I look the same and sound the same, but if you peel off the flaky paint, you find an illiterate cross-eyed peasant.'

Henriette almost laughed, before remembering court etiquette. Smiling into her fan, she watched him inch closer.

'When are you going to let me do another reading?' he asked. 'I hope I didn't scare you off?'

'Not at all. Give me some time to assess your predictions. I am waiting to see if any of it comes to pass.'

'Like an astronomer. Or an academic. So rigid and controlled, madame.'

'I must manage and direct my life, monsieur, or others will insist on doing it for me.'

'Direct your life according to what? A guiding star?' Romain smiled and took her hand.

Henriette withdrew her hand. 'According to my principles and morals, and guided by my faith.'

'Very commendable. As long as those morals are balanced by pleasure and joy in life.'

'This is true and difficult to achieve. Sometimes I feel lost and kindness helps me. Kindness to myself and to others. I know it sounds trite, but it never fails me. The duchesse detests me, did you know? We were friends, but now she won't even look at me, because

I had the audacity to support Letitia. I pay a high price, yet I press on, because to abandon the girl would be to abandon my principles. This would be betraying myself. Do you understand?'

Romain accepted a glass of brandy from a servant and took a small sip, considering her words. 'Yes. The duchesse is jealous, sad, and insecure,' he murmured in her ear. 'I must caution you, though, she will not yield. When she gets an idea in her head, she is determined. You could try talking to her?'

'Perhaps I will. You know, monsieur—'

'Call me Romain, please.'

'Romain,' she smiled at him. 'You are a good listener, and it's a relief to be able to confide in someone. I've felt so very alone, without allies. All the mistresses support Charlotte. I know Madame Franche-Bastien sympathizes with Letitia and I, but she has known Charlotte since childhood. There's...a risk I will be sent away.' Henriette twisted her hands in her lap. Romain placed his palm over hers, and this time she did not pull away.

'I am your ally, don't forget that. You're strong and good. I wish there were more here like you.'

'Thank you, Romain,' she whispered. 'Thank you so much.'

The marquis drained his second glass of brandy. Letitia stared at his broad shoulders, then looked away, a blush creeping over her chest. The few times she had been brave enough to meet his eyes, she was struck by the multitude of expressions in them. She imagined thoughts flitting through his mind like arrows. He seemed a man unaccustomed to waiting, yet he had an air of calm—a care in the way he moved and the words he chose.

'May I call you Letitia, mademoiselle?'

'Yes. How would you like me to address you?'

'If there are others present, Your Lordship. Anything more familiar would arouse suspicion. If no one is listening, you may call me Antoine.'

'Are you concerned about creating suspicion, Your Lordship? Have you something to hide?' Letitia blurted out, then cringed. 'I'm sorry, that was rude. My mother often says I speak before I think.'

'There is nothing rude about you,' Antoine said. 'You are all that is refreshing, beautiful, and honest. Frank speech is not something I come across at court, or amongst my friends and relatives. To answer your question, I do have something to hide, but not from you. I haven't been able to stop thinking about you since the day we met.'

Letitia felt heat in her cheeks. 'I have thought about you too, Antoine,' she whispered. 'But I don't wish to waste your time. There are so many women here at court who are free to be with you. Nothing can happen between us. I'm sure you understand.' Glancing sideways at him, the intensity of the marquis's expression made her catch her breath.

'In my mind, yes,' the marquis replied, his voice low and heated. 'In my heart, not at all. We can be discreet. No one need know.'

Letitia was silent for a moment. Her heart drummed in her chest and her mouth went dry. 'I need to see you again. God help me. Do not speak to anyone of this.'

Antoine placed his hand over hers. 'Do you know the hamlet of Renaud?'

She nodded. 'It's near the Château d'Amboise. The other side of the forest.'

'There is a path from the hamlet to the forest. It is used by the woodsmen. I will meet you there on Thursday morning at ten o'clock and we can ride together on the forest trails. Only the birds will see us. Will you come?'

She felt the warmth of his hand and his eyes. Her stomach swirled with pleasure. 'I will.'

Henriette returned to the château to discover the door to her rooms locked, and her daughter, pale-faced, waiting for her. She pressed down on the handle and the door rattled on its hinges. 'You need to fetch someone to fix this door, Solange. I can't open it.'

'Maman, it's locked. We have been given another room.'

'What do you mean?'

'Thierry moved all our things while you were out.'

Henriette pressed her fingers to her forehead, rubbing the spot between her eyes. 'It must be the duchesse. It's the only possible explanation.'

At that moment the head butler, Thierry, appeared at the bottom of the stairs. 'Good day, Madame d'Augustin.'

'Thierry, I must ask what is going on. Why have you moved my belongings without my permission?'

'The duchesse has asked to have access to your rooms for guests. You will be installed in an upstairs room. Follow me, please.'

The staircase to the top floor was narrow and dark. A dimly lit hallway came into view.

'Who lives up here, Thierry?'

'You are most fortunate, madame. No one lives up here. You and your daughter will have the floor entirely to yourselves.'

The air was musty and the carpets worn. This part of the château was devoid of art, fresh flowers, and inhabitants. Thierry opened the doors to a room the size of their previous sitting area. Within was a fireplace, a canopy bed, a velvet settee, and two armchairs. An immense mahogany armoire dominated one corner. The curtains were closed, and a draught filtered in from somewhere.

'It is a little smaller than you're accustomed to,' Thierry acknowledged, 'but I will send some maids to air it out and freshen it up.'

'Where is my daughter to sleep?'

'There is a mattress under the bed. Of an evening, your maid will pull it out.'

Henriette felt heat in her cheeks. 'This is an outrage. Solange is the duc's daughter. It is not appropriate that she sleeps on a mattress on the floor. And why do you speak of one maid? I have three.'

'The duchesse has relieved the other maids from your service, madame.'

Tears filled her eyes, but Henriette blinked them back. 'Goodness, Thierry. I'm surprised I've not been relegated to the servants' quarters.'

'There will be no need for that, madame. I'll send some maids immediately. Please, sit down. Would you like some hot chocolate?'

'Yes, thank you.'

Thierry scurried out, as if the room were infested with rats.

Solange sat on the bed and bounced. 'Don't worry, Maman. It's not that bad. We have a fireplace.' She jumped up and darted to the windows, dragging the curtain aside. 'Look, it's a long way down, but we have a nice view of the rose gardens and the orange grove.'

Henriette nodded, wrapping her arms around her daughter, staring down at the gardens. A tear ran down her cheek and dropped onto the crown of Solange's head.

They made their way down to breakfast, clutching the wall of the dark staircase. Henriette drew her shawl closer around her shoulders, as Solange leapt down the stairs three at a time.

'Careful, you might trip,' Henriette cautioned.

'I'm starving, Maman. The pastries go quickly and I don't want to miss out.'

The chatter of the women could be heard in the dining room as Henriette opened the door and ushered Solange inside. The room fell quiet and Charlotte nudged Céline, before picking up her cutlery and placing a forkful of scrambled eggs in her mouth.

Céline rose and approached them. 'Good morning, Henriette. I'm sorry to inform you, but you can no longer have breakfast here. Solange may stay.'

Henriette stood immobile, her mouth dry. Pain flared in her chest and she gripped Solange's shoulder. The other women pretended to ignore the scene unfolding before them, their eyes fixed on their plates. Only Letitia and Isabelle stared open-mouthed.

'Where are you suggesting I dine?' Henriette asked stiffly.

'In the kitchen. The servants will provide you with a meal there.'

'I'm not a servant. Why should I eat there?'

'Your status is in question. You flout the wishes of the duchesse and as a result, you are reaping the consequences of your actions. Please leave. Solange, you may accompany me to the table.'

Solange folded her arms, glaring up at Céline. 'I will go with my mother. I don't want to share a table with you.'

'Insolent child. Like mother, like daughter. Enjoy your breakfast. I believe the fare is rustic. Sardines, perhaps, or stale bread.'

Henriette gave her a caustic look. 'Céline, you are a minion of hate. Let's go, Solange.' She swivelled her daughter around and they left the room. Isabelle and Letitia stood, distress etched on their faces.

A maid guided them down another dark staircase, into the bowels of the château where they were welcomed by the head cook, Imogene, who gestured toward a table near the fire. Two maids kneaded pastry at a workbench along the wall and glanced furtively in their direction before resuming their labour.

'I have some fresh bread and butter and some apple turnover. Please, warm yourselves. I will boil the kettle for tea.'

Henriette spoke through clenched teeth, shivering despite the warmth. 'There has been a mistake. We won't be troubling you here tomorrow, rest assured.'

'You're no trouble, madame.' Imogene smiled, her cheeks round and pink, gleaming in the orange light of the fire. Her arms were plump as she laid some buttered bread on the table. Solange plucked some from the wooden board and took a large bite.

The bread was fresh from the ovens, the butter deep yellow and glistening. It was delicious. Solange abandoned her good manners and stuffed her mouth full. Her mother smiled. The turnover was served in earthenware bowls, piping hot and dusted with cinnamon. Imogene did not ask why they were there and chatted about her family in Normandy. They were soon informed about her six grandchildren and a childhood spent stomping on grapes. She interrupted her monologue to instruct the servant girls and stir the bubbling cauldron on the hearth.

After they had their fill, Henriette thanked Imogene. The woman beamed and wiped her hands on her apron.

'See you tomorrow.'

Henriette smiled back and decided not to contradict her.

'You may go and play now,' Henriette told Solange as they reached the entrance hall. 'I've something I must do.'

'Yes, Maman. But don't do anything silly. It was cosy in the kitchen. I quite liked it.'

Henriette frowned. 'That's not the point, Solange. Just because something is not unpleasant doesn't make it right. Rank and position are everything here and our honour is being sullied. Don't you see?'

'Maman, you are the most honourable and kind person I know. It makes no difference to me where you sleep, or where you eat your breakfast.'

Henriette drew Solange to her, stroking her hair. 'Darling, what a beautiful thing to say. I know it is hard for you to understand. For women, rank is the clearest indicator of their future. I'm responsible for your future, and I'll do whatever I can to make it a happy one.'

'*Je t'embrasse*, Maman. Just be polite. You're scary when you're angry.'

'Yes, darling. Now, off you go. No frogs today.'

'I can't promise that, Maman.'

Henriette turned to the grand staircase.

'Maman?'

'Yes?'

'Where will I meet you for luncheon? I suppose we're not to dine at the lunch table either?'

'We'll ask for it to be brought to our room today.'

The closer Henriette came to the duchesse's rooms, the quieter it seemed. She breathed in the scent of tuberoses and lilies and ignored the knot in her stomach.

Hercules greeted her, his gaze fixed over the top of her head.

He entered the room to announce her arrival, before emerging with Yolande. 'Her Grace is not here, Madame.'

'Yolande, I know she is there. Tell her I am prepared to sit outside her rooms until she comes out. I will not be deterred.'

'Madame, might I suggest you come back at another time? Her Grace is not in a good humour.'

'It's nothing I haven't seen before, Yolande. Please, it is of great importance that I speak with her.'

'As you wish.' Yolande opened the door and waved her inside.

Charlotte was stretched out on a grey silk sofa, sipping tea. She did not turn as Henriette approached, nor did she look up as the mistress stood before her.

'Why are you here?' Charlotte snapped. 'I have nothing to say to you.'

'Your Grace, why did you banish Solange and me from our rooms and the breakfast table? We have a right to be here and to be on the same footing as the other mistresses.'

'You have not listened to me, Henriette. I told you to demonstrate loyalty and you ignored me. Your actions have consequences, as perhaps now you understand.'

'Why do you hate me so, Charlotte? I can be both loyal to you and kind to Letitia. She has no one else.'

'She has my husband, does she not?' Charlotte said, her tone low and spiteful. 'I confided in you, Henriette. I introduced you to all the best people. I treated your bastard daughter as my own.'

Henriette's cheeks prickled with heat. 'I'm perfectly happy not to receive any more of your charity, Your Grace. I will speak to your husband of the matter. I'm sure he'll not want his daughter living in a musty attic room and eating scraps in the kitchen.'

'You really think so?' Charlotte replied with an icy smile. 'Hugo cares only about bedding his whore. Oh, and one more thing. Romain is a hopeless flirt who likes his women young, nubile, and preferably stupid. He befriends women of high status and wealth, from whom he can obtain spending money.'

'How very kind of you to advise me, Your Grace, but I have no interest in Monsieur de Villiers. But I must ask you, will my daughter and I be similarly disgraced at luncheon?'

'Yes. Go to the kitchens, or ask for your meals in your room. You must remember, madame, that you are entitled to nothing. Everything you had was a privilege. Accept the new arrangements, or you may find yourself searching for lodgings in town. Please go, you are giving me a headache.'

Henriette marched from the room, her face red. She muttered under her breath as she strode the hallway, tears blurring her vision.

Charlotte moved to the window seat, her eyes scanning the gardens below. Henriette emerged from a side entrance and walked toward the stables. Thibault and Raoul proceeded to attach a horse to an open carriage while Henriette waited, her figure partially obscured by the open door of the stables. Charlotte rang the bell for Yolande.

The maid rushed in from the next room. 'Yes, Your Grace?'

'Fetch Madame de Poitiers for me.'

Yolande bobbed in a quick curtsey and returned a few minutes later. Céline bustled in behind her, an eager glint in her eye. Charlotte sighed inwardly. She hated to admit it, but she missed Henriette's quiet dignity and calm demeanour.

'Good morning, Charlotte. I'm so pleased you called. I very much enjoyed the rosehip tea we shared the other day. And do tell me, did Madame Foulbret have gossip from court?'

'I will talk to you about it later, Céline. There is very little time, as I need you to do a favour for me.'

'Yes, what is it?'

'Go to the stables and ask Thibault to ready the smallest carriage. You are to follow behind Madame d'Augustin. I wish to know where she goes every Wednesday and why. Hurry—you need to go right now. Under no circumstances must she see you. Understood?'

'Understood.'

'Go! There is no time!'

❧

Céline dashed out of the rooms and broke into a run through the hallways. She yanked off her shoes to take the stairs. A maid clutching a pile of sheets ducked out of the way, eyes wide. Céline's hair escaped from its clasp as she sprinted toward the stables. In her peripheral vision, Céline could see the carriage passing through the gates and hear the crunch of its wheels on the gravel. Thibault watched her approach with alarm, her skirts hiked up and her cheeks inflamed.

'Thibault,' she panted. 'Please, get the smallest carriage ready, I need to follow Madame d'Augustin. Her Grace's orders.'

'Yes, madame.'

Thibault ran into the stables and called for Bénédict. They hurried to drag out the carriage and attach it to the horses, all the while bumping into one another and grimacing under Céline's piercing stare.

'There needs to be a safe distance between this carriage and the other—they must not know we're following them,' Céline added, allowing Thibault to help her into the carriage.

Bénédict climbed into the box and flicked his whip with a crack, and the horses lurched forward into a trot, then a gallop.

Céline gripped the armrest as the carriage hurtled down the road, watching as the fields passed in a blur of green and white. She inclined her head out of the window, holding a silk handkerchief over her mouth to shield it from dust. In the far distance she spotted a speck of brown—the open carriage. She exhaled with relief.

Bénédict left a good distance between them, as instructed. The carriage slowed to a more civilized pace and Céline reclined in her seat. The sun broke through the clouds and warmed her face as they passed through an avenue of plane trees, their trunks wide and knotted.

They took the narrow road around the edge of the town and the carriage slowed, allowing more space between them. Céline took her rosary beads from her pocket bag and fingered them. She thought about Charlotte's skin, as white as milk. Her low, conspiratorial laugh. The way her dresses fell on her slender frame. When Charlotte shared stories of her childhood, hiding in chests with Isabelle, Céline felt pangs of jealousy. Yet Charlotte paid attention to Céline now; she was the one who knew the duchesse's most intimate thoughts and feelings. After a lifetime of being ignored, Céline revelled in her new status.

'Repent, child,' her father, the Reverend Joubert, had rebuffed her. 'You are as wanton as Salome, as two-faced as Judas. Read Corinthians and purify yourself. Corruption of the soul is passed from the mother. Your mother died from inner dissolution.'

'You're wrong, Papa. Maman died from consumption. The doctor said.'

The Reverend drew himself up to his full height, and rapped his cane sharply on the wooden floor. 'Show respect, you deviant child! God punished your mother for succumbing to base desires. Do not make the same error. Read. Read and remember. You will recite it to me this evening.'

Céline shook her head, trying to dislodge the memory. Her father had met his God a number of years earlier, and even on his deathbed he had railed at her, his words dripping with scorn. Her decision to become a mistress was an affront to him, a final humiliation.

After crossing a stone bridge the carriage jolted to a stop before the rusted gates of the convent, Saint Bernard de Thiron. Céline could see Henriette's *calèche* standing within, the horse gnawing on tufts of grass. The driver dozed in the sun, half slumped in the box seat above.

'Bénédict, you'd best take the carriage around the corner, in case she comes out again. I shall go in.'

'Yes, madame.'

Bénédict opened the carriage door and took her hand as she

stepped out. Céline hurried through the grounds, anxious not to be seen from the windows above. She made her way along a stone wall, passed the side of the main building, and was soon concealed by a copse of sycamore and oak trees. A wooden gate divided the front from the back of the convent and she tried the latch. It was unlocked and she pushed it open with care.

Groups of young girls dressed in blue serge pinafores were scattered across the grounds, some strolling, others sitting on benches. Céline felt suddenly vulnerable. How was she to navigate the gardens without being seen? And if she were seen, what could she say to explain her presence? Darting behind an oak, she waited. The girls would disperse soon enough. A moment or two later, a bell sounded, its peals reverberating six times before fading to silence. The girls meandered inside, laughing and chattering. One remained, her slim body tense and angular. She sat on a bench near the steps, her hands gripping the edge and her gaze flitting everywhere before falling on her lap. She fidgeted with the hem of her dress and glanced back at the door.

Céline took the opportunity to slip further into the garden, making her way around the perimeter, before finding the enormous trunk of a sycamore, not far from where the girl sat.

As she took up her hiding place, the door swung open and Henriette emerged with an imposing woman in a black habit. Her white headdress shadowed her face and the two women appeared deep in conversation.

The girl watched as Henriette sat beside her on the bench and the older woman settled on a wooden chair to the side.

The girl was crying, her hands forming fists. 'You've been talking about me, I know. What have you been saying, Maman? That I'm evil, that I deserve to be here?'

Henriette reached for the girl's hand, but she snatched it away. Behind the tree, Céline's eyes widened. *A daughter!* She bristled with excitement. This was a gift from God.

'No, my dear, no one thinks you're evil. But you really need to stop harming yourself. What if no one came in time to help you? You could die, Amalia, don't you see?'

The abbess leaned in. 'Child, if you were to succeed in ending your own life, you would go straight to the braziers of hell. There is no heaven for those who take their lives.'

'I'm not trying to take my life. I'm trying to make the pain go away. The voices tell me to cut, and where to cut. They like to see my blood.'

Céline covered her mouth with her hand to stop from exclaiming aloud. *A mad daughter!* She pressed her fingers into the rough bark and remembered to breathe.

The abbess patted the girl's hand. 'Run inside now, Amalia. Go to the great hall for morning prayers. If Sister Théa is angry, tell her I kept you.'

Amalia folded her arms. 'I want to stay with Maman,' she insisted.

Henriette pulled the girl close, stroking her hair back from her face. 'I'll stay for a while, dearest. When you've finished prayers, we can have tea together. Off you go.'

Amalia fingered the brooch on her mother's dress, before rising and returning inside.

'Madame d'Augustin, the other girls are troubled by her behaviour. It's the cutting, the attacks of hysteria and madness, but also the way she lurks behind doorways, listening to their conversations. The nuns feel the same. I have, perhaps, had more time to acquaint myself with her ways and I am sure that underneath the extreme behaviour is a little girl longing for affection. I just don't know what to do with her. You do realize, madame, an asylum would be more appropriate for her?'

'Yes. But Abbess de la Fontaine,' Henriette pleaded, 'you must realize an asylum would be the death of Amalia. I call on your piety and compassion and ask that you continue to watch over her. I have no other option. *Je vous en supplie.*'

The abbess nodded, her fingers tracing the crucifix around her neck. 'Madame, of course. I will do the best I can. However, I will need a larger contribution to the convent. The upkeep of the roof and cloisters is becoming more expensive. I'm sure you understand.'

'Yes, of course.' Henriette wrung her hands.

Céline had to restrain herself from running as she emerged from the carriage. They had returned before lunch and Céline wanted to find the duchesse before she went to the dining room.

It was washing day and the maids weaved past her in the hallways with armloads of linen and baskets of soiled clothing. The sun was out, and they would wash outside, gossiping and splashing suds at one another. Céline had eavesdropped on them a number of times and discovered all manner of compromising snippets about the other mistresses.

Hercules announced her to the duchesse who stood by the window, a Bichon in the crook of her arm. Charlotte whispered to the dog, and Céline sat with her hands folded, waiting to be acknowledged.

'So. You have news for me?'

'Indeed I do, Charlotte,' Céline said with relish.

Charlotte kissed the dog, and released him to the carpet.

'Well, are you going to just stand there looking pleased with yourself, or tell me what you have discovered?'

'A daughter, Your Grace. Henriette has a daughter who lives in the convent just outside of town. Saint Bernard de Thiron.'

'Extraordinary,' Charlotte said, with a slow smile. 'Well done. I have a feeling there is more to the story. Go on, tell me.'

'Charlotte, the girl is completely mad. She cuts herself. The abbess thinks she should be in an asylum rather than a convent.'

'Good grief. I always thought Henriette had a secret. She has a deceitful quality about her. You know, this poor child has never met her sister or visited her mother's home. Don't you find that dreadful?'

'Scandalous,' Céline smirked.

CHAPTER 15

Henriette stood at the door of the seamstress's shop, an armload of dresses held in front of her. Pauline perched on a stool, inserting pins into the hem of a dress. She looked up and smiled, a question in her eyes.

'Good day, Pauline. I need to adjust these dresses; the necklines are the style from last year and the waistlines too. Unfortunately, I can't pay you. Can I perhaps help you with them?'

Pauline hesitated, smoothing the fabric on her lap. 'Have you sewn before? Do you have some skills, madame?'

'Yes, I've taken on sewing for others in the past. My eyes are good and I have deft fingers. I thought maybe I could help you with other dresses as well?'

Pauline nodded. 'I've many jobs this time of the year. I could use some help and if you learn quickly, I could pay you per dress. What do you think?'

Henriette beamed. 'It sounds perfect. I could come a few mornings a week?'

'All right. Let's have a look at those dresses. The fabrics are magnificent.'

Henriette sat down next to her and showed her the necklines, indicating with her hand on her chest where she thought they should be cut. Pauline asked Henriette to change into the first dress.

As the seamstress pinned the neckline, they chatted about the people who frequented the shop: The Comtesse de Vaubert, who was always accompanied by her six Pomeranian dogs; the Duc de Crancy, who wore so much pomade in his wig that it made Pauline sneeze; and the unforgettable Duchesse de la Trémoille who had once had a tryst with her lover behind the silk curtain of the change room.

Henriette frowned. 'I need you to teach me. How do you measure the adjustments?'

Pauline picked up a long strip of paper and a pair of scissors. 'With these. I mark measurements on the strip with scissors. Many of my clients have their own strips, which I re-use for other garments. By the looks of these dresses, they are all cut too high in the bust by about the same measure.'

'Well, you made them. Whose fashion sense has prompted the plunge in necklines, do you think?'

'The Duchesse de Fressange,' Pauline replied. 'She wished to tempt her lover.'

'Did it work?'

'Well, yes. They visited the change room just last week.'

Henriette smiled. 'You're very tolerant.'

'Perhaps. I do need to keep my clients happy. There. It's done. I'll pin one more on you and we will have one each to work on.'

Once the second dress was pinned, Pauline showed Henriette the small stitches required to sew the neckline seams, and they stitched together, the only sounds the squeak of carriage wheels and the muffled cadence of conversations outside.

Henriette was hesitant to show the seamstress her work, as her stitches looked haphazard, but Pauline smiled and said, 'It's not bad for your first effort.'

Henriette stared at her work and her shoulders drooped. 'It's terrible, isn't it? I'm sorry, it's been a long time.'

'We may need to unpick this one. Don't worry, you just need a little practice.'

～

Pulling her red cloak closer around her with one hand, Letitia steered her horse under the canopy, along the forest path. Her chest thudded with excitement at the thought of seeing Antoine.

Birds twittered and branches cracked beneath the horse's hooves as they trotted along the dimly lit path. A squirrel skittered past, its tail bouncing behind. The light dimmed as the foliage thickened around her, and Leitita shivered, nudging her heel into the horse's flanks.

She arrived at a clearing—it was as still and peaceful as a cathedral. White wildflowers dotted the forest floor and ribbons of light streamed through the trees, making patterns on the ground. She made a mental note of the types of trees surrounding the clearing, monumental oaks and birches, some with trunks the size of several men. Pulling on the reins, she pressed forward until she emerged at the outer edge of the forest. A rocky path wound ahead of her and beyond, the thatched roofs of Renaud nestled in a valley.

Letitia dismounted and waited for him, allowing her horse to nibble on the lush carpet of grass. Before long, Antoine arrived on a grey and black horse, wearing a long navy coat, his hair dishevelled from the wind. Smiling broadly he swung to the ground, reaching for her hand to kiss.

'Good day, Antoine.'

'Good day, Letitia. I'm so pleased you were able to meet me, I wasn't sure if you would.'

'I always keep my promises. Besides, I'd hate to think of you waiting here for me, only to be disappointed.'

Antoine dismounted and helped her back onto the saddle. She nodded toward the darkness between the trees.

'Come. I've found a special place.'

'Sounds intriguing.'

As they penetrated the gloom, Letitia could hear his horse snorting behind and sense his eyes on her back. The path skirted around a stream and several fallen logs before opening back up at the clearing. Her heart beat in her chest with a wild and strange kind of excitement as Antoine spread his coat at the foot of an oak. He caught her eye. She sat with her hands folded, her bravado fading to apprehension.

'Are you regretting your decision to come?' Antoine asked.

'No. Are you?'

'No regrets, no explanations, no apologies. The credo of my father.'

'Do you agree with it?'

'Not really. Well, I do sometimes have regrets, but put less stock in explanations and apologies,' he confided, taking her hand. He turned it over so the palm faced upwards, then traced a circle.

'Uh-oh,' he murmured, his brow furrowing.

'What?' Letitia arched an eyebrow.

'Eight children. You're going to have your hands full.'

'What on earth are you talking about?'

'Your palm. Our family's cook taught me to read palms; her mother was a gypsy. A large brood is foretold on your hand.'

She suppressed a smile. 'Do you want lots of children?'

'Maybe.' Antoine ran his fingertips down her jawline, before cupping her chin. 'It's beautiful here, isn't it? It feels…pure, somehow.'

'I know. I was struck by it as I passed. It was quiet then, but the birds are singing now.'

He leant forward and kissed her, his hand falling to her waist and clasping it. The kiss deepened and they drew closer, their arms and legs entwined.

The timing was perfect—Hugo stretched out beside her on the sofa, the light from the window forming a halo around his head. His eyes were half closed, his arm draped over her waist.

Letitia slipped her hand inside his shirt, playing with the soft hairs on his chest. He pulled her closer and opened one eye. 'What is it? You seem skittish.'

She traced the side of his face with her index finger and lowered her gaze, sliding her calf over his. Leaning forward, she knew the outline of her breasts was accentuated, falling from her low-cut gown.

'Hugo, I'm worried about Henriette. Did you realize the duchesse has moved her and Solange to shabby quarters on the top floor?'

'Arthur did mention it to me, yes.'

'Solange is your child. Do you think it appropriate for her to live like that?'

Hugo pushed himself up on his elbow and raised an eyebrow. 'Little Letitia, since when have you taken an interest in petty conflict? It's pointless. Honestly, leave it to Madame de Poitiers and my wife. They delight in it.'

Letitia, fighting to keep her voice low and calm, sat up. 'It may be petty, Hugo, but Solange is your daughter. Do you think Henriette deserves to be treated like a servant?'

Hugo sighed as he took her hand, stroking her palm with his thumb. 'By all accounts she is still being looked after.'

'Who is telling you such nonsense? Henriette and Solange have been excluded from both breakfast and luncheon, and are forced to eat in the kitchens, or in their room.'

The duc frowned, dropping Letitia's hand as he rose to his feet and moved to the window. Fog enveloped the gardens and the hedges emerged from the top like islands in a misty sea.

'Letitia, I am not interested in the arrangements and rivalries of women. Solange and Henriette are hardly at the poorhouse. Mind your own concerns. Now, are we going riding today or not?'

Letitia pouted and picked up her shawl, draping it around her shoulders. Her chin jutted forward as she pressed her feet into her shoes. 'No. I'm going to play with Solange and Tomas. We're hunting for frogs. I shall see you at dinner.'

'My love, don't sulk.'

'The meals, Hugo. At least fix that.'

'I'll think about it. My wife has already declared war on me, so it's difficult. Do you understand?'

Letitia's eyes glimmered. 'Yes. Thank you.'

Hugo sidled up to her and put his hand around her waist. 'Riding then?'

'Three o'clock. But only if this horrid fog clears.'

Henriette sat on the settee with Solange. Intent on their books, they both startled at the knock on the door.

'Come in,' Henriette called, marking her page.

Théa, the new servant, who was both shy and ungainly, entered and curtsied. Her cleaning skills consisted of limply running her duster along the windowsills whilst humming. Clementine still came to dress her hair, but not every day. Henriette missed her efficient bustle and warmth.

'Madame, Her Grace has requested your presence this afternoon in the salon, for afternoon tea.'

'Thank you, Théa. I'll need you to dress me.' Henriette said, avoiding Solange's curious eyes. The servant nodded. *The duc has forced the duchesse's hand*, Henriette thought.

Théa helped Henriette into a blue dress that she and Pauline had cut and hemmed to reflect the new fashion.

'Maman, what should I wear?'

'Your pink rose dress.'

'Ugh, I look like a fairy in that. It's too babyish.'

'*Chérie*, the other dresses need adjusting, and I haven't taken them to Madame Rolain yet. Besides, you look lovely in the rose.'

'All right, Maman, but you'd better fix the other ones soon. Tomas will tease me you know.' Solange pulled the dress from the armoire.

'You could dress later, just before we go to tea? We have plenty of time. Just go and play now for a little while.'

Solange did not hesitate—their new room was claustrophobic and the dust made her sneeze. She put on her shawl and raced out into the corridor.

The hours seemed to slow as Henriette waited, glancing at the clock on the mantel. The thought of being in the same room as Charlotte made her ill at ease and she picked up her sewing to distract herself.

Fifteen minutes before the appointed hour, Letitia knocked on Henriette's door as she was buttoning Solange into her dress.

'Good day, Henriette,' Letitia said warmly. 'I thought we might arrive together.'

'Thank you, Letitia. I'd like that.'

Solange fidgeted as her mother pinned up her hair and the three of them made their way to the salon.

'Charlotte's request is a little strange, isn't it?' Letitia asked.

'Yes, it is. I'm not allowed to lunch with her, yet she invites me to afternoon tea. Did the duc say anything?'

'No, he's not even coming as far as I know. Everything to do with the duchesse he dismisses as 'mistress politics.' I suppose he's right.'

Thierry opened the door of the salon and they entered. Héloïse sat between Isabelle and Estelle, and Céline had positioned herself next to the duchesse on the large sofa. A tiered serving tray filled with fruit tarts, dainty cream cakes and pastries took up the centre of the table, beside which rested a silver teapot and china cups. The women fell silent as Henriette, Letitia, and Solange sat down.

'How kind of you to ask us to tea,' Henriette addressed the duchesse in a neutral tone.

'It's my pleasure,' Charlotte replied coolly, eyeing the door.

The duc bustled in wearing his riding coat, his cheeks red from the wind.

'Dearest, how good of you to join us,' Charlotte said. 'Please have a seat.' She nodded at the two servants hovering behind them. One poured tea and the other placed pastries on small plates before distributing them among the ladies. Charlotte seemed inordinately cheerful; she beamed at the women who clustered around her and giggled at her husband's few comments. Her gaiety worried Henriette. She had assumed Charlotte had been awaiting Hugo's arrival, but the duchesse's gaze was drawn still to the closed door. Henriette, feeling a clammy sense of dread, wondered who else might be expected. Muffled voices and footsteps sounded from the hallway, and the door opened to reveal Thierry, who leaned forward to whisper something in the duchesse's ear. Charlotte nodded, a smile playing around her lips as she took a sip of tea.

Thierry withdrew and opened the door further. Henriette placed her cup and saucer on the table with a clatter, and rose trembling to her feet. Her heart pounded in her chest.

It was Amalia, her hair pulled back tightly, wearing the blue serge pinafore of the convent. Her eyes were huge in her pale face.

'Maman,' she stammered. 'I knew you would ask me to come one day.'

Thierry cleared his throat. 'Miss Amalia d'Augustin,' he intoned impassively.

The women gaped, their eyes moving from the girl to Henriette and back again. Solange spluttered and choked on her pastry, spitting it into a napkin. The duc stared at Amalia as if she were a ghost, then rose and approached the girl. 'Come, child, you may sit with us.'

'Amalia,' Henriette murmured, her voice shaking.

The girl's face brightened as she sat down next to Henriette.

'So, Maman, aren't you going to introduce me?' Amalia asked, her voice shrill.

Henriette felt the heat of blood in her cheeks.

'Solange, this is your half-sister, Amalia. She lives at the convent.'

Solange's mouth fell open as she examined the girl from head to foot. Her eyes brimmed with tears. 'How could you not tell me I had a sister, Maman?'

'That's an excellent question, Solange,' Charlotte smirked. 'One that begs for an answer. Tell us, Henriette, why keep this lovely child a secret from us all?'

'Most of us are merely trying to survive, Your Grace. The world is a harsh place. I kept Amalia's existence secret because otherwise, I would never have gained a place at the château.'

A stunned silence filled the room once more. To Henriette's alarm, the duc's face twisted into an expression of contempt.

Amalia was undaunted by the brittle atmosphere. 'Maman, I've been good, you know. I've not cut myself lately, and I've learnt the whole book of Job by heart.' As if in celebration of her achievements, Amalia snatched a cream cake and stuffed it into her mouth, grinning at Charlotte as she chewed, bits of cake and cream oozing out from between her teeth. Henriette felt her heart sink and her blood roar in her ears. Amalia wiped a smear of cream across her cheek.

Without hesitation, Amalia reached for another cake. Her mother seized her daughter's hand and placed it firmly in her lap.

Amalia glared at her. 'I'm allowed. That's what they're there for, to be eaten.' She turned to her audience, her smile hard-edged and manic. 'Maman is ashamed of me. She thinks she is better than her own daughter. Isn't that terrible? She tries to buy me off with dresses, but I show her what I think of that, don't I, Maman?'

Henriette's posture was rigid, her face crimson.

'I burn them. I burn them to ashes and one day, if she doesn't start to treat me with love, I'll burn Maman too!'

Henriette stood, her body trembling and her lips pressed together. 'That's quite enough, Amalia,' she said, striving to keep the tremor from her voice. 'Come child,' she grasped Amalia by her arm and pulled her upright.

Charlotte was triumphant. 'Oh, but she must stay. She's more entertaining than an opera ballet. Don't be so cruel, Henriette.'

The duc rose to his feet and let out a sharp exhalation, as if he had been holding his breath. Taking Henriette firmly by the elbow, he escorted her into the hallway. Amalia, dragged along behind by her mother, muttered, 'Bitch, bitch, bitch' under her breath.

Henriette felt the ache of dread in her stomach as the duc turned to look at her, his expression forbidding. He opened his mouth and shut it again, rocking slightly on his feet, before speaking, his voice low and heated. 'Henriette, you've been lying to me all these years. Dishonesty is something I cannot tolerate.' She tried to interject, but he stopped her with a raised finger. 'Don't speak. Nothing you can say will dissuade me. You are to pack your trunks. You have one week to find alternate lodgings. Solange is free to choose her arrangements—she is welcome to stay, or go with you. If she stays, she will live with Madame Franche-Bastien and Tomas, and you may visit her. I will also assume the cost for this child to remain at the convent, as a gesture of good will. But your deceit is a betrayal of my trust, Henriette.'

Henriette leaned forward to kiss his cheek; Hugo raised his chin and stepped back, his gaze distant. 'Goodbye, Hugo. Thank you for everything,' she whispered, her eyes filling with tears. Squaring her shoulders, she turned to climb the staircase. Amalia trailed behind her, singing to herself.

CHAPTER 16

The rain came down in sheets outside the window as Henriette and Solange sat together on the bed. The storm had begun as dusk fell, and Henriette felt that the weather was in tune with her emotions. Letitia, with a despairing glance over her shoulder, had taken Amalia to her rooms, and Solange hiccupped as she cried.

'Maman, I will not stay here without you. I need you. Please, don't leave me.'

'Dearest, I'll send for you after a while. I just can't afford to keep both of us until I'm making some money. You'll be safe and comfortable here, and Isabelle is good and kind. She will take care of you.' Henriette stroked her daughter's face and wiped her tears with her thumb. 'I'll visit all the time, I promise.' She pulled Solange into a tight embrace.

'Where will you go?' Solange's voice was a muffled whisper, her face pressed into her mother's shoulder.

'I'm hoping Pauline might be able to accommodate me and I can work in her shop. But you mustn't worry about me, darling girl. You know how resourceful your mother can be.' Henriette forced a smile. 'Besides, imagine how much fun you and Tomas will have, without me to rein you in. All the frogs you can catch! Goodness, I might come back to find you've actually turned into a boy.'

Solange buried herself again in her mother's chest, flinging her hand around Henriette's neck. 'How often will you come?'

'Several times a week. This is only temporary, Solange. Do you understand that?'

'Why didn't you tell me about my sister?'

'Some things are better left quiet,' Henrietta said. 'I didn't know where to start, Solange. How to even begin to tell you—'

'She frightens me, Maman. When she said she would burn you…'
Solange shuddered. 'And her eyes have a strange look to them.'

'Yes, she is troubled. I wish I could help her more.'

The bell tinkled as Henriette entered the dressmaker's shop. Pausing for a moment, she observed the immaculate state of the room—its shelves stacked with baskets of cotton and rolls of lustrous fabrics in neat piles against the walls. The light poured through the windows, illuminating the three mannequins that featured dresses in progress, as well as those in the window that displayed finished garments. Pauline was leaning over a mannequin, pinning the skirt of a dress. She glanced up and smiled.

'Why, Henriette, hello. You look flustered, what is it?'

Henriette wrung her hands. 'I have a problem and I'm hoping you might be able to help.'

'Please, tell me.'

'I've found myself without lodgings or any means of income. I hoped that you might allow…that is, could I…could I perhaps stay above the shop with you for a while?'

'Of course, I'd be glad to help,' Pauline said and rose to her feet. 'The room over the shop is small, but I could curtain off a space for you.' She frowned. 'But I'm afraid it will be far less grand than what you have been used to.'

'Oh, Pauline, I only need a bed,' Henriette smiled with relief. 'I'm indebted to you as I've no family here. I was so worried I would be left to the streets. There's one more thing. Can I work here every day, Pauline, to earn my keep and put a little aside as my skills improve? Please tell me if I'm asking too much.'

Pauline placed a hand on Henriette's shoulder and smiled. 'In truth, I could use the company. I won't be able to pay a lot, but I have some large orders coming up.'

'Oh, Pauline, thank you!' Henriette kissed Pauline on both cheeks, tears brimming in her eyes.

Both Letitia and Solange cried the morning Henriette left. Letitia helped Henriette pack, sniffling and withdrawn. Quiet sobs emanated from the corner where Solange sat, her legs drawn up, her face buried in her hands.

'You don't need to help me, Letitia. A servant is coming.'

'I want to. You know, I could speak to Hugo. Perhaps you should wait a little longer? Did he not give you a week?'

'He did, but I just want to go, Letitia. There's nothing worse than being in a place where you're not welcome.'

Henriette put the slip she was holding down, and put her arm around Letitia.

'But I'll be back in a week to check on you and see Solange. Come on, you two, this is hard enough as it is.' She kissed Letitia on the cheek and the younger woman gave her a weak smile.

'I'm sorry. I just miss you already.'

'Me too.'

Henriette crouched down next to her daughter, and drew her into an embrace, stroking her hair. Solange peeked up from between her hands, her eyes swollen and bloodshot.

'Now, now, my love. I'll see you in a week. Isabelle has promised to bring you into town every other day to see me, and I'll be coming here.'

Pauline set up a bed near the window in the room above her shop. A red-lacquered screen provided a little privacy in what was otherwise a sitting room. Doors, from a narrow hallway, opened into a small kitchen and a bedchamber. An elderly housekeeper, Jean, kept the rooms tidy.

Pauline scooped up an armload of Henriette's dresses and hung them in the armoire.

'I'm sorry. It's very small here. I imagine it will take a while for you to become accustomed to it.'

Henriette blushed. 'Please don't apologize. You are immensely kind to let me stay.'

On the first morning Pauline rose at dawn and Henriette woke to her footsteps. For a moment, Henriette was overcome by longing for Solange and wondered if she had done the right thing in leaving her daughter behind. From the trunk near her bed, she retrieved a blue linen dress with a lace collar.

Jean prepared a simple breakfast of eggs and buttered baguette. The sun streamed through the windows, casting broad stripes of gold on the oriental rugs that adorned the floor.

'I've never asked, Pauline, how you came to live here? Have you always lived on your own?'

Pauline smiled. 'I think you are asking if I've ever been married?'

'Well, yes, if I'm not being too intrusive.'

'Not at all, it's a common enough story. I was engaged to a man from Marseilles, but he was killed in battle a few months before our wedding. I stayed in Marseilles for a while, enduring pitying looks. Every time I left the house it was the same. I would buy bread, and the baker was sorry. I would go to church and people would whisper, then approach me to commiserate. My parents gave me my dowry, after which I moved here and set up this business.'

Henriette nodded. 'I lost my husband. He was a Huguenot and died in prison.' Pauline touched her hand and murmured her condolences. They ate in companionable silence, each absorbed in their own thoughts.

After breakfast, the two women descended to the shop and Pauline handed Henriette a basket of dresses that required hemming.

'I can help with the adjustments, too—I've been practising and my skills are improving.'

'I know, but work on those, then I'll challenge you in the afternoon.'

Henriette picked up the first dress and threaded a needle. The garment was already pinned and just needed a straight line of stitches. She became immersed in the work and the steady rhythm of her hands as she sewed. Pauline's presence was calm and reassuring, and

Henriette felt some of the previous day's tension begin to dissipate.

They stopped mid-morning for tea and almond biscuits before resuming their work. An elderly comtesse arrived soon after, bustling in with her manservant. Pauline and Henriette looked up as the bell sounded on the door, and a waft of frigid air entered the room. The comtesse handed her manservant her vivid oriental shawl, and peered at Henriette.

'Who is this woman?' she asked, her voice cutting the air like a lance.

Pauline rose and curtsied. 'Good morning, comtesse. May I introduce Madame d'Augustin. She is my new assistant. Henriette, the Comtesse de Reines.'

'A pleasure, comtesse.' Henriette curtsied and smiled.

'Good day,' sniffed the comtesse. 'My word, Pauline. Am I paying you so much that you can afford an assistant?'

'We are fortunate to have much business at present, comtesse,' Pauline demurred, with a smile at Henriette. 'Now, your dress is looking splendid. I'll find it and you may try it on.'

The comtesse touched her silvery hair and nodded her approval as Pauline retrieved a dove-grey silk gown from a row of finished garments hung on hooks along the wall.

'Thank you. It has come up well,' she said, examining the seed pearls and tiny crystals that adorned the neckline. The comtesse clicked her fingers and the manservant took the dress from Pauline and hung it in the changing alcove in the corner. He swished open the silk curtain and ducked inside for a moment before emerging and nodding at his mistress.

They both disappeared behind the curtain and there was much rustling and muttered exclamations as the man helped her undress.

'I have never known a manservant to have permission to assist with undressing before,' Henriette whispered.

'I think he has permission to do a lot more than that,' Pauline replied, with a grin and a wink.

'Not *here*, surely?' Henriette asked.

'I don't think so, no. But there have been times when they've taken much longer than necessary and the comtesse does sound like she's enjoying dressing a little more than one might expect.'

Shortly after, the comtesse stumbled out, tripping on her hem. She was resplendent in the gown and from the expression on her face, she knew it. 'Pauline, *c'est magnifique.*' She paused to admire herself in the floor-to-ceiling gilt mirror.

Pauline adjusted the sleeves and the skirt of the comtesse's gown. 'I just need to make the neckline a little tighter, so it sits flat on your décolletage.' She withdrew some pins from the cushion on her wrist and deftly inserted them near the lady's shoulders.

The bell on the door sounded again and in strolled Romain de Villiers. 'Good day, ladies. Comtesse de Reines, it's been a long time. Did you leave your husband in the end?'

'Delightful to see you, Monsieur de Villiers,' the comtesse replied, extending her hand to be kissed. 'No, the scoundrel left me by way of a bullet from his own gun.'

'I am terribly sorry to hear that, comtesse,' he cringed. 'How utterly dreadful.'

The comtesse pursed her lips, waving away his expression of sympathy. 'Fortunately he went to the forest and did not subject me or the servants to it indoors. Imagine the mess. Some people are not meant for the trials of this world,' she declared.

'What brings you here, Romain?' Henriette asked.

He looked sheepish. 'Well, I understand this is your first day here, but I wondered if perhaps you might take an hour to visit the bishop's palace gardens with me? Madame Rolain, with your permission.'

'Henriette is not my slave but my assistant. As long as she finishes her work, I don't mind her having breaks. Please, enjoy your stroll.'

'It was lovely to make your acquaintance, comtesse.' Henriette smiled as she drew her shawl over her shoulders and tied on her hat. The sewing had been exacting work, and her fingers were sore. The unexpected break lifted her spirits.

Henriette took Romain's arm, and together they left the shop.

The wind was bracing and buffeted Henriette's skirts as they made their way toward the outskirts of town. The bishop's palace was surrounded by terraced gardens that were meticulously planted and maintained by a battery of palace gardeners.

Romain held Henriette's elbow as they walked down the marble stairs to the main section of the gardens. In the distance the slate roofs of the houses gleamed silver in the afternoon sun, and the imposing stone structure of the cathedral rose against the blustery sky.

The gardens were defined by finely trimmed hedging and rectangular beds of perennial flowers and ornamental trees. A stone path followed the perimeter, and Henriette and Romain made their way around in silence.

'I heard about what happened,' said Romain, his expression solemn.

'Yes, it was horrible,' Henriette admitted with a sigh, 'but I've been fortunate. Pauline is allowing me to stay and to work.'

'How is Solange?'

'She's not happy. She wanted to come with me, but she's better off in the château for now.'

'You didn't tell me you had another daughter. You are an enigma.'

'It is really not as romantic as that, Romain. I am merely a survivor. I had no choice really. Amalia is…she has some difficulties.'

'What kind of difficulties?'

'Amalia is not quite right in her mind. Her moods change very quickly…'

A wooden bench came into view as they approached the far end of the garden. 'Let's sit,' Romain said. The wind scurried around them as they sat, lifting the hem of Henriette's dress.

'I'd like to meet your daughter,' he said quietly.

'And why is that?' Henriette asked, astonished. 'She'll most likely insult you.'

'That doesn't concern me. I'd like to meet her because she is yours. Everything about you I want to know.'

'You hardly know me,' Henriette said. 'What possible interest could you have in my troubled child?'

'Henriette, how do I explain?' In a sudden movement, Romain drew her to him and kissed her, his arm around her waist. Shocked, Henriette hesitated before leaning into him, her mouth opening against his. He smelt of vetiver and wood smoke, his chin rough with stubble. Henriette's heart pounded as she abandoned herself to his touch. His chest radiated heat and he broke away, panting.

'That was unforgivable of me. I…have I offended you?'

Henriette was mute, her hand captured in his, her breath erratic. 'No. No, you haven't.' Boldness came from nowhere. 'Do it again,' she said. His look of longing mirrored her own feelings. This time, she kissed him, her hand cupping his jaw.

Afterwards, they strolled back toward the town, sneaking glances at one another.

'I know you have other women,' she said in a soft voice.

'I won't. Not anymore. I promise.'

'Is there anything else I should know?'

'Nothing at all.'

Henriette's face was still flushed as he bid her farewell at the door of the shop. Romain tipped his hat and walked away, turning to grin as he shoved his hands in his pockets. She thought she heard him whistle.

Greeting Pauline, Henriette settled back in her chair, picking up the dress she had been working on.

'Everything all right, Henriette?'

'Yes, thank you. We had a pleasant stroll. The palace gardens are truly beautiful this time of year.'

'Good,' Pauline gave her an appraising smile. 'You might want to put that on a mannequin to finish it off. It will make it easier.'

'Yes. Yes, of course.'

Henriette pulled the dress over a spare mannequin, her mind alight with the soft inquisitiveness of Romain's lips.

ༀ

Sister Babette tied the leather strap around Amalia's upper arm and positioned the bloodletting bowl underneath. Amalia spat in her face. Babette reared back, wiping the spittle away with the back of her hand, her black eyes flashing.

'Little witch,' Babette hissed, yanking the strap tightly. In her other hand glinted the small paring knife she used for making the incision in the crook of Amalia's arm. Earlier that morning Amalia had smeared excrement on the walls and torn pages from her prayer book, and so the abbess had ordered a bloodletting, to purge the taint of madness from her body.

'Keep still or you'll go back in the storeroom,' the nun hissed, making a shallow cut in Amalia's forearm. A stream of blood arced into the bowl, and Amalia heard a tinkle on the china as she averted her eyes.

'*You're* the witch,' Amalia said.

'Hysteria,' the abbess had concluded. Amalia didn't know the meaning of the word, but could recognize an approaching attack in the heavy weight of fatigue, and the waves of emotion that followed. The nuns would watch in alarm as she alternated between violent sobs and gales of laughter, as if her body were an instrument for some malicious force.

The nuns would tie her hands behind her back and place cloth between her teeth so she wouldn't bite her own lips. When the attacks subsided she found herself unable to move from bed for days, utterly spent. She knew the girls who slept on either side of her pleaded with the abbess to change beds, worried she might hurt them in the night. As she lay there, her gaze on a crack in the ceiling, she wondered if the life force ebbed from her, like water from a leaking bucket. She was glad of the heavy weight of her body and the fog in her mind. The urges she had frightened her. Her immobility stopped her finding a knife and harming herself, or worse.

Madame Martine Foulbret and Charlotte sat in the glass pavilion near the orange grove. A silver pot of tea glimmered in the middle of the table, surrounded by a delicate array of custard tarts. Martine thumbed through a thick book. The duchesse sneezed as a waft of book dust tickled her nose. 'Goodness, when did you last read this, Martine?'

'Many years ago. Charlotte, I have been thinking that we should have a practice of the Mass.'

'No, Martine. I'm frightened enough attempting it once. Have you ever done a Black Mass before?'

'Yes. As a young girl I performed one with a friend. We used a pig for the sacrifice and one hundred candles. It was rather beautiful, in a macabre sort of way.'

'What were you seeking to gain with that Mass?'

'Why, my husband, of course. And you see, I now live at Versailles and my every comfort is assured.'

Charlotte felt the sun warming her back through the glass. Since Henriette had left, Céline had followed her around like an eager puppy. When Martine sent word of her arrival, Charlotte arranged for their conversation to take place in the pavilion, hoping Céline would not discover her there.

'Where is your shadow today?' Martine asked, reading her thoughts.

'Céline is a nuisance. I can't get rid of her,' Charlotte sighed. 'She has the impertinence to assume we are the closest of confidantes. I do, however, need her help and she is a loyal creature, in her fashion.'

'Good. We will be in need of her assistance.'

Martine poured them both more tea, before returning to her book.

'Let's see. Crucifixes must be inscribed on the soles of the feet. The celebrant should be cloaked in black, and naked beneath. The ideal animal for sacrifice is a goat or a pig. The vessels should be placed on the naked body of a woman...In place of consecrated bread, we must use a decomposed turnip, and the blood of the slaughtered animal replaces the consecrated wine.'

Madame Foulbret gave a wicked smile, her eyes glinting. 'I will kill the pig, having had experience at the task. Where is the best place for the Mass to be performed?'

Charlotte pondered the question, gazing out of the pavilion windows toward the orange grove, its symmetrical rows of trees stretching into the distance. The tree canopies were thick and their leaves glossy, casting dappled shadows along the gravelled pathways.

'The orange grove,' Charlotte replied. 'No one will see us amid all that foliage.'

Céline placed the pouch of coins in the man's hand. They stood near the château gates, hidden by a copse of trees. He emptied the coins into his palm and counted them.

'You're short five livres.'

'Come back next week, I'll have it then.'

'Monsieur de Poitiers has moved to a cottage with some other men. He said to tell you he'll make you live with him unless you send more.'

'He's a gambler. His reduced circumstances are his own doing.'

The man sniffed and picked his nose. 'Madame, he is your husband. In the eyes of both God and the law, you are obliged to help him or go back to him.'

'How can I return when our home is gone?'

'If you keep up the payments, he may be able to live there again soon.'

She bristled. 'Tell him I don't appreciate being threatened, and that this, and what I give next week, will be the last payment for a while.'

The man shrugged. 'Do as you will, but Monsieur de Poitiers is only claiming what is his due. He won't give up.'

Céline turned on her heel and stalked away.

Romain shifted restlessly as he stood at Giselle's door. She flung it open, beaming when she saw who stood on the threshold, her curves concealed in a diaphanous white dressing gown, her black hair curling around her shoulders.

'*Tu es si beau*,' she exclaimed, reaching for his hand. She pulled him into her room and next to her on the chaise longue. The light was blue-tinged through the curtains, the shadows pooled over the satin bedcover and rag rugs spread on the floor. A vase of yellow daisies on her dressing table brightened the room.

'*Ça va?* What is bothering you, my love?' she asked. 'You look grim. Let me see if I can make you happy.' In an instant she was kissing him, her leg enclosed his waist and her fingers raked his hair. He drew away, panting.

'Giselle, you've been so good to me.'

'Ah, I don't like the look on your face or your words.'

'I've fallen in love with a devout and virtuous woman, and our visits, as pleasurable as they have been, must come to an end. Do you understand?'

'I do, but it makes me sad. I'm so very fond of you. When you visit it makes my day beautiful. I'm discreet, Romain. I promise you, what happens here won't ever be known outside these walls.'

Romain came closer and stroked her hair away from her face. 'I'm sorry, Giselle, but I have to follow my feelings. I hope you won't turn me away if it doesn't work out?'

She smiled and looked up at him from beneath thick eyelashes. 'Never. I could never do that.'

Charlotte kissed her friend on both cheeks before Martine, with a hand raised in farewell, climbed into the carriage. Watching the carriage as it rolled toward the château gates, Charlotte went over the list of items she needed to gather for the Mass.

The duchesse carried the letters in her pocket and had decided to use only the two most passionate.

It was late morning, and Charlotte knew her husband often went riding with Letitia at this time of day. She pushed open the door to her husband's rooms and slipped inside. It had been months since she had seen his quarters, and the scent of gardenia faintly lingered in the air—Letitia's perfume. Mouth tightening, Charlotte went to her husband's sitting room and eyed his bureau. The obvious place. He used it every day for his correspondence. Picking up a crystal paperweight, she placed the letters beneath it.

Charlotte retreated to the door, hesitated a moment, and glanced back over her shoulder at the paperweight that glittered in a shaft of sunlight. Fear gripped her heart, and she considered retrieving them. Yet gardenia still lingered in her nose, and hatred roiled in her stomach. She closed the door and left.

A draught plagued the dormitory, whistling through the gaps in the window frames and sweeping beneath doors. The nuns wedged strips of fabric into the window frames and positioned fat rolls of fabric at the base of each door, but to no avail.

Amalia had been banished from morning prayers again. It was even colder in the chapel and she had grown restless listening to the drone of voices. As they recited the catechism, she had stood and interrupted with a passage from the Song of Songs.

'My beloved is to me a sachet of myrrh, resting between my breasts. My beloved is to me a cluster of henna blossoms, from the vineyards of En Gedi.'

Sister Régine slammed her Bible down on the desk. 'Amalia! I've had enough of your filth. We are seeking to purify ourselves, and you destroy our peace of mind with wanton recitations. Go to the dormitory and say one hundred Hail Marys as penance.'

'But Sister Régine,' Amalia replied with a sly smile, 'how can it be filth when it is from the Bible? Are the words of the Bible not consecrated?'

'Go now, or I'll add the Prayer for Daily Neglects and the Promises of the Sacred Heart. Quickly, child, disappear!'

Amalia had said her Hail Marys and still clutched her rosary, swinging her legs on the edge of the bed. Each metal bed had a wooden crucifix at its head, and white sheets stretched tight over the mattresses. When the girls rose at dawn, they were expected to make their beds, the sheets tucked at right angles, the grey blanket folded at the foot of the bed. If the sheets were not smooth, the girls were punished with extra prayers and cleaning duties. A broom would be thrust into their hands and instead of eating breakfast, they would sweep the hallways until their fingers blistered.

Amalia heard footsteps outside her door and rose, her heart pounding. The door groaned open and Brother Deniel's stout form appeared. His oily dark hair hung over his forehead and his tiny eyes glimmered as he locked the door and walked toward her. The rosary dropped from her hands and clattered to the floor.

'Please leave me alone,' she said, her voice barely audible as he sat next to her. The springs squeaked under his weight.

Brother Deniel's round cheeks had a wholesome flush. His black habit strained over his girth. He placed a hand over hers and smiled.

'Sit on my lap, my dear. I've missed you.' He grasped her waist and pulled her to him as she whimpered. Reaching under her pinafore, he squeezed the inside of her thighs, his fingers edging closer to her crotch. He shuddered with pleasure, closing his eyes.

'Now child, don't cry,' he crooned. 'I am expressing God's love.' He fingered her as tears trickled down her neck and she gasped in pain.

'You can't tell anyone about this. No one would believe you anyway. They all think you're crazy, Amalia.' He murmured and licked his lips.

'I will tell them,' she sobbed. 'I hate you, I hate you, I hate you.'

Brother Deniel slapped her hard with his free hand and gripped her neck. 'You won't tell. If you do, you'll regret it!'

Amalia's vision went grey, and she fell back on the bed, unconscious.

Brother Deniel kept his room at the seminary cold. He was a hot-blooded man and had been advised by the bishop during confession to douse the flames with frigid air, prayer, and a whip. He removed his shirt as soon as he returned from the convent, opening the window, his teeth clenched as he whipped himself. He felt the pain as a thousand knives, as if rats were gnawing the flesh from his spine. He mouthed a prayer: 'Count not my transgressions, but my tears of repentance. Remember not my iniquities, but my sorrow for the offenses I have committed against You.'

Hugo had been surprised to feel pangs of guilt since Henriette had left. He knew, of course, that his wife was behind Amalia's visit. While petty secrets were unavoidable in such a large household, concealing a secret child was a breach of faith. If Henriette were allowed this much, what might the other mistresses then keep from him?

A small knock came at the door. 'Yes?' he answered.

'*C'est moi,* Papa.' Solange poked her head around the door, her eyes swollen.

'Come in, child.'

She raced over to him and threw her arms around his waist. Hugo patted his daughter's head, as if she were an overzealous dog. 'What is it, Solange?'

'Papa, why did you have to send Maman away? She wouldn't take me with her. We've never been apart. You have to let her come back. Please, Papa.' Her eyes filled with tears and she gripped his hand.

Hugo sighed. 'Now, now. Your mother lied to me, Solange. I can't trust her anymore and it's better if she starts a new life. I'm sure when she's established herself elsewhere, she will send for you.'

Solange gripped his hand tighter. 'Papa, I'm lonely without her. I'm having nightmares, and Madame Franche-Bastien sleeps so deeply, I can't wake her up.'

Hugo nodded and withdrew his hand, placing it on her shoulder. 'Things will get better, Solange. Now I need to get on with my correspondence.'

'Do it for me, Papa. Not for my mother, but for me. Children need their mothers. I'll be your spy and find out everything you need to know in the château, so you'll never be duped again.'

Hugo suppressed a smile. 'That's a kind offer, Solange, but we're going to have to leave things as they are. I'll spend more time with you. We can go into town for cake tomorrow. Would you like that?'

Solange pouted. 'I'm not three, Papa. I can't be bought with cake.'

'Run along now, Solange. I'll come for you tomorrow.'

Hugo sat down at his bureau, hoping a letter to his mother would distract him. Picking up his quill, he noticed two folded sheets of parchment under the crystal paperweight. Lifting it from them, he broke the seal of the first one with an ivory knife.

He read Letitia's words in disbelief, a pain thudding in his chest. Then reread them, before opening the other letter. It was from the Marquis d'Urveilles, expressing deep love for Letitia. He clenched his fist, his fingernails digging into his palm.

'Arthur!' Hugo bellowed.

At the courtyard near the orange grove, whoops of delight rang out. Letitia, Tomas, Solange, and Estelle crouched on the ground. Tomas had marked the start and finish points on the stone flagstones, and the frogs leapt toward the finish line. Thomas nudged several errant frogs back onto the track with his foot as they jumped to one side.

Estelle clapped her hands, laughing as her frog gained the lead.

'I'm the winner! What's my prize, Tomas?'

Tomas gave her a pat on the shoulder. 'Congratulations, Estelle. A *bilboquet*. Here you are.' He withdrew the cup and ball toy from behind his back.

Estelle grinned. 'Thank you. I'm good at this.' She tossed the ball in the air and it landed squarely in the cup. Her cheeks were flushed, her eyes sparkled, and her hair gleamed in elaborate braids around her head. Letitia felt a stab of envy—Estelle would marry well, with little risk of being sold as a mistress.

Rapid footsteps sounded on the gravelled pathway and Arthur appeared. He was out of breath and took a moment to compose himself. 'Mademoiselle du Massenet, His Grace wishes to see you.'

'See you soon,' Tomas said, gathering up the frogs and placing them in a large glass jar.

Letitia gave her companions a wave and disappeared inside.

Hugo sat at his bureau, his posture stiff. He held two sheets of parchment in his hand and gazed out of the window.

'Good day, Hugo. I wasn't expecting to be summoned until later.'

His voice was icy. 'The Marquis d'Urveilles. Are you acquainted with the man?'

Letitia's body turned cold and she shivered. 'Yes. I met him at Versailles.'

Hugo had still not looked at her. 'I believe you've met him on other occasions. I have the love letters you've written to each other. One from you and one from him.'

Unable to speak, Letitia felt her legs tremble. 'I have never written to him and he has never written to me. I hardly know him. Please believe me.'

'It is useless to lie to me, Letitia,' he said coldly. 'I have the letters.'

'Hugo, this is Charlotte's doing,' Letitia cried. 'Don't you see? She has not been satisfied with trying to take my life, but now must seek to further discredit me. She has always been jealous of your affection for me, Hugo, which is all the more surprising given her own dalliance with—' Letitia broke off.

'What do you mean?'

'I saw her in a compromising position.'

'Come on. Tell me what you mean?'

'Maybe you should ask her.'

The duc's voice hardened. 'Tell me.'

'I was in the garden, and I glanced up and saw her being intimate with Romain de Villiers.'

Hugo groaned and stood, slamming his fist down on the bureau. His cheeks reddened. 'I knew there was something between them—

the rogue. He'll pay for this. As for you, I don't know what to think. I trusted you. Now, I can't work you out. Have you seen this man in private?'

'No, Hugo. I wouldn't do that to you.' Her hands shook so she held them behind her back, her mouth dry. She hesitated, shifting from foot to foot.

'What is it?'

'I suppose you don't wish to see me later today.'

'That's correct. I need to think. You may have the face of an angel, but I'm not sure you speak the truth. Perhaps Monsieur de Villiers can enlighten me. In the meantime, you are not to leave the château grounds. Please go.'

He dismissed her with a wave of his hand.

Hugo whipped his horse, Zephyr, and the animal raced after the hounds on the scent. The tails of his blue hunting coat streamed out in the wind. His two friends, the Vicomte du Mauré and the Comte du Ponsardin, followed behind along with his huntsman, Guillaume.

The hounds leapt into the forest and Hugo steered his mount to pursue, his blood hot with the thought of the kill. He could always sense when the boar was close. The hounds would run faster, their barks louder and more urgent. A branch scratched his face as he and Zephyr galloped on, the trees dense around them before clearing to a small path. There it was. A grunt and a squeal and a brown flash as the boar barrelled ahead, the dogs at its heels. Hugo pulled on the reins, watching as the hounds circled the boar, which screamed and reared back. Hugo raised his musket and fired. The boar dropped to the ground, writhing and squealing. Hugo swung himself down from his horse and strode over to the boar. Taking his dagger from its sheath, he sliced into the tender skin beneath the boar's neck. Dark blood spurted out, wetting his boots and breeches.

CHAPTER 17

Romain, grinning, chased Tomas in the orange grove, his shirt billowing as he ran. 'Run, run!' Estelle and Solange yelled, as Tomas weaved around the rows of trees, clods of earth flying behind him.

Romain reached out, seized Tomas's sleeve and swivelled him around. 'Got you! You rascal. Don't worry about the bet.'

'You're fast, for an old man,' Tomas gasped, his eyes glinting.

The girls clapped and giggled before turning to see an armed guard from the gates approaching. He was dressed in a red uniform with gold epaulettes, his hand on the hilt of his sword.

'Monsieur de Villers,' the guard said, 'the duc wishes to see you.'

Romain followed the guard through the orange grove to the stone stairs that marked the entrance to the château, where the duc waited.

The duc dropped a brown leather glove at Romain's feet. 'I hope you are enough of a gentleman to understand my meaning?' he said.

Romain swallowed, turning pale. 'I understand you are challenging me to a duel, but I do not understand how I might have offended you, Your Grace.'

'How about bedding my wife, monsieur?'

'I will leave immediately, Your Grace. It was a single occasion, one we both deeply regret.' Romain felt light-headed, his blood pulsed in his ears, and his body was rigid.

Hugo laughed, the expression in his eyes unyielding. 'Only one occasion, you say? As if that excuses your behavior! In *my* château with *my* wife—you dog. We will fight with swords to first blood. You will leave the château within the hour and I will inform you of the time and place of the duel.'

'Your Grace, I offer my apologies and hope that we may resolve this matter another way.'

'This is the only way. If I see you again today, we will duel on the spot. Find yourself a second. If it's the Marquis d'Urveilles, perhaps I can stab him too.'

Hugo turned and strode inside. Romain waited until he disappeared before sitting on the steps, his face cradled in his hands.

It was late afternoon and honeyed light pooled on the wood floors of the shop. Henriette and Pauline had been working to complete a large order from an aristocratic family with three daughters who were to be presented at court the following week. Henriette was flustered, her skills not quite ready for the rapid and intricate sewing required.

Pauline's hands were hidden beneath the voluminous skirts of a white gown as she sewed the hem. 'Henriette, you look exhausted. Just complete the lace collar and you can finish for the day. You've done very well.'

'I hope I've helped rather than hindered.'

'Of course,' Pauline smiled. 'I couldn't have done it without you. The duchesse will be very pleased.'

Henriette flushed with pleasure. 'Thank you. I've just realized this is the first time I have felt truly appreciated, other than by my daughter. It's new for me.'

'I appreciate your help as well as your company.'

The last stitches done, Henriette placed the gown over a mannequin, arranging the elaborate sleeves across the shoulders. The bell jingled over the door and Romain walked in, his face solemn.

'Good afternoon, Madame Rolain, Madame d'Augustin.'

'Monsieur de Villiers, did you wish to walk?'

Romain smiled uncertainly. 'Yes, yes I would, if Madame Rolain permits?'

'Yes,' Pauline replied. 'Henriette has just finished for the day.'

Romain waited as Henriette retrieved her coat, and helped her into it.

'Would you like to go back to the bishop's palace gardens?' he asked.

Henriette nodded, taking his arm. They walked without speaking, his arm stiff beneath her own.

At the gardens, Henriette and Romain walked around the perimeter, before sitting on a bench. Romain slipped out of his coat and draped it across his knees. A robin flitted in and out of the rosebushes, his body a flash of red as the scent of turned earth filled Henriette's nose. She covered his hand with her own, and waited for him to look at her.

'What is it?' she asked.

'The duc has challenged me to a duel.'

'Why?' she gasped.

'I was seen,' he admitted at last, 'with the duchesse.'

'We were together, intimately. Just once. We were seen. We were lovers in our youth, you see.'

Henriette's vision blurred as her eyes flooded with tears. 'Why didn't you tell me?'

'I'm sorry.' Romain touched her shoulder, gently turning her to face him.

'I need to go,' Henriette pulled away from him, wiping her eyes with the back of her hand. 'I need to think about this.'

Romain took her hand. 'I want to be worthy of you, Henriette.'

Yanking her hand away, she rose and stood shaking before him. He rose to his feet, his coat falling to the ground, a rectangle of folded parchment sliding from the pocket.

Henriette noticed the name 'Antoine' written above the wax seal and reached down to pick it up. Romain snatched it away.

'What is it, Romain? Give it to me.'

'It's just a letter.'

Henriette gritted her teeth. 'Let me see it.'

He sighed and placed the letter in her outstretched palm. She opened it and scanned the words, frowning.

'I have been acting as an intermediary for the Marquis d'Urveilles and Letitia.'

'Why, Romain?'

'The marquis is a friend of mine.'

Henriette shoved the letter into his chest. 'I'm leaving. Just let me be for a while.'

'I'll be at my aunt's house, rue des Rosiers,' Romain called after her retreating figure. 'It's the one on the corner, if you need me!'

Romain watched her hurry up the steps and out of the garden, the letter a crushed ball in his fist.

Henriette hired an open carriage to take her to the château, and as it approached the elaborate iron gates, she felt a twinge of sadness. She was now a mere visitor at the château, and an unwelcome one at that. The coachman delivered her to the entrance, where she pulled the rope to sound the brass entrance bell.

Thierry opened the door to admit her. 'Good day, Madame d'Augustin. Are you here to see Mademoiselle Solange? She will be delighted.'

'Yes, Thierry. But I would like to see Mademoiselle du Massenet first. Do you know where I can find her?'

'Mademoiselle du Massenet is writing a letter in the library. Follow me.'

Thierry opened the door to the library to reveal Letitia, bent over the desk, absorbed in her writing.

'Letitia,' Henriette said. 'Sorry to interrupt you at your writing. Do give the marquis my regards.'

Letitia looked up, startled, dropping her quill. 'Henriette! Oh, it is so good to see you. I've missed you so. Why would you think I was writing to the marquis?'

Henriette sat on an armchair and motioned for Letitia to join her.

'It is indeed strange,' said Henriette, 'as I've just seen a letter of yours, written to the marquis and in the possession of Romain de Villiers.'

'The marquis somehow believes the same,' Letitia exclaimed, pacing the room. 'Not only have I *never* written a letter to the marquis,

I've never received one from him. It is the duchesse's handiwork, Henriette. She left forged letters on Hugo's bureau for him to find, I just know it. She couldn't manage to kill me, so now she seeks to utterly ruin me in his eyes. What can I do?'

'Romain is involved in all of this, Letitia. He is not on our side.'

'Maybe Romain forged the letters from me.'

'He kissed me, last week, Letitia,' Henriette confided. 'I was starting to fall in love with him. It's been so long since I've had feelings for someone…since I've felt such tenderness.'

'I know you have feelings for him, Henriette. I'm so sorry. I could be sent away too, now Hugo suspects me of an affair.'

'I don't wish homelessness on you. Something has been happening between you and the marquis though, hasn't it?'

Letitia blushed. 'Yes, we've met a few times, in the forest.'

'Letitia, you are playing a very dangerous game. You'd better stay away from him.'

'Yes, I will. I'm not permitted to leave the château in any case. Henriette, Romain relies upon the duchesse to retain his place at court, as you know. Perhaps, since you have fallen out of favour, Charlotte may have pursued him, sensing the attraction between the two of you. Romain may have had little choice but to submit to her desires.'

Henriette laughed, a short and bitter sound. 'You make Romain sound as if he were a blushing girl, Letitia, instead of a courtier well practiced in the arts of seduction.' Henriette pressed her fingertips to her forehead and sighed. 'I've been so naïve, Letitia. I feel foolish, as if perhaps they've been laughing about me together.'

'Romain wouldn't do that, Henriette. Come, let's go and find Solange. She's been missing you desperately.'

Marianne stirred a cauldron of soup on the fire whilst Romain sat at the table in her parlour. Shrieks of delight could be heard from Romain's cousins who played in the street. Through the streaked window, Théa, Marianne's eldest daughter, hung washing on a rope strung between two walls.

'Have some soup, Romain.' His aunt spooned the thick vegetable soup, seasoned with paprika, into a bowl and placed it before him. Romain stirred the soup, then pushed the bowl away with a sigh. Marianne watched him with concern. Her face had filled out after her illness, and her eyes had regained their gleam.

'Thank you, but I can't possibly eat,' he told her. 'Let the children have it.'

Marianne frowned, dark curls of brown hair escaping from beneath her cap. She wiped her hands on her apron before taking a seat next to him.

'What's ailing you, Romain? You're so quiet. I'm used to you telling me so many things—news from the court, news of your readings. You're pale and hardly eating. The twinkle has gone from your eyes. What is it?'

'I must fight a duel against the duc.'

Marianne gasped. '*Mon dieu*, a duel! The duc is known for his expert swordsmanship. Romain, you must leave. You must run now. I have a friend in Marseilles who can take you in—'

'No. I must think of my honour. I won't leave.'

Marianne shook her head and pushed his bowl closer to him. 'All right. You should eat first, Romain, to keep up your strength. And then we can figure out what to do.'

They jumped at a sharp rap to the door. Romain opened the door to a young servant boy from the château. 'Good day,' he said. 'Are you Monsieur de Villiers?'

Romain nodded, apprehension swirling in his stomach. The boy held out a folded piece of parchment, sealed with red wax.

'Thank you,' said Romain, pushing the door closed with his shoulder.

Scanning the curlicued script, he made note of the time, date and location of the duel. It was to be held in one week, in the field behind the château. Romain felt nauseated. He wondered who could be his second. The duc had mentioned his animosity toward the marquis, and Romain surmised that Hugo knew something of his friend's dalliance with Letitia. Yet, there was no one else he could ask.

Romain wandered through the bustling streets of the town. It was market day and stallholders stood by their trays of foie gras, rounds of cheese, sacks of spices, and baskets of fruits and vegetables. The cream façades of houses rose behind the stalls, their black iron balconies hung with washing or decorated with flower boxes. Henriette's face kept appearing in his mind and he found himself walking in the direction of the dressmaker's shop.

He could see Henriette bent to her work through the shop window, her hair glossy in the shafts of afternoon light, her expression one of intent concentration. Around her lay bundles of fabric, baskets of thread, lace, and buttons, spilling onto the floor. His heart beat a frantic rhythm in his chest.

As he entered, the two women glanced up from their work, and Henriette reddened.

'Romain, what are you doing here?'

'I must speak to you privately.'

'I won't be a moment, Pauline,' Henriette apologized, before making her way to the door and stepping outside. 'I have found employment here and I don't need you to risk it for me,' Henriette snapped. 'I have work to do. What do you want?'

'Henriette, I...'

'What about the letters, Romain? You lied to me. Letitia never wrote them.'

'I forged them, Henriette,' he admitted, his face flushed. 'The ones from the duc were real. But what choice did I have? Charlotte demanded I cooperate and keep silent on the matter. She threatened to have my aunt and her children evicted—'

'I don't want to hear anymore.' Henriette's hands shook and she avoided his eyes. 'I thought you were better than this, Romain.'

'I am, Henriette. I will show you. Let me show you.' Romain reached for her hand and she took a step back.

'Please. Please don't try to see me. Goodbye, Romain.'

The field outside Blois was cast in shadow as clouds scudded overhead. The two men parried and lunged with a clang of steel, each damp with sweat despite the cold. Romain cursed as Antoine thrust forward, the point on his sword touching his chest.

'I'm a dead man,' Romain sighed.

Antoine wiped his forehead with the back of his hand. 'You're actually better at swordplay than I expected.'

'The last time I fought, sword in hand, was with you, when we were boys.'

'That's right,' Antoine said. 'Remember my fencing master, Gilles? His pompous affectations? He had that ridiculous silk handkerchief poking out of his pocket. Once I managed to draw it out with my sword. He wasn't impressed.'

Romain laughed, before his expression quickly became sober.

'So will you do it, Antoine? Be my second?'

Antoine fingered the hilt of his sword. 'Yes, although he'll probably demand a second round with me.'

'One duel at a time.'

Antoine raised an eyebrow. 'How reassuring. The duel is to first blood?'

'It is. Only I am afraid that in the heat of the moment he will become murderous.'

'Ah well, if that's the case he might fight me too. Then we can both fly up to heaven together.'

Romain raked his fingers through his hair. 'Henriette doesn't want to see me anymore.'

'So, she's discovered you're a lovable rogue?'

'Not lovable, unfortunately. The reason for the duel is the same reason she now hates me.'

'Don't worry,' said Antoine, clapping him on the shoulder, 'she'll come around if you mend your ways.'

Romain nodded. 'I might just have to grow up a little. Come on then, let's go again. I'm ready.'

Both men readied themselves for another round then parried back and forth, the grass swishing around their calves.

Marianne's door was ajar. Romain found her on her hands and knees, picking up shards of porcelain. The older children swept up straw from ripped mattresses. His aunt glanced up at him, her face blank with shock. 'Some men came,' she explained in a faltering voice. 'Three of them; they asked for money. I gave them the little I had. But they said it wasn't enough and they smashed our dishes and slashed the mattresses apart.'

'I'm so sorry,' Romain dropped to his knees beside her. 'How much did you give?'

'Two livres.'

'I'll pay you back and buy some new mattresses. And china.' He set fallen chairs upright, picked up cutlery, and mopped up water that had spilled from an overturned bucket.

'Marianne, I have debts, but I have enough money to pay. I promise you, this won't happen again. May I stay here? I'll understand if you would prefer I leave.'

'Of course you must stay. But please, pay them, as I don't want another visit.'

Carmine piped up. 'I hid under the dresser, Tati. They were very loud and very angry.'

Romain ruffled her hair. 'I'm sorry, Carmine. I really am.'

Solange insisted on accompanying her mother to visit Amalia. Spring had arrived and the plane trees on the street leading to the convent were sprouting fresh leaves. Soon it would be Holy Week and Henriette's favourite service, Tenebrae.

Henriette had arrived at the château earlier that morning to visit the chapel before collecting Solange. She flicked holy water on her forehead and murmured prayers, clutching her rosary. The priest asked her if she wished for absolution, but Henriette shook her head and replied, 'It is not I who needs it.'

As they descended from the carriage at the steps to the convent, Henriette adjusted the collar on Solange's dress and gripped her hand.

'Now, just remember, Amalia might be unpleasant toward you, my dear. She may insult you, but remember it is not about you. Amalia has…difficulty understanding appropriate behaviour.'

Solange peered up at the building that rose in marble hues from the gravel road, neatly lined with boxwood hedges. Inside the bell tower, the bell glinted gold in the morning sun.

'It's beautiful, Maman. Do you think the bell might ring whilst I'm here?'

Béatrice opened the door to their knock and ushered them inside. She led them through a series of narrow passageways and out to the yard, where the girls had just been released from morning prayers. A group of them descended on Solange, eagerly asking questions and playing with her hair.

Amalia crept up behind her mother, touching her arm. Henriette swung around. 'Amalia!' she exclaimed. 'I'm happy to see you.' She kissed her daughter on both cheeks, noticing that Amalia seemed thinner, her face pallid, with dark circles beneath her eyes.

'Come, let's sit down. Solange will come over in a minute. She's very excited to see you again.' Henriette and Amalia sat on the stone bench, overlooking the girls who shrieked as they played, chasing each other around trees, hair streaming behind them.

Henriette frowned and took Amalia's hand in her own. 'You're not well, I can see. Has something happened?'

Amalia was silent for a moment, her gaze darting around the garden as if she were seeking answers. 'Brother Deniel visits me, Maman, and does disgusting things. Abbess de la Fontaine doesn't believe me. No one does.'

Henriette flushed and clasped her hand tighter. 'Amalia, you need to tell me exactly what he does.'

'He touches me on my private parts.'

Henriette's hand flew to her mouth. 'Mother of God,' she muttered. 'Amalia, why have you not told me this before?'

At that moment Solange skipped over and leaned in to kiss Amalia, whose face reddened. 'Hello, Solange,' she said. 'How do you like the convent?'

'It's lovely. The girls are very friendly. They all want to write to me.'

Amalia's eyes were soft as she regarded her sister. 'They're lonely. They want to know about places outside these walls. We can't leave until we're of age.'

Solange eyed her mother before responding. 'That's sad. Maybe we can go for a picnic another day, all together.'

Amalia reached out and touched the lace on Solange's dress. 'Maman gave me a dress like that too, but I burnt it. It's so pretty.'

Abbess de la Fontaine appeared at the top of the stairs that wound down to the garden; she shaded her eyes and raised a hand in greeting before descending and crossing the grass to them. With a warm smile, she arranged her habit in the chair opposite.

'Béatrice is coming with the tea. Now, you must be Solange,' the abbess said, reaching out to touch Solange's hair. 'Your mother has spoken very highly of you, my dear.'

Solange beamed. 'Thank you. Mothers are biased, I think.'

'No, not true.' Amalia's blue eyes flashed. 'Maman has never spoken highly of me and I, too, am her daughter.' She drew her gangly knees up and rested her chin on them.

Henriette pressed her lips together and shot the abbess a look. 'Oh, Amalia, of course I am proud of you. Your Bible recitation is excellent.'

'What about me as a *person*?' Amalia scowled at her mother. 'That's not really something to boast about, is it? It's a sly whispered thing, like a dead mouse starting to smell.'

Henriette sighed. 'Why don't you two girls go for a little walk, get to know each other? The abbess and I must talk privately.'

The two girls eyed each other with uncertainty, before walking toward the trees. Solange tucked Amalia's arm into her own, and chattered as her half-sister dragged her feet alongside, casting dark glances over her shoulder at her mother and the abbess.

'Abbess de la Fontaine, I need to speak with you about Amalia. She has confided in me about something very troubling.'

'What was it?' the abbess asked with a frown.

'She said that Brother Deniel has been touching her inappropriately.'

The abbess flushed. 'Yes, she has spoken of this before. Brother Deniel has been providing us with spiritual solace for five years. Before that time, he assisted the Bishop Delacroix in Avignon, who recommended him. He is a most pious man, committed in his devotions.'

'I understand that, but I am concerned and think this matter needs to be investigated. It must be brought to the attention of the church.'

'No, madame. Your daughter is not in her right mind, as you know. I won't risk staining the reputation of a respected man of God, on the claims of one mad girl.'

Henriette bristled. 'In my opinion, this is not one of her delusions. Amalia seems genuinely upset. I understand your wish to protect his reputation, but you have a duty to protect the girls.'

'I'm sorry, madame. I will look out for the child, but I won't cast aspersions on Brother Deniel without proper evidence. I trust this won't have a negative effect on our good relations?'

'No, Abbess. But perhaps you can uncover whether Brother Deniel has behaved in this manner toward any of the other girls.'

'Of course madame, and I will watch for anything suspicious.'

CHAPTER 18

As the weather warmed, Letitia spent more time with Tomas and Solange, playing hide and seek in the orange grove, racing sticks down the forest stream, and taking cloth bundles of cake into the gardens for outdoor tea. On other days, she spent hours riding alone in the forest. Every day she woke and wondered if she would be sent home humiliated, never to marry, a burden to her parents.

One morning after her maid had departed, Letitia sat at her desk to compose a letter to her mother, a letter she knew she would never send. Writing of her troubles relieved her anxiety. She wrote of her feelings for Antoine and her concerns about her position and honour. Folding the parchment, she threw it into the fire and watched as it was engulfed by flames.

She called out for Adele, who came and dressed her, before attending to her hair. Once dressed, she made her way downstairs and outside. The amber sun was low and the morning chill less severe. She walked toward the orange grove.

Solange and Tomas tugged on Letitia's arm as they walked through the rows of orange trees. The three of them sat in the shade of a tree, heavy with fruit, and devoured the ripe oranges, the juice running down their chins. 'We have to watch out for the gardener,' Solange said, with a wink. 'He doesn't like us to pick the oranges.' They had waited a long time for the trees to bear fruit, eagerly watching the blossoms bud and open and the green nodules of fruit emerge, then the ripe oranges, the colour of a setting sun. For a moment Letitia and Solange forgot their troubles as the juice filled their mouths.

The morning of the Tenebrae service arrived, and Henriette dressed in a dove-grey silk gown and a pearl pendant. The duc had given permission for her to attend the service at the château. Solange would be waiting for her at the chapel.

The hired open carriage waited for her outside, the coachman wearing a felt hat that hid his eyes. As the carriage traversed the dirt road out of town, thoughts of Romain crowded Henriette's mind. The passion aroused by his kiss and her anger at his deceit mingled together. She crossed herself.

The coachman pulled on the reins and the carriage came to a halt near the chapel. Looking out the window, Henriette caught sight of Solange and felt a thrill of happiness course through her veins.

Henriette clambered down from the carriage and rushed over, enfolding Solange in her arms. Her daughter's tears wet the fabric of her gown. They remained in a tight embrace for a while before Henriette held her at arm's length, admiring, through her own tears, Solange's white lace dress and braided hair.

'Is Isabelle taking good care of you?' she asked.

'Yes, but I need you, Maman. I have bad dreams, and I don't like to wake her.'

'My poor darling, it will get better, I promise. We need to go inside now.' Henriette took Solange's hand and together they entered the chapel.

The chapel blazed gold with candlelight, emanating from an immense wrought-iron candelabra set in the middle of the altar. Feeling the stares of the congregation, Henriette and Solange found a seat near the back. The dark blue candles on the candelabra would be extinguished after each reading, until only the large white one, representing Christ, remained. Then it, too, would be snuffed, symbolizing the end of his life.

Henriette did not recognize all the men and women in the congregation, but she knew they were connected to the duc and duchesse in some way. She reached for Solange's hand and stroked it, relieved to be in her daughter's company. The door to the chapel opened and the duchesse and Céline entered. As they passed along the aisle, the duchesse nodded at several people. Henriette attempted to catch her eye but Charlotte stared at a fixed point above her head, refusing to acknowledge her.

The priest made the sign of the cross and began the service with communion. One by one, people filed up to him to receive the sacraments. A small child cried out at the back of the chapel and was shushed by her mother. Henriette watched the flames waver and smoke before rising with her daughter to join the queue. As the priest placed the wafer in her mouth she silently asked for forgiveness. *May God cleanse me of desire and fill me with divine spirit,* she implored, crossing herself. She sipped from the brass goblet of wine and returned to her seat.

The duchesse gave the first reading from Psalms. Her clear voice resonated through the small space. She was the picture of virtue in a dark purple gown. A pearl and diamond brooch was pinned near the high neck, her fair hair swept up with tortoiseshell combs. She wore no powder or lip colour and crossed herself, giving the priest a solemn nod as she finished the reading. Taking the silver snuffer from him, she held it over the first candle until it went out.

She looks as if she's in training for the convent, pure and virginal, thought Henriette. An ache of bitterness formed in her throat.

As others rose and gave readings Henriette allowed the ceremony to soothe her. As each candle was put out, the chapel dimmed until only one candle remained. Solange whispered in her ear.

'It's me, Maman. I'm reading from Matthew.'

Henriette glowed with pride and watched her daughter stand at the lectern, her face half in shadow.

'You have heard that it was said, "You shall love your neighbour and hate your enemy." But I say to you, love your enemies and pray for those who persecute you, so that you may be sons of your Father who is in heaven; for he makes his sun rise on the evil and on the good, and sends rain on the just and on the unjust."'

Henriette stared at Solange in wonder. She had chosen the reading to enlighten her mother, to show her the pointless nature of her antipathy. *It's true*, she thought. *The passage from Matthew*—'*Out of the mouths of infants and nursing babies you have prepared praise.*' Her daughter had wisdom that she herself was only beginning to learn.

Solange extinguished the candle and beamed in her mother's direction before stepping down and taking her seat. Henriette squeezed her hand and wiped a tear from her eye.

The priest recited Psalm Twenty-Two, his voice rising with emotion.

'My God, my God, why have you forsaken me? Why are you so far from saving me, from the words of my groaning? O my God, I cry by day, but you do not answer, and by night, but I find no rest.'

He crossed himself and put out the white candle, casting the chapel into near darkness. Drapes were pulled over the stained glass windows and the only light came from beneath the door. Henriette let her tears fall, her chest rising and falling with suppressed sobs. She prayed fervently, holding fast to her daughter's hand.

Antoine collected Romain from his aunt's house in his carriage on the morning of the duel. Tiny white wildflowers dotted the edges of the road leading to the château. They passed beneath giant plane trees and Romain stared out at the farmhands planting wheat, their backs bent to their tasks. They turned a corner and the carriage climbed the hill leading to the château. Romain's heart thudded as he saw the iron gates glinting in the distance.

The sun was still low on the horizon, and above Mont Pinçon, heavy storm clouds billowed. Romain frowned, running his fingers over the engraved hilt of the sword Antoine had lent him, perspiration beading on his forehead. Thunder murmured in the distance, growing to a threatening rumble. The carriage stopped at the main entrance and the coachman stood at the door as they stepped out. Thierry was waiting for them on the steps. 'Good morning, gentlemen. His Grace is waiting in the field behind the château.'

Romain nodded. 'Thank you, Thierry.'

Antoine and Romain walked past the front of the château and along the side to the field. A flash of lightning brightened the sky and Romain felt several drops of rain on his face. He sighed. 'Rain. That will make matters even more difficult.'

Antoine turned his palm upwards as the drops became heavier. 'Perhaps, perhaps not. It makes the fight more difficult for your opponent as well.'

Three figures were visible at the far side of the field. As the two men approached, Romain recognized the Comte du Ponsardin and the valet, Arthur, standing with the duc. Arthur held an umbrella over the two men. In front of them, on a table with a white cloth, lay a selection of swords. Thunder clapped once more, louder this time.

Romain nodded at them. 'Good day, Your Grace, Your Lordship.'

The duc's stance was rigid. 'You've a nerve coming here as a second,' he snapped, glaring at Antoine.

Antoine drew himself up. 'I'm not sure what you mean.'

The duc examined the swords on the table, hefting a few and drawing them through the air in figure eights, making a swishing sound. Romain felt the draught from the swords fanning his face.

The drops of rain came faster, hitting his head in cold needles. The duc still refused to look in Romain's direction. He settled on a small sword with a golden hilt studded with rubies. The Comte du Ponsardin measured it against Romain's sword to ensure both swords were of the same length and nodded his approval.

'Are you ready to begin, gentlemen?' the comte asked.

The two men nodded their assent. Arthur helped the duc remove his coat and undid the ties on his white shirt. Another rumble of thunder made them start. Romain took off his own coat and handed it to Antoine. 'Lift your shirts, please,' instructed the comte. The duc and Romain raised their shirts to show they were not hiding any other weapons.

The comte stepped forward, the wind howling as his voice rose to a shout. 'This duel will be fought to the first blood, in order to satisfy the offense against the duc. Gentlemen, we will begin. Walk to the middle of the field.'

Romain withdrew his sword from its scabbard. It glinted in the light, its tip sharp as death. He strode to the middle of the field, determined to get the ordeal over with.

The two men faced each other. '*Allez*,' said the comte, holding his hand in the air, before bringing it down, indicating the duel should begin.

The two men lowered themselves into the initial fencing position, moving back and forth on their heels, swords raised to the offensive. The rain pelted down, drenching their clothing. Their faces glistened as their swords connected, the metallic twang echoing through the field. Romain was forced to take backward steps as the duc advanced, his strokes sure and adept.

The duc lunged, and the swords clashed; Romain stepped forward and parried, trying to arrest his backward movement. His sword sliced the duc's shirt, but no blood appeared. A jagged streak of lightning cut through the sky with a loud crack. Distracted, Romain was pushed back further. The roar of rain accompanied the clang of their swords. Romain thought of Henriette, and a sudden jolt of aggression coursed through him. This man had humiliated her. He dodged the duc's sword and moved forward, trying to strike a blow to the other man's chest. Instead, he lost his balance, and his sword fell to the ground. The duc gave a grim smile and lunged once more, his sword making contact with Romain's chest, striking a diagonal blow. Romain cried out and clutched the wound, feeling the warmth of his blood as it seeped through his shirt. Antoine ran to him as he sank to the ground.

&

At the edge of the field, Letitia waited, half concealed by a birch tree. When she saw Romain drop to the ground, her hand flew to her mouth, and she rushed to the front of the château. She raced through the entrance hall and upstairs to her rooms. At her desk, she composed a letter and gave it to Adele. 'Take this to Madame d'Augustin. Right away.'

❧

Pauline hung completed dresses on hooks, casting worried glances in Henriette's direction. Henriette knew her employer was concerned about her—she had pricked her finger several times that day and barely touched her breakfast.

She could think of nothing but Romain. Her emotions pitched and soared, her mind returning to him again and again. It was impossible not to wonder what else he had obscured, held back. The idea of his involvement in the duchesse's plot sickened her. She sighed and pinned the bodice of a gown draped on a mannequin.

Pauline touched her shoulder. 'Henriette, why don't you take a walk? You'll just drop stitches when you're like this.'

Henriette turned around, startled. 'Oh, I'm sorry, Pauline. Forgive me.'

'It's Monsieur de Villiers, isn't it?'

'He's fighting a duel today.'

Pauline's eyes widened. 'Do you know if it's to the death or first blood?'

'No, I don't know anything.' Her lip trembled and she pressed her fingertips to her forehead.

The door tinkled and Adele burst in, out of breath.

'Good day, Madame d'Augustin. I have a letter for you, from Mademoiselle du Massenet.'

Henriette jumped to her feet and took the parchment from the maid's outstretched hand. 'Thank you, Adele. Pass on my regards to Mademoiselle du Massenet.'

'I will, madame.'

Henriette's hand flew to her mouth as she read Letitia's note.

Dearest Henriette,

I am sorry to tell you that Monsieur de Villiers has been badly wounded. I'm not sure where he is, but I would suggest you go immediately to his aunt's house; the duc may have taken him there. At the very least she may be able to tell you of his whereabouts. He fought bravely but was not strong enough for the duc's swordsmanship. I so wished to be able to deliver this news myself, but the duc has confined me to the château. My prayers are with you.

Letitia.

'Pauline, Romain is wounded. I need to find him and I may need to stay with him. Do you mind? Can you do without me for a few days?'

'Yes. Please, do what you must.'

'Thank you. I need to get a few things from upstairs.'

Henriette rapidly packed a leather bag with a change of clothes and some rosewater. Retrieving her shawl, she tied on her hat and hastened downstairs.

CHAPTER 19

An older woman opened the door to the house on rue des Rosiers. 'I am Marianne,' she introduced herself. 'You have come to see Romain? Come in, please. He's stopped bleeding, but he's very weak. The physician has just left.'

Henriette felt tears prick her eyes as she spotted Romain's familiar form, covered by a thin blanket. Several children lingered near him, their expressions grave.

'Children, go and play outside. The lady needs some time with Romain.'

'Romain? It's Henriette.' He tried to turn and moaned in pain. 'Stay there, don't move.' She knelt down in front of him, stroking his damp hair. His face was colourless and had a sickly sheen.

He gave a pained smile. 'Henriette, I—'

'Don't try and speak. It's all right, Romain. It's going to be all right.'

She glanced up at Marianne. 'Where is the physician?'

'He will be back later this afternoon.'

'And the marquis?'

The woman wrung her hands. 'He will return tomorrow and take Romain to his château in Orléans. He said Romain will be more comfortable there.'

'What did the physician say?'

'He's lucky to be in this world. The sword struck a hair's breadth from his heart, but he will recover.'

'Thanks be to God,' murmured Henriette, crossing herself.

'Henriette, you're here,' Romain managed, his voice a ragged whisper. 'I wasn't sure if you'd come.'

'Of course I'm here,' Henriette said, taking his hand. 'I'm going to help you get well.'

❧

Romain's torso was tightly bound with bandages under his shirt. He sat propped up in the carriage, his face grey and clammy. Pain flared as the carriage jolted over potholes and stones. His joy at Henriette's presence was tempered with shame at his enfeebled state. She sat next to him at the window, Antoine opposite.

As they approached the Château d'Auverge at Orléans, Romain heard the lowing of cows outside. Antoine had told him the land surrounding the château was a working farm. He smelt dung and hay as he sat up, wincing and clutching his chest. He watched the château appear from behind oak trees dotted throughout the grounds. Plantings of daffodils and dahlias were surrounded by willows. The front of the château was dominated by giant columns, and a team of servants stood to either side of the stairs in black and white uniforms. The effort of looking tired him and Romain sank back into the padded seat.

The coachman opened the door and Antoine signalled for him to assist. They grasped Romain under the arms and lifted him as far as the stairs. Two male servants then carried him inside. Exhaustion blurred his vision as he was lifted up an immense flight of stairs and everything turned black.

❧

Hugo's elation after the duel was short-lived. He retreated to his rooms, his thoughts consumed by Letitia. Arthur had announced her presence a number of times, but the duc refused to see her. After several days of reclusiveness, Charlotte burst in, waving away Arthur, who hovered behind.

'What in the world are you doing, Hugo? The servants are gossiping. You can't have all your meals in here. What's wrong with you?' Her blue eyes were dark with concern.

Hugo sat on a chaise reading Racine. He sighed and put the book down, patting the space next to him. 'You need to be announced,' he said sternly.

'I'm your wife. I haven't needed to be announced before.'

'You hadn't betrayed me before. I don't know what to make of anyone these days, Charlotte. Sit down, please.'

Charlotte gave a tentative smile and obeyed, angling her knees toward him. She stroked his hair back from his face. 'Hugo, I've missed you so.'

'Why did you betray me, Charlotte?'

He watched her chest rise and fall, tears brimming in her eyes. 'I wish I knew, Hugo. I'm so sorry.'

He took her hand and brought it to his lips, kissing the palm with infinite tenderness.

Hugo and Charlotte remained in his rooms for the rest of the day and night. Servants brought them dinner under silver cloches. They laughed and fed each other morsels of pheasant, toast with terrine, and chocolate tart, before climbing beneath the sheets. Charlotte felt like the girl beneath the tree, and in her husband's face, she saw the young man he had once been.

His blue-grey eyes still held the same warmth, and his body felt nearly the same as he pinned her to the bed, kissing her neck. A silver cloche clanged as he kicked it to the floor. A wave of pleasure engulfed her and she wondered how long the miracle would last.

Just after dawn, Charlotte brushed her lips over her husband's as he slept. She swung her legs over the side of the bed, pushing herself upright with care. She put on her silk dressing gown and returned to her rooms.

Yolande was asleep on a chaise, and Charlotte tapped her on the shoulder. 'Yolande. Help me get dressed.'

Yolande helped Charlotte with her slip, stockings, petticoat, pocket bags, and stays. The maid tightened Charlotte's laces and eased a coral-coloured gown over her head. Then, she pinned the duchesse's upswept hair with mother-of-pearl combs. She reached for the powder but Charlotte waved her away.

'I'm ready now. You may leave me for a while.'

Charlotte waited until the maid had departed, then made her way through the hallways to the double doors of Letitia's rooms. Giving three sharp raps on the door, she waited.

Letitia opened the door in a thin silk dressing gown.

'Get dressed,' Charlotte spat.

Letitia drew herself up, scowling. 'And why should I obey you?'

'If you don't obey me, I'll show the duc the rest of the letters in my possession.'

'That is ridiculous. I never wrote a single letter to the marquis.'

'You can't prove that,' Charlotte replied with a tight smile. 'The duc already has doubts. You can't afford to make things worse. Besides, he and I are close again. Ring for your maid.'

Letitia shut the door and rang the bell to alert Adele in the next room. Charlotte sat in a gilt chair and waited as Letitia was dressed. A clock ticked on a side table and she drummed her fingers on her lap. When the girl emerged, Charlotte rose to her feet. 'Follow me,' she said.

The two women walked along the hallway to a narrow staircase that led to the upper floor. As they approached the doors to the dusty room vacated by Henriette, Letitia's eyes widened.

'You've gone mad. I'm not staying in there.'

Charlotte raised an eyebrow. 'I rather think you don't have a choice,' she said as she shoved Letitia inside, locking the door behind her. Muffled screams and thudding on the door caused her to smile. 'Be quiet,' she said, 'or this will become a permanent arrangement.'

The room was dim, the drapes partially drawn. Henriette sat at Romain's bedside, gently touching his brow with a damp linen cloth. His face was ashen and he appeared smaller than his usual robust size, tucked in the enormous canopy bed. A maid had filled a vase with roses and their scent filled the air. The old physician, Doctor Frette, came every morning and seemed happy with his patient's progress.

Romain stirred, and Henriette placed a hand on his chest.

'The doctor said you need to stay still, Romain. Until the wound heals. Would you like some water?'

He nodded, his warm gaze enveloping her. She brought the water glass to his mouth and he took a sip. 'Thank you,' he muttered. 'You're beautiful....'

'Shhh.' She touched his lips with her index finger. 'We can talk when you're better. Rest now.'

He reached for her hand. 'I'm so happy you're here.'

'Someone has to be,' she replied. 'I'll be gone soon.'

CHAPTER 20

Just after breakfast, Isabelle cornered Thierry in the hallway, glancing around to make sure they were alone. 'Thierry, I haven't seen Mademoiselle du Massenet for some days. Is she unwell?'

Something flickered in Thierry's eyes before his face resumed its usual inscrutable expression. 'No, madame. She has gone to visit her parents.'

'Oh? When did she leave?' Isabelle asked.

'On Thursday. She left very early, before dawn.'

'Thank you, Thierry.'

Isabelle waited until the manservant was out of sight before climbing the stairs and wandering through the hallways. *Where is she?* she thought, unease fluttering in her stomach as she made her way back to her rooms. She could hear Tomas and Solange laughing from the hallway.

Isabelle opened the door to find them frog racing on the Persian rug. Solange sprang up, her cheeks flushed. 'Sorry, Madame Franche-Bastien. It started to rain outside.'

Tomas gave his mother a crooked grin. 'Sorry, Maman.'

Isabelle smiled at them. 'It's all right. Put them in their jar now and listen. I have a job for you. Mademoiselle Letitia is missing. I can't find her. Go and do your spying, and see what you can come up with. Thierry says she's gone to see her parents, but I don't believe him.'

The children nodded, their faces solemn. Solange twisted a ringlet around her finger. 'I heard voices the other morning. Letitia and the duchesse.'

Isabelle held her breath. 'Of course. Whatever has happened, you can be sure Charlotte is behind it. Go now.'

The two children nodded and rushed out the door, their faces bright with excitement.

❧

'I'll go to the top floor,' Solange murmured. 'You can do downstairs. I'll meet you in the middle floor.'

'All right. But what are we looking for?'

Solange smiled. 'Some looking, but more listening. I bet the duchesse has hidden her somewhere, and I promise you Letitia wouldn't bear that quietly. See you soon.'

She strode along the hallways until she reached the narrow staircase leading to the upper floor. It was unlit and she clutched the balustrade, her eyes adjusting to the darkness. The stairs creaked under her weight. At the top she turned right, listening as she walked. A faint knocking sound reached her ears.

'Letitia?' she cried, breaking into a run. 'Where are you?'

'Here! I'm in your old room!'

The double doors rattled and Solange stood in front of them, unsure what to do. 'Letitia? Is that you?'

'Yes, it's me. You need to tell Madame Franche-Bastien that I'm here. Quickly. I think the duchesse is planning to send me away. The duc needs to know.'

Solange placed her hand on the door, wishing she could comfort her friend.

'Don't worry. I'll be back soon, all right?'

She sprinted back through the hallway and down the stairs. She burst into Isabelle's room where the mistress waited.

'Letitia is in Henriette's old room! She says the duchesse is going to move her somewhere if we don't get her out of there. You need to tell the duc.'

'Thank you, Solange. You've done an excellent job. Go and find Tomas now, he's probably looking for you.'

'But madame, there's something you should know.'

'What, child? Quickly.'

'I saw Madame de Poitiers in Letitia's room before she was wounded. I think she put something horrible in her stays.'

Isabelle frowned. 'Thank you for telling me. Run along now.'

Solange nodded and did as she was told. Isabelle rushed to the duc's rooms at the other end of the château, pinching her cheeks as she went. Arthur, as always, waited outside the duc's door.

'Good day, Arthur. May I speak with His Grace?'

'Just a moment, madame. I will see if he is able to receive you.'

Isabelle waited impatiently, straining to hear the murmur of voices from within.

Arthur returned with a slight smile. 'You may go in, madame.'

The duc sat at his bureau. He rose to greet her, kissing her on both cheeks. 'What a pleasant surprise, Isabelle. What can I do for you?'

'Thank you, Hugo. Letitia has been locked in Henriette's old room on the top floor. We need to let her out as soon as possible. She seems to think your wife is planning on sending her away.'

Hugo blanched. 'Good grief. Why would Charlotte do such a thing?'

Isabelle sighed. 'Jealousy, I assume. She and Céline have tried to exclude Letitia at every opportunity. And now Solange has told me she thinks Madame de Poitiers put something in Letitia's stays, something that caused her injuries.'

Hugo walked to the window, muttering to himself. 'She was never like this as a girl. She was kind. Imperious but kind. I don't understand why she has become this way.'

Isabelle touched his arm. 'Hugo, we have to let Letitia out, whether you understand or not. Life changes people. If they don't get what they want, or even if they do. Sometimes they change for the better and other times not. Please, we have to go.'

Hugo ran his hands through his hair and grimaced before meeting Isabelle's eyes.

'I'm sorry, yes, of course, we must let her out.'

They found Thierry at the door of the drawing room.

The duc addressed him. 'Thierry, we need you to open the door of the room where Madame d'Augustin last resided. Can you get the keys?'

'Yes, Your Grace. Immediately.'

Thierry strode toward the servants' quarters and returned with the keys. Together, they marched upstairs. Just before they reached the locked room, the duc called out to him. 'Thierry, stop for a moment.'

'Yes, Your Grace?'

Hugo examined him. 'You knew about this, didn't you?'

Thierry's face flushed and his gaze dropped to his polished shoes before returning to his master. 'Her Grace swore me to secrecy. She said I'd lose my position.'

'And you will, if you ever follow such an order again. If she asks you to do something questionable, you will report it to me. Understood?'

'Yes, Your Grace. Forgive me.'

'Carry on. We must free Mademoiselle du Massenet.'

Thierry rushed to the doors and unlocked them. Letitia flew out and into Isabelle's arms.

'It's all right, dear. Have you eaten? Goodness, you're pale.'

Letitia shook her head. 'Not much, some bread and butter.'

The duc stood by and waited. Letitia approached him, her eyes flitting up to his and down again.

'Letitia.' He enfolded her in his arms, stroking her hair. 'We need to talk,' he whispered.

Hugo sat next to Letitia on the sofa. Letitia wondered if she should speak, but decided to remain silent. Hugo always chose his words with care and she understood he was forming them, like an intricate jigsaw puzzle.

'You've been wronged, Letitia. My wife has evidently been persecuting you, more than I realized.'

Letitia's mouth was dry and her voice shook. 'Hugo, I'm sorry. The truth is I'm drawn to the marquis, but I won't be seeing him anymore. I hope you can trust me again.'

Hugo reached out and seized her chin, pulling her face toward his. His fingertips dug into her flesh. 'I could throw you out on the street for that. To think I believed you were different, above other women. I will let you stay. But if I have the slightest suspicion that you've seen that man again, you will be sent away immediately. Do you understand?'

Letitia blinked back tears and wrenched her chin away. 'Yes, I understand.' Her voice was barely above a whisper.

Dawn had just lit her rooms when the arrival of her monthly blood sent Charlotte into a fury. The bloodstain on her sheets reminded her of the thimble of chicken blood she had released onto the sheets on their wedding night. In a fit of rage, she threw a vase at the wall, then the glass by her bedside, and a ceramic water pitcher at the marble base of the fireplace. Yolande cowered in the corner of the room and the dogs hid under the furniture, waiting for the explosion to dissipate.

Yolande brought her tea and Charlotte calmed enough to take her usual morning stroll in the orange grove. The orange trees had flowered, the scent of their blooms sweet in her nose. One of the Bichons scampered by her side, sniffing the fallen flowers and bounding after butterflies. She reached up and twisted the blossoms from their stems and placed them in a small basket. She would float them in bowls of water in her rooms.

I'm not yet with child, but at least Hugo favours me again, she thought, a faint smile on her lips. Children's voices sounded out in the distance. *That tomboy Solange,* she mused, *always spying on everyone like a thief.*

The sight of Tomas's wavy brown hair made her breath catch. She longed to know him, to hold him, but it wasn't possible. It would never be possible.

Her pace quickened.

Solange, Tomas, and Estelle were chasing each other, darting in circles and laughing with a fourth figure Charlotte couldn't identify. As she approached the group, her heart thudded and her mouth went dry. The fourth figure was Letitia, giggling and reaching out to tap Tomas on the shoulder.

Solange saw the duchesse first, nudging Tomas and pointing. They stopped running and stood panting as she approached.

'Good morning,' Charlotte said.

Estelle's chest rose and fell. 'Good morning, Maman.'

Letitia scowled and ground orange flowers into the dirt with her shoe, avoiding Charlotte's eyes. Tomas looked from Letitia to the duchesse and frowned. 'Good morning, Your Grace.'

'Tomas, you're a scamp,' Charlotte said. 'Your clothes are all muddy.'

He blushed. 'I'm always muddy. It's what I do best. Well, other than catching frogs.'

Charlotte wrinkled her nose. 'Very soon you'll be old enough to be presented at court. You'll have to swap your muddy clothes for a clean coat and breeches. You'll not be allowed frogs in your pockets, and the courtiers will expect fine manners.'

'Yes, Your Grace.'

Charlotte nodded at the group and walked on, grinding her teeth, and wondering how Letitia had been freed. She discovered Thierry at the library door.

'How did she get out?' she hissed.

Thierry flushed. 'His Grace found out and I was forced to free her. I'm sorry, Your Grace.'

'Who told him?'

'I cannot say....'

'You will say or you will pack your bags.'

'Only His Grace has the power to dismiss me, Your Grace.'

'You're being impertinent, Thierry. His Grace would not approve. Tell me!'

Thierry's lips trembled. 'Madame Franche-Bastien.'

'Thank you.' Charlotte smiled icily. 'And where is my husband?'

'In the library, Your Grace.' Thierry opened the door for her, sweat beading on his forehead.

'Ah, darling, there you are.' Charlotte approached Hugo and kissed him hard on the lips.

'Hello, Charlotte,' he said, his voice cold.

She stiffened. 'Ah, I see. Our marital happiness is already finished then. Just a brief honeymoon, was it?'

Hugo scowled. 'Charlotte, you can't just lock people up. What were you thinking?'

'What was I thinking? Let's see, that the mistress who has my husband in her thrall is nothing but a whore? How about that? She doesn't deserve to be here, Hugo.'

'I'll be the judge of that. You've gone mad, Charlotte. I don't know who you are anymore. Where is the gentle, sweet girl I once knew?'

'Maybe that girl is tired of sharing her husband. Maybe she needs to feel wanted and loved.'

Hugo's gaze dropped to his feet. He opened his mouth and shut it again. 'I don't know, Charlotte. I don't know if I can give you that.'

Charlotte's heart thudded in her chest. Tears stung her eyes.

'You're my husband. Who else can love me?'

Hugo was silent, his face pale. 'You will go to the estate in Normandy, after the forest banquet. I've made my decision.'

She paled. 'For how long?'

'Permanently.'

Charlotte stared at him in disbelief then staggered from the room, tears streaming down her face.

At her bureau, she scrawled a note to Martine and handed it to Yolande.

'This needs to be taken to Versailles immediately. Take it to the stables and instruct Thibault. Now!'

Abbess de la Fontaine carried an enormous ring of keys as she traversed the barrel-ceilinged halls of the convent. She went into her study and hung the keys on a nail next to the door. The room was on the second floor, its windows looking down on the garden. Her mahogany desk gleamed. Neat stacks of papers sat on its surface, awaiting her response. There were always applications; they came every day. Orphans, girls accidentally with child, and girls who were troublesome. She could not accept them all, but considered every case with as much compassion as she could muster.

From the hallway she heard the clanging bucket of the new servant girl. Glancing through her open door, the abbess could see Brielle, wielding the cleaning rag on the floor as if it were a mortal enemy. The girl was from the colonies, as dark as molasses, and with an impertinent tongue. The wood floors glistened with haphazard patches of water and the abbess trod with care. When Brielle had first started cleaning the floors, Abbess de la Fontaine had slipped in a puddle of water the girl had left behind, landing hard on her hip, and she did not wish to repeat the experience.

'Brielle! What have I said to you about cleaning the floors? You need to wring out the rag in the bucket, or else you make puddles!'

The girl studied the abbess with limpid black eyes, her full lips puckered.

'I wring it out, but the bucket has a hole in it and makes puddles, abbess.'

'Go and get another bucket then.'

'Storeroom locked. I bang, bang, bang on it, but no one inside. In Senegal, there were no locks. Why lock, when all there is to steal is millet?'

'Brielle, I don't wish to hear about Senegal and millet. The floors are awash with water, it's like Noah's Ark in here and someone is going to break a leg. Go find Béatrice and ask her to open the storeroom to fetch you another bucket. Hurry up, and stop pouting like a child.'

Brielle jutted her chin and laid down the rag. 'I go and find her, but she no like me. She says I'm a black devil. Once she made me cry.'

The abbess glowered and pointed the way. Brielle shrugged and sauntered off. The floor in the other direction was dry. The abbess had been idle at her desk for hours, so she walked along the hall. Her legs had been stiff with gout. On the days she did not walk, she was immobile with pain in the evenings, soaking them in a metal tub full of hot water.

The girls were at afternoon prayers and their dormitories were quiet. The only noise was the sparrows chirruping outside. A strange sound met her ears. It was a low groan and was coming from the dormitory to the left. She crept to the door and placed her ear on it. Beneath the groans of a man, the abbess heard the plaintive weeping of a girl. Her heart raced as she turned the door handle, careful not to make any noise. The hinge of the door was oiled and it did not squeak. The abbess stood frozen in place, trying to comprehend the scene before her.

Brother Deniel and Amalia sat on one of the narrow beds. Her skirt was hiked up and he had his hand at her crotch. A half smile curved his lips as he moaned.

Amalia sobbed quietly, her head turned in the opposite direction, her torso angled away from him. The abbess gasped and took a step back, her hand flying to her mouth. Brother Deniel jumped to his feet as if he had been scalded, his eyes wide. Amalia cowered, her face flushed.

Abbess de la Fontaine drew herself up to her full height. 'What is going on here?' she spat, her eyes locked with Brother Deniel's.

The man smoothed his hair and adjusted his habit. His voice was syrupy.

'Can we please speak alone, Abbess?'

The abbess nodded. 'Amalia, wait outside, please.'

The girl scurried out, her chest heaving.

'I've made a mistake, Abbess. Please keep this to yourself. Amalia is a temptress; she lured me in here and exposed herself. I'm just a man, with human weaknesses. May God forgive me.'

'What utter rubbish,' the abbess snapped. 'That girl wouldn't lure anyone. Your time here is finished. I will be speaking to Bishop Delacroix about you. Whatever happens, you will not be around young girls again. Go and pack your bags. I do hope that God forgives you, because I won't.'

'But Abbess, I ask for your compassion. My life is in your hands.'

'You will not inflict your perversions here or elsewhere. I will make sure of it.'

Brother Deniel scowled. 'You don't have as much power as you think. His Excellency will never believe you.'

'We'll see about that. Get out. Now!' The abbess pointed to the door, her posture rigid.

৵

Charlotte had chosen the night of the full moon for the ritual. In her dressing room, she stared at her naked body in the full-length mirror. Other than the silvery marks on her lower abdomen, her skin was unblemished and powder white. Her breasts were small and full, the nipples pink. She imagined her body laid out for the ritual. Madame Foulbret had pressed her to act as the host, to offer her form as consecration. Charlotte had been hesitant, but she did not wish to involve anyone else in their plans. The older woman had procured most of the items they needed and had cautioned against asking any nobles to participate—courtiers were notoriously loose-lipped.

Charlotte tried to ignore the risks, but at times her heart would beat too fast, and she would feel as if she were breathing underwater. Martine had asked her what she wished to achieve and Charlotte had replied, 'Harm.' As for the level of severity, she told herself she wanted her enemy injured. In her heart, the truth sat like a stone— she wanted her dead.

The night before, Charlotte had sat outside Hugo's rooms in her dressing gown, a candle flickering in a holder by her side. She listened as he made love to Letitia. Tears coursed down her chin and drenched the collar of her nightdress. She was no longer angry but tired and numb. In her mind, she tried to focus on what she had left, but could only see her loss. She would never hold another baby, and her husband did not value her. These two facts were irrefutable. A constant pain ached in the middle of her chest and acid burned in her throat. All that remained was a certainty, a knowing. The Black Mass would take place.

The following day she drifted around the château like a phantom. She took her breakfast and luncheon in her rooms and asked Yolande to keep any visitors at bay, other than Céline. Martine was to arrive that evening.

Yolande fluttered in after lunch, her cheeks flushed.

'Your Grace, Thierry tells me there is a funny man waiting at the side entrance with a baby pig. He wishes to know what you want done with it?'

'It's to be slaughtered for a special dinner, Yolande. Tell Thierry that the man should take it to the stables to be placed in one of the empty stalls. Please ask that he keep it quiet—it is a surprise for my husband.'

Charlotte watched Yolande shift from one foot to the other. She was not normally excitable and the duchesse was irritated.

'Well? Why are you still standing there?'

'Sorry, Your Grace. But Madame de Poitiers would like to see you. She is outside the door.'

'Send her in.' Charlotte waved her away.

Charlotte sighed inwardly as Céline strode in, breathing heavily.

'I have the decomposed turnip, Charlotte. I've hidden it in my rooms. Did Martine say she'd bring the candles?' Céline smiled. 'Are you nervous? I'm beside myself!'

Charlotte narrowed her eyes. 'You should pull yourself together, Céline—the servants might suspect something and the other mistresses, too. Turn that excited face into a mask of calm.'

'I'll try. Can I please have some of that lovely floral tisane of yours? It might calm me a little.'

'Certainly. Ask Yolande to make it for you. I'm having a rest. If my body is going to be used as a host, I need to be ready.'

She put her feet up and lay down on the cushions. Céline reluctantly rose to her feet, calling out for Yolande.

The duchesse called out. 'Drink it in the entrance hall. I need to be alone.'

⌀

Yolande dressed Charlotte's hair for dinner and painted her lips dark pink. The duchesse imagined the different questions her husband might ask, the ways in which she might gain his attention and deflect anything unpleasant. Letitia was less of a problem. Her fate would soon be sealed, so at the evening meal, Charlotte decided, she would be civil, even kind.

'Which necklace shall I retrieve, Your Grace?' asked Yolande, inserting a mother-of-pearl comb.

'The one with the pear-shaped diamonds and sapphires.'

Yolande adjusted the sleeves of the pale blue silk dress and withdrew a key from her pocket bag to open the shagreen jewellery box on the mantel. Retrieving the necklace Charlotte had requested, she brought it over and fastened it around her mistress's neck.

'Yolande, I wasn't being entirely honest with you. The pig is for a ritual I'm performing with Madame Foulbret. I'm going to need your help in taking some items to the orange grove this evening. I must ask that you not speak about it with anyone. If I find that word has spread, I'll assume it's your doing and you will no longer have a position here. Do you understand me?'

Yolande curtsied and blushed. 'Yes, Your Grace. I'm discreet.'

'I know you are, Yolande. Thank you.'

CHAPTER 21

Martine held a lantern high as she led them along the path to the orange grove. She wore an ink-black cloak with a hood and carried a basket. Charlotte also wore a cloak, but it was deep blue. The cool night air entered through a gap in the cloak and brushed against her thighs. She shivered. Behind her, Yolande carried the piglet. It wriggled in her arms and snorted, its hind legs kicking her forearms. Céline was the last in line, wearing a black lace dress, holding another lantern and a bucket. The two lanterns cast shafts of amber light on the path, shifting as they walked.

The full moon flooded the grove with muted light. The trees' leaves were bathed in silver, their trunks casting indigo patterns on the ground. The women walked in silence, listening to the rustle of birds in the trees and the low call of an owl. As they approached the farthest corner of the grove, a grey shape came into view. Céline had set up a table.

Charlotte's skin prickled. She rubbed her arms and looked back towards the château. Her heart hammered in her chest, and her hands shook.

Martine touched her shoulder, her face cast in shadow. 'Are you all right?'

Charlotte nodded and attempted a smile. 'It's a beautiful night, Martine, maybe that's a good sign.'

'I believe so.'

Martine spread a dark cloth over the surface of the table and lit black candles with a taper from the lantern.

Yolande cursed as the piglet struggled in her arms. 'I can't hold it,' she exclaimed. 'How much longer?'

'Soon,' said Martine. 'You may take off the cloak now, Charlotte, and lie down on the table.'

The duchesse untied the bow at her throat and let the cloak slip to the ground. Trembling, she climbed onto the table and lay on her back. Her blonde hair shone in the moonlight, cascading over the side. Martine gave her two candles to hold, one in each hand. The length of her body was tinged blue in the darkness.

Martine painted the air with her finger, making the shapes and signs of various symbols for the Black Mass. Picking up a quill, she drew on the soles of the duchesse's feet. All the while, she sang in Latin, her voice low, her arms extended over Charlotte's body. The duchesse closed her eyes, her body stiff with fear and cold.

'*Dies irae, dies illasolvet saeclum in favilla: teste David cum Sibylla. Quantus tremor est futurus, quando judex est venturus, cuncta stricte discussurus!*'

From her basket Martine withdrew several small gold pentacles, which she positioned on each corner of the table. Beckoning to Céline, she whispered in her ear. Charlotte felt warmth emanating from the pentacles, and she flinched as Céline placed the rotten turnip on her chest. The piglet screeched as Martine's voice enveloped her, the Latin words hypnotic. Charlotte heard a rushing sound in her ears, as if a multitude of voices were all speaking at once. Gripping the edges of the table, she bit her lip hard until she tasted blood.

Opening her eyes, Charlotte saw a flash of metal and the legs of the piglet pedalling over her, its squeals distressed. Céline held the animal as Martine wielded the knife, slitting the animal's throat. The piglet's blood appeared black as it gushed out, covering her torso in a hot rush. The metallic smell filled her nose and Charlotte retched, turning her head away and writhing on the table. The urgent cries of the animal seemed endless as they became weaker, then ceased.

Martine's melodic chant grew louder as she formed symbols with her hands, consecrating the blood and the turnip. Charlotte's face was wet with the blood of the piglet. It seeped into her mouth and she spat it out, wiping her lips with the back of her hand. Glancing up, she saw the piglet's eye, close to her face, glazed in death. Grimacing, she held in a scream.

Something silky was placed on her belly. Charlotte peered down and saw Martine place a lock of blonde hair on her stomach. It absorbed the blood, turning red. *Letitia's hair*, she thought with satisfaction.

Martine touched her shoulder. 'It's over, Charlotte. You may rise.'

Charlotte accepted her hand and swung her legs over the side. Her body felt heavy and sluggish. Her head throbbed.

Martine handed Charlotte her cloak and she pulled it around her shoulders, hastening to the cover of trees near the grove. Once hidden, she disrobed and cleaned herself with a bucket of water Martine had provided. 'Shameful,' she whispered. 'Hideous and shameful.' Her lip trembling, she crossed herself and mouthed a prayer.

❧

'Romain.' Perched on the edge of the bed, Henriette touched his shoulder. Romain grunted and opened one eye, his hair askew.

'I was dreaming about you,' he croaked, reaching for her hand.

'I have to go back to Blois, Romain. I've had word that Solange has been going into town, checking to see if I've returned. Will you be all right?'

Romain pushed himself up on his elbow, wincing. 'Yes, I understand. Solange needs you. There are so many servants here; I'll be well looked after.'

Henriette nodded. 'The doctor said you could travel back in a week or so. I'm leaving in an hour.'

There was a faint tic near his mouth. 'So soon.'

Behind them the fire crackled and spat in the hearth. A sliver of light from a gap in the curtains illuminated his pale face. 'Well, thank you for everything.'

'Get well, Romain.' Henriette stood, touched his shoulder and gathered her shawl.

❧

Solange was waiting in the workroom with Pauline when Henriette returned. The girl beamed as her mother walked in and she flung her arms around her waist. 'Maman, I can't live at the château anymore. I won't. I'll live here with you and Pauline.'

Henriette's gaze flitted to Pauline and she gave a hesitant smile. 'There's not room here, Solange. Besides, what would you do all day while I'm working? For now, the best place for you is the château. You've got Tomas to play with and all your toys.'

Solange pouted, her eyes downcast. 'Can I stay with you until dusk? Madame Franche-Bastien said it was all right.'

'Yes, but I need to start work, my dear. You'll have to amuse yourself.'

Pauline rummaged in her straw basket, withdrawing some spindles and an assortment of silk ribbons.

'Would you mind helping me, Solange? I have a terrible mess of ribbons that need to be sorted and wound onto these spindles. Perhaps you can sit on the stool next to your mother and do this?'

Solange nodded and held out her hands for the pile. She sat on the stool and placed the ribbons at her feet. Her tongue poking out the corner of her mouth, she set to work. Henriette smiled at Pauline and mouthed her thanks.

The hired coachman pulled the reins, halting the open carriage near the stables at the château. Solange wiped her eyes with the back of her hand and composed herself before stepping out. Her mother had taught her the importance of hiding emotions from the servants. Every time she thought about her mother being in town, her chest would contract with pain. At night, she cried herself to sleep, her pillow damp beneath her cheek. She'd thought about putting a raw egg on the duchesse's chair at breakfast, but decided against it. Perhaps she, too, would be locked in the upstairs room.

At least she had Tomas and she was fond of Madame Franche-Bastien. The woman embraced her often, drawing her into her ample bosom which smelt of lilac.

The sky was tinted apricot and rose as the sun slipped behind the top of the château. Solange dawdled, idling near the stables before walking toward the field. A ripe smell filled her nose, sweet and cloying. She stopped and sniffed, wondering where it was coming from.

As she reached the back corner of the stables she saw a mound of earth. She crouched down and peered at it before reaching out and brushing off the top layer of earth. A gap in the dirt revealed something pink and black. Solange gasped and reared back, panting. The rank smell was stronger this close.

Solange stood and sprinted in the direction of the gardeners' shed. Inside it was dingy and airless. Terracotta flowerpots were stacked in one corner and spades and other implements hung on hooks on the wall. Sacks of earth were piled under the dust-covered window. She picked up a small trowel from a hook and returned to the stables.

Scooping away the earth, Solange fought back the urge to retch. It was a dead piglet, legs curled beneath its small body, filmy eyes staring into nothingness. Patches of burnt flesh dotted its flanks. She guessed there had been a hasty attempt to burn the animal, before the more expedient option of burial had been taken.

Solange wiped a tear from her cheek. She covered the corpse and made her way back to the château.

Charlotte watched and waited. Martine had assured her the Mass would work. In the days following the ritual, she wandered the hallways late at night and was relieved to find her husband sleeping alone, his rooms silent.

On the third night she slipped inside, pulled away the coverlet and climbed into his bed. *I can't leave everything up to magic*, she thought, stroking his chest.

'Letitia?' he mumbled.

Charlotte tensed. 'It's me, your wife.'

'Ah, it's you.' Hugo pushed her onto her back and parted her legs, removing his nightshirt with the other hand. He entered her, his touch slow and deliberate. Joy flooded her and she clasped his back, listening to the rasp of his breath as they moved faster. Afterwards he rolled onto his side. She slung her arm over his waist.

He edged away. 'I'd prefer to sleep alone,' he said, his voice expressionless.

Charlotte sat up, hugging herself. 'You would dismiss me, like a whore?'

'No, Charlotte. I just want to sleep without being disturbed. Thank you for visiting.'

In the darkness she reddened. 'Visiting? I'm your wife, not a dinner guest.'

'Don't be like that. I'll speak to you in the morning. Have some rest, you'll feel better.'

She flung the bedclothes aside and lowered her feet onto the rug, feeling for her dressing gown.

Tears pricked her eyes and her hands shook as she tied the dressing gown around her. In the distance she heard the clock chime three in the morning. She was as cold as a corpse.

Céline sat on the edge of the tabouret, facing the duchesse. Charlotte was wan with crescents of grey beneath her eyes, her lips tinged blue.

'You look cold,' said Céline. 'Would you like me to fetch your fur wrap?'

'No, thank you.'

'I expect Letitia might fall ill or be shunned any day now.'

'Perhaps.' Charlotte stared out the window, her eyes vacant.

'What's wrong, Charlotte? We did it. We actually performed a Black Mass.'

Céline leaned forward and rubbed the duchesse's arms; they were icy to the touch, the veins visible beneath her ivory skin.

Charlotte pulled away and frowned. 'What do you want, Céline?'

Céline felt a pain thud in her chest and flinched. 'Nothing, I...I was just worried. You seem so distant and you don't look well.'

The duchesse met her gaze and Céline felt it as a cold draught.

'You lurk about me like a ghost. I can't seem to rid myself of your presence. Just because you've helped me doesn't make us friends.'

Céline's hand fluttered to her mouth and she stumbled toward the door, her cheeks aflame. She was grateful Yolande had gone to the kitchens and had not witnessed her humiliation.

The door clicked behind her and Céline leant back against it. Touching her face, she realized her cheeks were wet. Her legs weak, she sat on the floor and grimaced, keeping her wails inside. She recalled her father's words. 'You're hard, Céline. No one will ever love you. You have hungry eyes and a hungry mouth.'

At the same time, Céline worried for Charlotte, sensing a slow unravelling, a sullied heart. *I am stupid,* she thought. *Stupid to think I could help her and be her friend. Maybe she didn't mean it. Maybe I just need to prove my affections.*

Céline rummaged in her bureau drawer, averting her eyes from the stack of letters scattered upon its surface. They were from her husband, each one more threatening than the last. Inside the drawer, beneath her parchment, was a blue velvet box.

Céline opened the box and the watch brooch gleamed on its bed of blue silk. Tiny pearls were set around its onyx face; the numbers and hands were mother of pearl and it hung on a heavy gold chain. She admired the watch and returned it to the drawer, dabbing at her eyes with a handkerchief.

At the duchesse's rooms, she gave a light rap on the door. When nobody answered, Céline turned the handle and made her way inside, through the vestibule and into the sitting room. The mantel clock ticked and the goldfinch trilled from his copper cage in the corner. A barely audible moan came from the bedroom. Charlotte was sprawled on the bed, wearing her silk dressing gown. Her face was as colourless as a full moon, her hair spread out in waves on the feather pillows.

Céline edged closer, looking for signs of life. Her heart pounded and she covered her mouth.

'It's all right, Céline,' Charlotte rasped. 'I'm still here.'

Céline leaned over the bed to stroke a lock of hair from the duchesse's face. Charlotte's arm was smeared with blood, the source a gash on her wrist. Blood stained the quilted grey coverlet and streaked across her gown.

From the marble washstand, Céline seized a stack of linen towels and raced back to the duchesse. She tied one around her wrist, tears blurring her vision.

'How did you do this?' Céline asked, her voice catching.

'How do you think? A knife. I hid it after dinner last week.'

The duchesse's lips were bloodless, her eyes glazed over.

'Charlotte, you mustn't do these things. You could have died. If I hadn't come—'

'Yes, why did you come? Most inconvenient.'

'Did you mean what you said? Do you really dislike me?'

'No. I just don't like anyone very much. Not even myself.'

'You're beautiful. Even when you've cut yourself. Even when you're crying or angry. You have me.' Céline brought the duchesse's injured wrist to her cheek, and kissed the palm of her hand. She smelt the metal of blood mingled with tuberose.

Charlotte's face softened. 'Do you think I'll be all right for the forest banquet?'

'Yes, I'll make sure of it.'

The duc had arranged a banquet for the following Saturday. Various courtiers had been invited and the Duc d'Orléans, who was unable to attend, had loaned his chef.

'I've chosen your dress. You'll be needing long sleeves,' said Céline, her fingers tracing Charlotte's jaw, the elegant line of her neck, and her décolletage. In her mind, she hummed.

'You're a strange woman, Céline. But I cannot deny your loyalty.'

'Do you want me to arrange for Doctor Mouret to come and see to your wound?'

'No. I'm perfectly fine.' Charlotte's eyes rolled up into her head and she fainted.

CHAPTER 22

There was a hill near the château that was adorned with cornflowers. Letitia and Henriette sat on a blanket and ate buttered bread with hunks of goat's cheese. Several sheep grazed nearby. Each day was warmer than the last. They tipped their heads back and felt the sun on their faces. For a moment, Letitia was content. Henriette glanced sidelong at her friend. 'You seem troubled. What is it?'

Letitia wound the stem of a cornflower around her finger. 'I miss Antoine. When I'm with the duc, I feel like an actress playing a role. It's not real, Henriette.'

Henriette touched her hand. 'Maybe not, but what choice do you have? The marquis hasn't promised you anything. You could end up with nothing.'

'If only I could see Antoine. I need him to know how I feel.'

Letitia grasped Henriette's arm, her eyes imploring. 'Help me see him, Henriette, please. Monsieur de Villiers can arrange it. Maybe here where no one can see us?'

Henriette sighed. 'It's dangerous, Letitia. I think you should stay away from him, at least for now.'

❧

'Maman?' Estelle's blue eyes were enormous and frightened, staring down at her mother. Her upper lip quivered. 'What's wrong, Maman? Céline told me you hurt yourself.'

It was late morning. Charlotte had waved Yolande away when she arrived with her hot chocolate and drifted back to sleep.

Estelle clasped her shoulders and guided her into a sitting position. 'Maman, you need to breathe some spring air. I'll help you dress.'

Charlotte groaned. 'I want to sleep, *chérie*. I want to dream of other times.'

Estelle gasped at the bandaged wound on her mother's arm. 'Why did you do it?'

Charlotte's smile was bitter. 'I hope you never have to understand. You'll marry and your husband will worship you. That is my one wish, Estelle.'

'Nothing is certain, Maman.'

'Maybe not, but I'll scrutinize your suitors. I will watch their manners, their every move.' She swung her legs over the side and raked her hand through her hair, the gold dulled to dark yellow as it hung limply over her shoulders. 'Fetch Yolande, my love. It is not a daughter's role to dress her mother.'

Once dressed, Charlotte descended the stairs with Estelle. They passed Héloise, who gave a small curtsey. A look somewhere between pity and delight crossed her features before she walked on.

At the stables, Estelle found Raoul and requested he take them to Blois.

'Do you have errands in the town?' he asked as he saddled up the horses.

'You will take us around the perimeter,' she replied, 'and the ride must be smooth as my mother is feeble today.'

Charlotte felt a cool breeze touch her face as they set off in a *calèche*, her hand slotted into Estelle's. The girl smiled at her and leaned her head on her mother's shoulder.

'See, Maman dearest? Don't you feel better already? It gets so stale inside, and boring. Look, baby lambs!'

Charlotte's throat ached with emotion and she patted Estelle's soft curls with her free hand. 'Are you reading the red volume of Racine I gave you?'

'Yes, it's delightful. Some of the scenes make me giggle.'

'I enjoyed it too. Oh my goodness, I must have been inside for too long. I had no idea there were so many new lambs already.'

'You've been all cooped up since the Tenebrae service. Did it upset you seeing Madame d'Augustin?'

'Not really. Your papa and I have had some problems, but nothing you need to worry about. Men are selfish and inconsiderate. The sooner you learn this, the better. If your expectations are low, my dear, you won't be disappointed.'

'I don't understand. You said you wanted to find me a husband who would adore me.'

'And he will, darling. We'll find you the least selfish one possible.'

The fields were a vivid green, the grasses not yet cut. A group of farmers ambled alongside the carriage, pitchforks slung over their shoulders. They tipped their hats as the vehicle rolled past. The sun was pale yellow and high, its beams warming Estelle and Charlotte beneath their parasols. The blue dots decorating Estelle's parasol reflected on her cheeks. She clutched the tortoiseshell handle and squeezed her mother's hand.

Charlotte was sure her husband knew about her injury, yet he did not come to her. She remained in her rooms in the days leading up to the banquet, surrounded by feather pillows and the warm bodies of her Bichons as she reclined in bed. She wrote a list of instructions for Céline to give the kitchen staff and visiting chef. Her limbs felt heavy, her mind disconnected, floating from memory to memory like stepping stones over a raging river. The happy recollections jarred against those of lost babies and an indifferent spouse.

On the afternoon of the banquet, Céline appeared just as the room was filling with golden light. Over her arm, she held an indigo dress with a high neckline encrusted with pearls and long sleeves.

Charlotte raised an eyebrow. 'An old woman's dress?'

'No,' Céline said, 'the dress of a beautiful woman who is thin in the chest and has a cut on her arm. You'll feel better once you have it on, I promise.'

Céline helped the duchesse out of bed and tightened the strings of the stays at her back. The duchesse held onto the edge of the table and gritted her teeth against the discomfort. She was sure Céline's eyes had lingered on her breasts.

'Usually Yolande helps me to dress...' the duchesse murmured, her arms in the air as Céline lowered the garment over her head.

'Well, we're all the same without our clothing, and I am happy to be of service to Your Grace.'

Charlotte remained silent as Céline buttoned the dress. Elegant folds of silk caressed her skin and she did feel better.

'What is it, Céline? You look like you've swallowed a pebble. Have you something to say?'

Céline put her hand in her pocket bag and withdrew a blue velvet box. 'I wanted to give you this, as a token of my affection and loyalty.'

Charlotte opened the box. A watch brooch glimmered from the silk interior, its gold chain catching the light. 'But Céline, you may need this. It is a lovely gesture and a beautiful piece. I'm touched. I'm just not sure I can accept it.'

'I insist that you do.' Céline took the brooch from the box and fastened it to the bodice of the blue dress.

'Céline, you're quite mad. We women have our trinkets as insurance. Nothing else, other than children, to keep the wolves at bay. Are you sure you wish to part with it?'

'It's so stunning on you, I knew it would be. I just want to cheer you up.'

'Cheer me up? It will take a lot more than a bauble to cheer me up.'

Céline's face fell and Charlotte patted her hand. 'I'm sorry. It really is beautiful. It's just...I received a letter this morning from Martine. It seems she completed the painting of my feet *before* the sacrifice, when it should have been after. Do you understand what this means, Céline?' Charlotte's voice had a manic edge. Céline shook her head. 'It means the Mass may accomplish something completely different to what was intended. You see? It's a complete disaster. The little whore will most likely be fine.'

Céline paled. 'It was a waste of time?'

'Maybe, maybe not. I suppose we shall see. Can you imagine, Céline? I have placed my soul in peril, betrayed my God, and for what purpose?' She smoothed invisible creases from the skirt of the dress. 'Please, go and prepare yourself. The banquet starts in one hour. I will need you at my side.'

Letitia pretended to read the Bible, the vellum smooth under her fingertips. The frigid air of the church made her shiver and she pulled her shawl closer around her shoulders.

Incense burned in the censers lining the walls, interspersed with stands for candles lit by the faithful. Daylight coursed through the stained glass windows, refracted colours playing on the wood of the pews. After Henriette had refused to help, Letitia had bribed a servant to send a letter to Antoine and explain her absence to her maids as a walk in the woods.

She smelt Antoine before she saw him, a heady combination of musk and polished leather. He sat next to her and crossed himself. 'Are you a believer, Letitia? An interesting choice of meeting place.'

'I am, of a sort. The sort that practises irregularly. What about you?'

'I attend church on the significant days in the calendar. I confess when I feel ashamed of myself, which is not often.'

'I thought I'd be unlikely to be seen here this early in the morning. It's only the very elderly who come at this time and their eyesight is bad.'

Antoine reached for her hand and covered it with his own. Her stomach swirled with pleasure at the warmth of his fingers.

'I've missed you,' she said in a whisper.

He leaned over and brushed the side of her neck with his lips. 'There has not been a single moment when you were not in my thoughts. What are you doing? Why are you still at the château? All you need to do is pack some dresses, walk out the door and find your way to Blois. Hire a carriage to take you to Orléans. If I expect you might come, I'll stay there for as long as it takes.'

She trembled. 'What about Versailles?'

'Versailles is an amusement, a distraction. Orléans is where I go to clear my head of the falseness that pervades the court.'

'Antoine, are you asking me to be your mistress?'

'I'm asking you to be my wife. Of course, I would support your parents as the duc has done.'

Beneath her stays, Letitia's heart raced. 'How can you ask me that when I belong to the duc? He could kill you. You're mad.'

'Perhaps I am mad, but perhaps that is why you love me.'

She flushed. 'You're right, of course. I do.'

'So? Will you come?'

Letitia frowned. 'Antoine, I need to think. I promised the duc I wouldn't see you. Give me some time, please, to make a decision.'

The duc sighed and withdrew his hand. 'I'm risking my life to have you, offering you my love. You say you need time? I've never felt like this about anyone. This isn't a decision, Letitia. What is between us, is. It exists.'

Letitia's cheeks glistened with tears. 'For a woman, everything is a decision. Even love.'

The duc had hired two dozen woodsmen to create an artificial clearing in the middle of the forest. A full moon hung low in the blue-black sky, casting the field in silver. Céline held Charlotte's elbow as they followed the crowd. On either side of the procession of guests, servants held flickering lanterns. Only a select group had been asked from Versailles, along with a number of nobles from Blois. The party of sixty were in good spirits, singing and chattering as they approached the darkness of the trees.

Charlotte pressed her fingers into the crook of Céline's arm as the foliage closed around them. Something skittered past her calf and she jumped.

'It was probably just a squirrel,' said Céline, placing a warm hand over hers. 'It's not far. I asked one of the serving girls.'

Charlotte tried to slow down her breathing. Her chest hurt. 'I'm perfectly all right.' She stared up through the black pattern of leaves and saw a glittering swathe of stars, like diamonds on a bed of velvet. Letting out a breath she took cautious steps, holding tightly to Céline's arm.

As they approached the clearing, Charlotte could smell meat cooking and felt a stab of hunger. This was a surprise—since the ritual her appetite had deserted her. She had craved only melon and slivers of white fish.

Someone tapped her on the shoulder, and in the dim light she turned to see the deep-set eyes of Martine. Beneath her cheekbones were dark hollows, giving her a sinister appearance in the gloom. She kissed the duchesse on both cheeks.

Charlotte's tone was chilled. 'I received your letter.'

'Good evening, Charlotte.'

'Your Grace.'

Martine raised an eyebrow. 'Since when must I address you as a stranger?'

'You told me you were experienced with the ritual,' Charlotte hissed, her body taut.

Martine was silent, measuring her words. 'I was sure at the time. It was only later when I reread the text that I realised the error.'

'What does it mean then? What will happen?'

Martine shook her head. 'I can't answer that. The dark forces will do what has been requested.'

Charlotte bristled. 'Requested? What does that mean?'

'The sequence of the ritual determines the request. Someone may die or sicken, but I'm just not sure. We must wait and see. I'm so sorry. Forgive me.'

'At this moment, madame, I cannot be in your presence. Leave me.'

'Of course. Your Grace.' Martine dipped her head, her face slack with distress, and withdrew.

Charlotte paused to allow Céline to join her and walked on. Ahead of them the procession snaked, cloaked in fiery light. The man-made clearing came into view and several of the guests gasped. Flaming torches had been placed around the rectangular space and tables were set with linen cloths and silver candelabras. Sparks from the torches leapt high into the sky. A lone cellist played Bach, his head bowed to his instrument. Ten liveried staff stood in line to one side. Blue and white chinoiserie pots were placed at intervals, filled with white hyacinths. To one side stood a striped tent where the chef and kitchen hands laboured over a wood-fired stove.

The scent of pine and whale oil filled the air and Charlotte gestured toward a Moor she recognized from the château, who came forward to escort them to a table.

The crowd fell silent as the duc approached with Letitia at his side. She wore a simple white gauze dress, the waist tied with a blue silk cord. Her pale hair was braided around her head and around her neck hung a large sapphire on a thick gold chain.

Charlotte recognized the necklace as an heirloom piece which had once belonged to his maternal grandmother. She twisted a napkin in her hands.

Her husband took his place at the table with Letitia beside him and cleared his throat. 'Welcome esteemed guests. We have gathered together for a banquet to celebrate the onset of spring, and you have all been invited because you are important to my family. I trust you will enjoy the cuisine created by the Duc d'Orléan's chef, François Massialot. You may be seated.'

Charlotte caught Isabelle's eye and her childhood friend looked away. The duchesse forced herself to greet the other guests at the table, attempting to quell the nausea that rose in her throat. It was incomprehensible—Letitia was seated next to her husband whilst she was on the opposite side of the table with Céline on one side and Estelle on the other.

'Maman, isn't it beautiful?' Estelle asked. Yet, young as she was, Estelle knew of the slight to her mother. Charlotte watched her daughter's blue eyes flicker from Letitia to her. Under the table Estelle took her mother's hand and stroked her palm.

'Yes, beautiful,' Charlotte replied, withdrawing her hand and pointing to her glass as a waiter passed. He returned with a carafe of red wine and filled her glass.

'I've changed my mind,' she said.

'About what, Maman?'

'Marriage. It makes no difference, Estelle. You'd do just as well to be a mistress or to join a religious order. I need to protect you, darling.'

'Maman, you're just upset. I promise to marry a man as different from Papa as possible. How is that?'

Charlotte did not hear her. She gulped her wine and watched the duc whisper in Letitia's ear. A bemused smile spread across the young woman's lips. The sound of Héloise and her incessant chatter merged with the other conversations. Charlotte heard snatches of sentences, disjointed and jarring.

'...and she kept it from him all this time! I know, scandalous...A skirt the size of the ocean in a cheap satin...Heaven forbid!'

Charlotte's throat felt closed. Her chest ached. She took a large sip of her wine, pretended to listen to Céline, and averted her eyes from Letitia.

'Charlotte? What do you think?'

'Hmm?'

'My maid. I think she's been stealing from me. What should I do?'

'Goodness, I don't know. Which one do you have again?'

'Marie. She has shifty eyes.'

'Oh yes, Marie. We did catch her once but gave her another chance. You have to catch her, Céline. Leave something tempting out and then walk in at the exact moment. Not easy, but possible. Then I give you permission to send her on her way.'

Trays of truffle and mushroom soup arrived. Steam curled from the bowls and obscured the faces of the servants. Charlotte lifted her spoon and dipped it in her bowl. Her stomach contracted as she brought it to her lips and she set it down. Her gaze drifted back to Letitia, now laughing at something her husband said.

Someone touched her shoulder and she swung around, startled.

'Your Grace, so lovely to see you.'

'Comtesse de Vaubert, a pleasure indeed. You remember my daughter, Estelle?' She made to stand up but the comtesse gestured for her to stay seated and greeted Estelle. A young brunette with a thin, angular face, she was known for her considerate nature and witty stories.

'Are you staying in town, comtesse?' asked the duchesse.

'Yes, I have a friend just outside of town, in the country. It's very quaint. She even has ducks and chickens.'

'You should have come and stayed at the château. I'm embarrassed.'

'Ah, don't be silly. It is good to be reminded of normality. I'm so accustomed to the excesses of Versailles.'

'Have you seen Monsieur de Villiers lately?' said Charlotte, her tone casual.

'Yes, in fact he did a reading for me just the other day. He's so charming, sometimes I wonder if he's making my future sound better than what he sees in the cards.'

'I wouldn't be surprised,' said Charlotte. 'Has he recovered from his injuries?'

'Yes, it seems so. A lady called Madame d'Augustin nursed him back to health. Wasn't she once a mistress in your household?'

'She was, until we discovered she had a secret daughter.'

'Heavens above, really? You never know about people, their histories. It was the right thing to send her away, otherwise the daughter might insinuate herself into your household. Just last week an urchin boy knocked on the doors at court, claiming to be a long-lost cousin of the Vicomte du Rousseau. He got as far as the Hall of Mirrors before a butler intercepted him and asked him why he was there. The scamp announced with utmost gravity his far-flung connection to the Vicomte. The butler said, "Yes, and my great-aunt once met the king, but am I permitted to sit on a tabouret in His Majesty's presence? I think not. Be on your way."' She tittered and glanced at the duchesse's soup. 'Oh dear, I'm sorry to interrupt your entrée, duchesse. Please, eat and I will speak with you later in the evening. I hope you're all right?' The comtesse patted Charlotte's shoulder, her expression solicitous.

'Of course I'm all right. Why wouldn't I be?' She sucked in her cheeks and wondered how many at court knew of her predicament.

'I'm glad. Husbands can be so beastly.'

'I really don't know what you're talking about.' Charlotte swivelled around. Her stays pressed on her chest and for a moment she struggled to breathe. Her soup had congealed at the edges and she gestured to a waiter to remove it. In any case, she was not hungry.

'Maman, stop looking at them,' Estelle said quietly. 'Try to think about something else. I don't think she loves him, you know.'

'How do you know that?'

'I can see he's more absorbed in her than she is in him. His eyes are always on her, but look at her, Maman. She looks almost bored.'

'What does it matter if she's bored, child? Your father is besotted. That's the problem.'

Estelle sighed and watched the servants emerge with the main course.

'It matters, Maman, because that means it won't last.'

Charlotte smirked. 'Goodness, darling. Since when have you been so knowledgeable about adults and feelings?'

Estelle shrugged and picked up her knife and fork, ready to devour her lamb ragoût. The duchesse took some small forkfuls before she laid down her cutlery and played with her wineglass, swirling the liquid around and holding it up to the light. Pain flared in her chest and she had a fervent wish to be alone in the quiet of her rooms. With difficulty, she averted her eyes as Hugo drew Letitia close, his arm draped around her shoulders.

Estelle tried to eat slowly as her mother had instructed many times. Yet the ragoût was infused with rosemary and thyme, the lamb tender. She wished Maman treated her less like a child. For a long while, she had understood things—why people behaved badly, how they spoke when they were in love, the way they blushed and glanced away when they lied. She kept to herself and observed everyone. She knew they underestimated her and that was how she liked it. In the pages of her books she learnt about love and contempt, and at the château, she watched these emotions play out as if on a stage.

At that moment Estelle wanted to hold her mother, to stroke her hair and soothe her with the right words. She could not do these things, so she just watched her. Later in the evening, when her mother looked as if she might break, or scream, or run into the forest, Estelle took hold of her hand and did not let go.

The duchesse seized Martine's sleeve as they walked through the forest near midnight. A light mist dampened Charlotte's face, disguising her tears. 'I need to know how to use the liquid you gave me. The one for emergencies. Do you remember?'

'No, Your Grace. Please, what are you planning?'

'It's of no concern to you. Tell me how to use it.' She gritted her teeth and clutched Martine's arm, feeling her daughter's presence close behind.

'Milk. You put two teaspoons in warm milk.'

'Thank you.' Charlotte walked on with her head down, shielding her face with her hand. Estelle hurried to catch up with her, calling her name.

The guests stared as mother and daughter rushed ahead through the foliage, the duchesse snapping twigs underfoot and waving away a servant who approached with an umbrella.

CHAPTER 23

It was just after sunrise. The gardeners were at work outside and Charlotte could hear the metallic swish of their scythes as they cut the grass. She was dressed and her body prickled with energy. For the first time in months she was cheerful as she picked up the blue velvet box and left her rooms.

Thierry stood near the entrance doors, his face impassive, his hands folded in front of his navy silk coat.

'May I have a word, Thierry? In the drawing room.'

'Good morning, Your Grace. Yes, of course.'

'I need some information about Mademoiselle du Massenet; particularly her habits in the evenings.'

'Your Grace, with all due respect, I am uncomfortable with your question. As head butler in this household, it's my job to show propriety. Divulging the habits of one occupant to another is hardly appropriate. Imagine, for instance, if I were to reveal your habits to Mademoiselle du Massenet.'

Charlotte nodded and tapped her foot on the parquetry. The clock on the mantle chimed. 'I admire your decency, Thierry. This is why you have been in our employ for many years. Discretion, tact, and decorum. However, my question is important and I will reward your cooperation.'

She held out the box and placed it in his white-gloved palm. He opened it and his eyes widened.

'It's a very handsome piece. Are you giving it to me, Your Grace?'

'I am. Assuming you're able to help with my enquiry.'

'Certainly. Let me consult with mademoiselle's maid and I will speak with you later in the day.'

'As soon as possible'

'Yes, Your Grace.'

As Charlotte made her way back to her rooms she saw Isabelle. The duchesse gave a sardonic smile.

'Good morning, Charlotte. You're up early.'

'So you're speaking to me again. Am I forgiven?'

Isabelle fidgeted with her hands and glanced around before meeting Charlotte's eyes. 'You locked Letitia up, Charlotte. It was inhumane. I've been worried about you, though. You're so thin. We could talk further, if it would help? Over tea, perhaps?'

Charlotte's laugh was brittle. 'There's nothing to talk about, Isabelle. I have the most wonderful marriage and an old friend who supports my enemies. What could I possibly be upset about?'

Isabelle touched her forearm. 'You're not well, Charlotte. I've never seen you like this. Talk to Hugo; talk to me. There's nothing that can't be resolved.'

Charlotte withdrew her arm. 'Dear Isabelle, always the optimist.' For a moment her face softened and her eyes filled with tears. 'My sweet friend.' Charlotte reached out with a shaking hand and tucked a brown curl behind Isabelle's ear.

'If I've wronged you, I'm sorry. I have to go.'

Charlotte, picking up her skirts, retreated up the stairs.

Thierry was ushered into Charlotte's quarters, the glittering brooch pinned to his coat.

'Well?' Charlotte asked, raising an eyebrow. 'Have you come to pay condolences or to tell me what you've discovered? You look mournful. As far as I know, everyone is alive at the château?'

'Yes, Your Grace. I made some enquiries. Mademoiselle du Massenet, unless there is a formal dinner, eats in her rooms at seven o'clock in the evenings. She embroiders, discusses the day with her maid, and reads. At ten o'clock, she is brought a hot chocolate to aid sleep, or, if she is visiting His Grace's rooms, she is provided with a small glass of spiced wine.'

Charlotte winced and he paused. 'Continue,' she said.

'She visits the duc at eleven o'clock, usually for two hours before returning to her rooms.'

'Bravo, Thierry. You have done an excellent job. One more question. How many servants are in the kitchen at ten o'clock?'

'In addition to the cook, no more than three, Your Grace.'

'Thank you. You may go.'

Céline arrived soon after, bearing a tray of watercress and salmon. 'I've found some lunch for you. You need to eat something.'

'You know, Céline. I think I might just eat something. It looks delicious.'

The two women sat down at the table, linen napkins spread over their laps. The sun warmed them through the windows and a bird chirped outside. Charlotte ate with care, finished her salmon, and slid her plate away.

'Tonight,' she said with excitement, 'we will enact a plan that will fix our previous failure.'

'Please explain, Your Grace.'

'You, Céline, will be my foot soldier. At a quarter to ten tonight you will go to the kitchens where the maids will be making a hot chocolate for Mademoiselle du Massenet. You will pour two teaspoons of the liquid I have in my dressing table into her drink. You will ensure no one sees you.'

Céline coughed nervously. 'And what will my reason be, for being present in the kitchens?'

'That you're hungry. Ask the cook for some smoked ham. As she retrieves it from the pantry, assuming the drink has been made, you will pour in the liquid.'

Céline hesitated, her gaze flitted to the window and she touched the gold crucifix at her neck.

'So, can I trust you?' asked Charlotte.

'The liquid, does it take life?'

'Yes.'

'It's a sin, Charlotte. You're asking me to act against my beliefs. My soul will go to hell. Do you realise what this means for me?'

'Yes, I do. You're the most loyal friend I've ever had and I adore you for it. My gratitude is so great I cannot even begin to express it.' She leaned forward and embraced Céline, their cheeks together. The duchesse edged back and at that moment the other woman manoeuvred so their lips met. Céline grasped the side of her face and drew closer, her lips pressed hard.

In an abrupt movement Charlotte sprang back, her face inflamed and her gaze on the floor.

'You may go. Thank you, again. Your intentions are good and God will understand.' Her voice was breathless.

'I'm sorry,' said Céline. 'I don't know what happened.'

'It's all right. Just help me tonight. Please. You'll be rewarded handsomely.'

'Yes, of course. You may rely upon me, Your Grace.' Céline scurried away, her shoulders hunched.

'Have you finished the lilac dress?' asked Pauline.

'Almost. Just a few more stitches to bring in the waist.' Henriette's expression was intent as she sewed, the light from the window framing her hair in a red aureole. She had been working hard in an attempt to keep Romain from her mind.

The atelier was warm despite the open window, and Henriette felt perspiration bead on her upper lip.

Pauline adjusted a dress on a mannequin. 'I'll finish it. The flowers are drooping. Why don't you go for a walk to rue du Foix and buy some more from the flower seller there? '

'Thank you,' Henriette smiled, 'I'd like that.'

Outside, she wandered along the cobbled street, enjoying the fresh air on her cheeks. As she turned into rue du Foix, she spotted Romain walking toward her. He smiled broadly as he approached.

'What a lovely surprise,' he said.

Henriette allowed him to kiss her hand, but drew back when he tried to embrace her. They strolled past the shop windows toward the flower seller with his baskets of blooms in riotous colours. Henriette avoided his eyes. 'I need to buy flowers. Can you wait a moment?'

'Of course.'

She selected some yellow chrysanthemums, pressed coins into the hand of the seller, and waited as he tied the stems with string. They continued walking in silence.

'How are you?' she asked finally. 'You look better, but still not yet yourself.'

'I'm feeling better each day. Let's stop for tea at the Café Victoire,' he said and she nodded.

'It will have to be quick, though. Madame Rolain is waiting for me.'

The café was quiet with only a few patrons, an elderly couple, and a mother with her small boy. They sat on grey velvet armchairs and examined each other surreptitiously over the linen tablecloth. A waiter came and took their order.

'Something's wrong,' he said.

'Not exactly. I've just been thinking.'

'Oh dear, what about?'

'You. Me. I don't think our relationship is a good idea.'

Romain winced, averting his gaze as the waiter brought a pot of tea on a silver tray. As the waiter withdrew, Romain's eyes met hers. Their blue had darkened and his face had lost all colour.

'Why?'

Henriette took a sip of her tea and placed the cup back on its saucer. Her shaking hand made it rattle. 'I'm disturbed by how much I didn't know about you and your actions. I worry that deception is part of your character. I have a responsibility to Solange to make sure anyone I bring into her life is above reproach. I can't risk it, Romain. I'm sorry.'

Romain clenched his jaw and pushed his tea away. 'You don't understand me at all. I'm a good person. I would never hurt you. Never. The things I've done were wrong, I admit. Yet meeting you has changed me. I love you.'

'I can't, Romain.'

'Henriette, please. I want you to come to Versailles with me, to be my wife. I'm trying to acquire a room there. I'll speak to Madame Foulbret and she might arrange another room, for you. They need a seamstress. There is much demand for one, to supplement the work of Madame Rolain. There would be space for you and your daughter. Think about it, that's all I ask.'

'I will think about it, thank you, but I cannot be your wife.'

'I understand.' His face was a mask, all emotion gone.

By the time Romain spotted Hervé's stocky figure at the entrance to the tavern, it was too late. Hervé stood up straighter and stared in his direction.

'Good day, Monsieur Fillon.' Romain tensed and shoved his hands in his pockets.

'Ah, Monsieur de Villiers, just the man I was looking for. I have some problems with unpaid debt. It seems there are certain folk who do their best to avoid me.' Hervé's red cheeks glistened as he rocked on his heels.

'I have nothing for you.'

In a swift movement, Hervé grasped Romain's neck cloth, his breath reeking of sour ale and tobacco.

'I may not be a man of letters, but I'm not stupid, de Villiers,' Hervé sneered. 'My patience is running out. Pay your debt within the week or I will send another man to your aunt's house.'

Romain did not have time to duck before Hervé swung his fist and made contact with his nose. Romain crumpled to the cobblestones, warm blood gushing from his nostrils. 'I'll pay, I'll pay,' he wheezed, cradling his head in his hands as Hervé kicked him viciously in the ribs.

'Very good,' said Hervé and brushed his hands together. He entered the tavern and the door slammed behind him.

Romain met with Martine Foulbret two days later. He had liberally dusted his face with powder and worn a black velvet coat and ruffled shirt, hoping to distract her from his swollen nose.

'Madame, I have found myself in reduced circumstances. I'm sure you know of my duel with the duc. I can no longer conduct readings at the château.'

Martine's rooms were small, but comfortably furnished with blue and grey silks on the walls and windows, a sofa, and overstuffed armchairs. Portraits of her relatives in gilt frames adorned the walls.

'Yes, I've heard of your misfortune and the events that provoked it. Your charm seems to land you in trouble. How may I help, monsieur?'

'I need new readings as soon as possible.'

Martine poured him tea from a silver pot. 'I could arrange something for next week.'

'I need it to be this week.'

She raised an eyebrow. 'That's more challenging, but I will see what I can do. Was there something else, monsieur?'

'Yes. I'm living with my aunt, but I cannot prevail much longer upon her hospitality. You had mentioned a small room here at Versailles? I don't take up much space. Even a large broom cupboard would do.' He gave what he hoped was his most charming smile.

'I'll make some enquiries, monsieur. '

Céline sat in her rooms, turning the glass bottle the duchesse had given her over and over in her hands. Her stomach roiled with rising anxiety and she muttered prayers under her breath.

As afternoon turned to dusk, her heart hammering in her chest, she went to the small cupboard in her dressing alcove to retrieve her bottle of brandy. A frantic knock came at the door, followed by a slurred male voice.

'Céline! I know you're in there! You haven't answered any of my letters and you won't see me.'

She heard her maid's voice, pleading.

Céline, with a sigh, opened the door, and Arnaud de Poitiers barrelled inside, his finger pointing like a sharpened knife. 'You're too good to speak to your husband now, are you? Bitch.'

'Lovely to see you, Arnaud. What can I do for you?'

'I'm broke. I can't eat. I can't play faro. A thug came yesterday. If I don't pay up I'll be thrown out of the dismal cottage I'm living in. Where's that watch brooch? I need it. Give it to me.' He approached her, his face ruddy and menacing.

'I don't have it, Arnaud. I lost it. I'm sorry.'

Arnaud seized her neck and she flinched. She gripped the edge of the table and kept her face calm.

'You're lying, whore. I know it's here. Where did you hide it?' He let go of her throat and she wheezed with relief, bent over. Arnaud roamed through her rooms, tossing clothing in disordered heaps behind him. He peered within a glass vase, then flung it against the wall where it shattered into thousands of pieces. Céline mused that it was a pretty sound as she withdrew into herself, watching the scene with a strange detachment.

After a while Arnaud tired of his hunt and turned to her with a scowl. He raised his finger once more, inching close. 'You find it. I'll be on the street soon, Céline. If I'm on the street, I'm dead. You don't want a dead man on your hands. You're already a *putain* in God's eyes. I'm sure you wouldn't wish to be a murderess too.'

'I'll look for it. Just go, please go,' she whispered, her voice trembling.

After the door slammed behind him, Céline slumped on a chair and poured brandy until the glass almost overfilled. She took a large sip and waited for night to fall.

As Céline approached the kitchen, the bottle secreted in her pocket, she heard the animated voices of the staff. A swishing sound, regular and slow, echoed in her head. Her skin burned and perspired.

Imogene greeted her as she entered and Céline forced a smile. As expected, a young maid was preparing Letitia's hot chocolate, stirring the pot over the fire.

'Good evening,' said Céline. 'I'm rather hungry. Might I have some smoked ham?'

'Of course, madame,' said Imogene, wiping her hands on her apron as she bustled over to the pantry.

The maid poured the hot chocolate into a dainty porcelain cup and placed it on a saucer. Céline's hands shook as she waited. A crash and a flurry of curses came from the scullery, and the maid raced to see what had happened. It was perfect timing. Céline withdrew the bottle, unscrewed it, poured some liquid into the spoon and stirred it into the cup. Then another spoonful. In a quick movement she put the two items back in her pockets.

Imogene returned with some slices of ham on a plate.

'Thank you. I have such a craving for ham.'

Céline left the kitchen and dashed toward the staircase. In the washroom beneath the stairs, she closed the door behind her and retched.

Rosalie had been serving Estelle for long enough to predict her needs. She sensed her mistress's agitation and knew she would find sleep difficult. As she passed the stairs she heard a gagging noise from the washroom. *Strange,* she thought. Imogene was such an angel. She always slipped her a biscuit or some other tasty morsel.

She entered the kitchen and inhaled the comforting smells. A vanilla tart had just been placed on the counter.

'Good evening, Imogene. Estelle is having difficulty sleeping and I wanted to bring her a hot chocolate. I see there's one here. May I take it?'

'Ah, yes,' said Imogene. 'Adele hasn't arrived for it yet. We can pour another as there's plenty more in the pot. But you're not allowed to leave until you've tasted my vanilla tart.'

'*Bien sûr,*' she replied, her cheeks dimpling.

༒

'Ouch!' said Estelle, as she sat at the dressing table in her nightgown, the new maid wrenching a brush through her thick locks.

'Where's Rosalie?'

'She went to fetch your hot chocolate.'

'Oh yes, of course. That's enough brushing. I only have half my hair left.'

'Sorry, mademoiselle.'

'It's all right. Can you please ready my bed? I'm going to read.'

Estelle's blue taffeta armchair was her favourite reading place. Settling into the soft upholstery, she picked up a volume of Molière.

Rosalie entered with a tray and stood near her mistress.

Estelle mouthed the words as she read. It was a particularly beautiful monologue about love.

'Thank you, Rosalie. Put it down on the side table here, please. Thank you both and goodnight.'

The maids curtsied. 'Good night, mademoiselle. Have pleasant dreams,' said Rosalie.

'Thank you,' Estelle murmured, engrossed in the passage.

After a few pages she lifted the cup of chocolate to her lips. The milky sweetness was laced with something bitter, and Estelle wondered if perhaps the chocolate had been sitting in the pantry for too long. She made a mental note to ask Imogene about it. *Best to drink it quickly,* she thought, *then I won't notice the taste.*

Laying her book to one side, Estelle's thoughts turned to her mother. The duchesse wandered like a ghost through the château, her unhappiness evident and unnerving. On this night and many others, sleep evaded Estelle as she tried to think of a solution to her mother's troubles. There was no use going to her father; it seemed he had abandoned responsibility. *The priest might help,* she thought. *Someone has to do something. Maman might die from all this heartache.* Tears welled in her eyes and she wiped them away with her fist.

Swallowing the rest of her chocolate, Estelle picked her book back up after replacing the cup in the saucer. The words blurred on the page and an odd knife-like pain lanced through her stomach. *Too much lamb at dinner*, she mused and put the book down. She rubbed her eyes and leaned back in the chair. The pain pulsed again, stronger and higher. Estelle groaned and tried to stand, but her legs lost their strength. Her vision was grey and unfocussed. One more stab ripped through her torso and she lost consciousness, folded over the arm of the chair.

☙

A body covered in white satin lay on the table, the face obscured. Charlotte edged closer, both desiring to see the face and fearful of it. Candles glowed in wrought-iron candelebras around the table. In a quick movement she drew away the fabric and the air left her body.

Charlotte gasped so deeply she could not breathe. She jolted upright in bed and tried to regain control. Her daughter's face was serene and angelic in the nightmare, but her spirit was gone. Charlotte considered rushing to her daughter's room but thought better of it. The sky was black beyond the windows, and Estelle would be fast asleep.

Sleep came but it was light and fitful. When Yolande opened the curtains at dawn, Charlotte was alert in an instant. She asked for her dressing gown.

'Your Grace, don't you wish to dress?'

'No, not yet. I'm going to see my daughter.'

As Charlotte traversed the hallways she felt as if a wind carried her, with urgency in her limbs and throat and a throbbing pain in her heart.

A sound of wailing reached her ears from the hallway ahead. Charlotte broke into a run, through the doors and into Estelle's bedroom. Rosalie and another maid were locked in an embrace, their sobs guttural and panicked. Charlotte heard a high-pitched scream unfurl from her own mouth as she launched herself at her daughter's still, grey form lying on the floor. Estelle's face was tinged blue and already cold. Her large blue eyes stared at the carpet, her hand flung out. Charlotte grasped her and rocked. She keened and sobbed, cursed God and asked him to take her. Her grief sharpened and cut with a million points until there was nothing to do but fall. She fainted to the floor; the corpse of her daughter tumbled with her. That was how the duc found them minutes later.

∂

The news spread rapidly. Townsfolk whispered of Satanism and dark practices in the night; of poison sent to the wrong person. By all accounts the duc and duchesse were inconsolable, locked away in their rooms. Only one message came from the château—a letter from the duchesse to Henriette, asking her to come as soon as possible.

Henriette studied the letter, standing by the window in the atelier. For a moment she wondered if it was a trick. Then reason told her a bereaved mother would be in no humour for deceit.

After Henriette and Pauline had finished their sewing for the afternoon, Henriette hailed a driver and carriage to take her to the château. The sky was slate grey, the clouds thick and impenetrable as they raced across the sky, propelled by the wind. She imagined how it would feel to lose a daughter—a part of you ripped away, never to return. Shivering, Henriette watched the patchwork of fields out the window as the carriage jolted along the dirt road.

Inside the château the air was stale and cloying, filled with the overpowering scent of lilies. The curtains were drawn. Thierry was pale and morose as he led Henriette to the duchesse's rooms.

'Her Grace is very fragile,' he murmured. 'It seems you're the only person she wishes to see.'

Henriette found Charlotte slumped in the window seat.

'Your Grace?'

The duchesse looked up, her face puffy, her eyes red-rimmed. Without a word she rose and clutched Henriette in a tight embrace, her chest shaking with sobs.

'Please, sit down with me,' she begged.

Henriette could see the bones on Charlotte's chest and the tremor in her hand as they sat.

'I've committed an indecent act, Henriette. My soul is in deep peril. It was my fault, you see? There was a ritual that went wrong. We knew something would happen but I never imagined....' Charlotte gasped, tears streaming down her face. 'I've killed her. The poison was meant for Letitia and it somehow ended up in Estelle's drink.'

'And why am I here, Charlotte? You did everything to ruin me, and now you call me back? For what?'

'You know God. You know what it is to be aligned with Him. I need you to tell me what to do, how to withstand this hell. I can't live with this, Henriette.'

'You're right. No mother could survive this if her life remained the same. No person of faith. Tell me, if you examine yourself and the situation, what would you do?'

Charlotte's face transformed. A light came to it and she glowed, her gaze meeting Henriette's. 'You are wise and I understand. Take me there, Henriette. Take me to the convent.'

'Not yet. You need to grieve. To have a funeral. To think a little. Would you like me to attend the funeral?'

Charlotte nodded. 'Please. I need you there. I'm so sorry for what I did to you.'

'I forgive you. There's something I need to ask.'

'Of course.'

'What was Romain's involvement in the plot against Letitia?'

Charlotte sighed. 'He forged letters from Letitia and brought me letters the duc wrote in reply. I asked Romain to put lye in Letitia's stays, but he refused. Romain was in debt. I threatened him and promised large rewards, the majority of which he has since spent on our son, Tomas.'

Henriette gasped. 'Your son?'

Charlotte smile was bittersweet. 'If only I could have had another, perhaps my marriage would have been happy.'

Henriette shook her head. 'I don't know what to say. It's a lot to take in.'

Charlotte took her hand. 'Perfect virtue is a rare and precious thing. I'm not convinced it even exists. For any of us.'

The two women stood and kissed one another other on both cheeks. Tears shone on their faces as they parted.

Three days after their daughter died, Hugo burst into Charlotte's rooms and stood tense before her, his face grey, and his eyes red and swollen. 'You were behind this. I'm sure it was an error, but I see your hand in it. Did Madame de Poitiers carry it out for you?'

Charlotte knew better than to try and embrace him. She rose and faced him, her features calm.

'Your suspicions are correct. Céline carried out a poisoning that was meant for Letitia.'

'You need to get as far away from me as possible, I'm sure you realize. Take that monster of a mistress with you, too,' he sneered.

Charlotte swallowed the pain in her throat and blinked back the torrent of tears. 'I will never forgive myself. My hatred killed Estelle. I will leave straight after the funeral. You never have to see me again.'

The duc's face remained hard and implacable. 'I did love you still, right up until the moment I found my daughter cold and lifeless. You offend everything in me. Every belief, every principle.'

Charlotte's voice shook. 'Maybe. Yet have you acted with complete honour? Forcing me to be second rank to a mistress? Perhaps one day you will see your part in this.'

He bristled. 'I will keep this affair quiet, not for you, but for the family name. This is the last time we will speak.'

'Yes, I know. I hope you find happiness.'

'There will be none. Not ever. You've made sure of that.'

For three mornings in a row Céline hammered on her door, her sobs echoing through the hallway. 'I'm sorry, Charlotte! Please, please let me in and I can explain.' Her voice was hoarse and desperate.

On the third morning Yolande gave her mistress a questioning look.

'For goodness sake,' said the duchesse. 'Tell Thierry to escort her to her rooms. And tell my husband to do what needs to be done.'

Yolande curtsied. 'Yes, Your Grace. I'll see to it.'

The butler hooked his hand under Céline's armpit and manhandled her down the hallway to her rooms. Left alone, Céline found her embroidery and picked apart a badly constructed flower. The mantel clock ticked and a feeling of dread crept into her stomach.

Some hours later, the duc arrived at her door, his face inflamed. He tried several times to speak before the words came out. Céline rose and bowed her head, waiting for the onslaught.

'Madame de Poitiers,' he enunciated with sickening relish. 'Paragon of Christian values and virtues. Handy with a bottle of poison.' He withdrew the bottle from his pocket and brandished it before her. 'This is yours?'

'Yes, Your Grace.'

'And you used it, to murder my daughter.'

'It wasn't meant for her.'

He nodded for too long. 'Does it matter? She's dead, lying in the drawing room, her skin blue. Have you seen her body?'

'Will I go to prison?' Céline asked, her voice trembling.

'No. That would be too good for you. You would look penitent, and people might feel sorry for you. You're going into town, and you'll have to find a way to survive.'

Céline shuddered. 'Please, Your Grace. I want to be punished. I want the judges to sentence me. It's the right thing.'

'No one must know of this. Get out of here. Pack your things.' The duc turned and slammed the door.

Céline was unable to stem the flow of tears as she threw clothes into a bag. Her breath caught in her throat as she sobbed.

Descending the stairs, she noticed that the door to the drawing room was ajar. The room was infused with gold light from flickering candles, and she glimpsed white satin covering the shape of a foot.

Céline crossed herself, her hands shaking. Thierry stood rigid at the door, his gaze impenetrable. She glanced at him and a pain twisted her heart. On his coat gleamed the watch brooch, its gold and pearls bright against the navy velvet. She pressed her lips against the scream lodged in her chest and slipped out the front door, her leather bag heavy at her side.

At the gates a horse whinnied. Raoul sat in the driver's seat of a carriage and tipped his hat. Smoke curled from his pipe.

'You'll be requiring a ride, madame.'

'Thank you, Raoul. Take me to rue Gallois, please.'

Her last journey from the château was peaceful. She stopped crying and watched the dappled shade of the plane trees on her forearms. Raoul yanked the reins as they arrived in rue Gallois. His brown eyes were gentle as he helped her to the ground.

'Will you be all right, madame?'

'Yes, thank you.' She pressed a coin into his hand.

'No, madame. You keep it. God bless.'

The street that led to Madame Rochas's was steep and Céline paused to catch her breath. As she stood at the entrance a woman burst out, reeking of spirits, her bosom straining against a checked dress, her mouth a slash of red. From upstairs, raucous laughter erupted. Céline turned and walked back down the hill. The river glinted below, its waters brackish green. She detoured past brick houses, washing lines, and gardens planted with vibrant petunias and daisies. At the edge of the river she murmured a prayer and crossed herself.

Céline stepped into the water, and within minutes she was up to her waist, her skirt floating to the surface. She shivered, her feet sinking into the mud, the icy water lapping against her skin. Looking upwards, she saw a flock of geese traverse the clearing sky, their wings outstretched against a banner of vivid blue. She sank into the cold, brackish darkness, the words of the prayer unfolding in her mind until it too, went black.

CHAPTER 24

Three months later

Charlotte smoothed the vellum under her fingers as she read the biblical passage in which Peter questions Jesus about forgiveness. The sun was hot on her back as she sat on the bench in the garden. From the dormitory she could hear the sound of the girls reciting the catechism. She fingered the wooden crucifix that hung from her neck.

Many nights she woke drenched in perspiration, the vision of Céline floating on the surface of the water clear and accusing. Charlotte's regret was a palpable, living thing that left an ache in her chest. Interwoven with regrets for Céline were thoughts of her daughter. Her faith dulled the pain, as did the girls of the convent and the gentle attentions of the abbess.

Someone tapped her on the shoulder. Charlotte turned and saw Amalia's smiling face. Her hair was braided and her cheeks flushed.

'Aren't you meant to be with the others?' asked Charlotte.

'The abbess said I should come and keep you company, Sister Charlotte. You didn't come down for breakfast this morning. She's determined to fatten you up.'

'Sit with me for a moment.' Charlotte handed Amalia the Bible. 'You read the Psalms so beautifully, Amalia. Please, I can think of nothing better than listening to you and watching the leaves sway in the wind.'

'Maman said to thank you.'

'Whatever for?'

'For keeping an eye on me.'

'Dear child, I think you're keeping an eye on me just as well. Now start here.' Charlotte pointed to the top of the passage, her hand on Amalia's forearm. The sun broke through the gaps in the trees, making patterns on the page.

Isabelle managed to coax the duc out of bed and into some clothes. He sat stiffly at his bureau and frowned. She flung open the drapes and neatened the room, folding clothes and lining up items on his dresser.

'You're on a mission. What is it?' he muttered.

'First of all, I want to make you feel normal again. It's going to take some time. And there's something else.'

'Ah, Isabelle, you always have a plan. I'm lucky to have you around.'

'It's Letitia. I'm sure in your misery you haven't noticed, but she is utterly bereft. Let her go, Hugo. She loves the Marquis d'Urveilles. What use is there in keeping someone around who doesn't wish to be here? You're not such an old fool that you believe she loves you, surely?'

Hugo's face was forlorn, with deep shadows under his eyes and furrows at the sides of his mouth.

'I'd be angry with you, except you're right. I've tried to hold onto her, hoping she'd care for me. Love me even. Tell her to come to me one last time. I'm sure she won't begrudge me an embrace.'

Isabelle's face lit up. In a moment of ebullience she flew at him and kissed him hard on the lips, then blushed.

'You're a good man. Sometimes.'

Hugo gave a caustic smile. 'Be off with you.'

Isabelle dashed out the door and returned with a beaming Letitia.

'I hear we must say our goodbyes?' he asked and beckoned. She went to him and he folded her into his arms. 'What of your parents? Will your marquis look after them as I have? Are you sure he'll be faithful?'

'Yes, he said he would support them. He'll be faithful as he's waited a long time. Thank you for everything you've done for me. I'm truly grateful.'

Letitia's face glowed and she shifted on her feet.

He gave a weary smile. 'You're impatient to leave. I wish you the best.' He kissed her on both cheeks and watched hunched over as she darted away.

Antoine and Letitia sat in the field above the town and gazed at the slate roofs and the bustle of people in the streets. The distant sound of the market vendors mingled with the song of the crickets. The air was warm on their skin. Antoine reached for Letitia's hand and turned it over, tracing her palm.

'I wasn't sure if I'd see you again. When I heard the news, I thought he'd keep you closer than ever, like a talisman against grief.'

'He did, for a while. Then Isabelle helped. I think the poison was meant for me.'

'Do you think the duchesse was behind it?'

'Yes, there have been whispers of it amongst the servants. Charlotte hasn't been right in her mind for a while, not thinking clearly. I feel sorry for her.'

Antoine was incredulous. 'You could have died, and you feel sorry for *her*?'

'Some people are wretched. They don't understand the consequences of what they do. I have missed you,' she said shyly.

Antoine leant over and pressed his lips to hers with slow tenderness, his fingers at her jaw. 'And I you. I'm here for a couple of days and then back to the château. I want us to marry as soon as possible. There is a guesthouse in the grounds where you can stay until you are my wife.'

'I will come with you. Nothing would make me happier.'

Pauline gave Henriette a spectacular pale green dress with a lace collar.

'Put it on,' she commanded.

'Why?' asked Henriette.

'You're going to Versailles to speak with Romain. If his words are unsatisfactory, then you may return and you won't have lost anything.'

'I told him I couldn't be with him. You know this.'

'You're unhappy. Go to him.'

Henriette sighed, 'All right, but I'll be back soon.' Pauline buttoned the back of her silk gown as Henriette looked in the mirror, wide-eyed.

'It's a marvel. Truly beautiful.'

'It becomes you,' agreed Pauline with a smile.

Settling into a hired carriage, she unfurled her parasol as the driver flicked the reins, urging the horse down the street toward the edge of town.

As she watched the fields of flowers and crops she felt the warmth of anticipation in her chest. She had tried not to think of Romain these past months, but he was always in the corner of her mind jostling for attention.

When the giant gilt-tipped gates came into view, she paid the driver and thanked him before moving through the main entrance doors. A butler led her to the Galerie des Batailles. Through its arched ceiling, swathes of light beamed down from curved windows, illuminating the parquetry and vast paintings that lined the walls.

Romain stood waiting with a delighted smile.

She approached and kissed him on both cheeks. 'Why this halfway point? There are no chairs.'

'No one will pass here,' he replied, 'other than servants. I want to speak candidly and look at you openly.'

'Are you well?'

'Yes,' he said. 'Although after our last meeting I went into hiding for a while. It was…unexpected.' He was pensive for a moment, a darkness flitted across his face.

'I'm sorry. I've been thinking about what you said and why you were part of the plot against Letitia. Charlotte told me about Tomas and your desire to help him. I find this admirable, although not your methods. Perhaps my judgements are too harsh. Maybe there is room for something in between, that is altogether more uncertain.'

Romain's gaze was warm as he took her hand, his expression urging her to continue.

'Your intentions are more often good than not. Your heart is true. I would like to trust that you won't disappoint me again. And that if you were to make an error it would be one of judgement rather than malice. Because we all live in a place that is unknown, where the results of what we do aren't always apparent until it's too late. I am, after all, only human, like you.'

Tears spilled from Romain's eyes as he drew her close, his lips at her neck. 'Henriette, I want you to come and live here with me.'

She kissed him, inhaled his scent, felt the solidity of his chest and the softness of his lips. A sense of release filled her, the heavy months without him lifted and scattered. 'I'll return to Blois and ponder some more. I'll talk with Solange. Be patient. I think yes, but I can't promise.'

They embraced again, fervent and whole. In the Galerie, the vivid battle paintings were like silent witnesses. What lay between them flickered and danced.

ACKNOWLEDGMENTS

A number of people have been instrumental in bringing this book to life. I am so thankful to you all.

To the members of the Women's Fiction Critique Group—Gail Cleare, Jackie Bates, Ann Warner, Muriel Canfield, Jennie Ensor and Nancy Hopp for their invaluable insights and assistance with my early draft.

To my other early readers—Kali Napier, Cindra Spencer, Peter Campbell, Sheena Macleod, Sebnem Sanders and Tabatha Stirling.

To my editor and publisher, Jaynie Royal, for her belief in this book and expert guidance and to the team at Regal House Publishing. To my agent, Sarah McKenzie, for her unwavering support of both this story and my writing in general. To my husband, David, and my mother, Pat, who are my steadfast cheer squad and listen to everything I need to say. Finally, to my children, Anika and Sebastian, whose love is plentiful and constant.